By Douglass Wallop

The Good Life

DOUGLASS WALLOP

The Good Life

ATHENEUM New York

Part One

1

In the year of his *idée fixe*, Albert Miller was zeroing in on the mid-century mark and already tired of life as he had known it. The years had become an untidy blur. Every time he looked up, Christmas was coming at him again, followed almost immediately by Ground Hog Day and then, before he knew it, by Flag Day. The year gave him no quarter.

Small of eye, protruding of ear, and fast going bald, Albert had all the usual marks of the good life, including a home with a mortgage and two cars with liens, yet he felt himself more slave than owner. To the house, to the cars, to the many chattels which filled his house and garage, to insurance companies, to tax collectors at various levels and substations —to all of these he was little better than an indentured servant, and when he brooded upon it, when he discussed it with his wife or with his God, he was inclined to crave change.

A good enough citizen in his churlish way, Albert nonetheless began to feel steadily waning enthusiasm for his country's socio-economic system, particularly for the aspect of *ownership*. At trifling moments, he would daydream of a

3

gimmick, of a way to beat the system, of a way to have his cake and eat it.

Albert could not have said for certain whence his idea sprung, although he rather thought it was from standing around at cocktail parties, not listening. Like all great ideas, it was remarkably simple and even rather obvious.

Over the years, not listening, he had heard enough to know for certain that in present-day America there was a severe shortage of so-called domestic help. Matrons of his acquaintance discussed the problem largely in moans and groans, betraying no interest in the socio-economic aspect, chattering instead in purely personal terms—of maids they had once employed, maids they now employed, maids they had fired, maids who had quit with or without notice, and even of maids who, behind the cloak of friendship, had been stolen from beneath their very noses.

If one believed the ladies, there was simply no domestic help to be had, at least from domestic sources. One had to reach beyond the border, extend a plucking hand over the blue Caribbean, into Trinidad perhaps, or Jamaica, pay the plane fare north and then, relying on haphazard means of recognition, meet the quarry at the airport and drive her home, conversing in pidgin English. "Me, employer. You, maid. Telephone rings, you answer. 'Maid speaking.' Paste wax—paste wax, not squirt can. Rub."

Jewels, Albert knew, came mainly from the Antilles, although a few arrived now and again from the Scandinavian countries, and one, to his knowledge, from Brazil—a plump, jolly girl, jungle-born, convent-trained, who, as a child in her native village, had seen the chief's smallest wife swallowed by an anaconda. Imported at understandable expense, highly

4

prized for her good nature and the skills taught her by the nuns, she was, two weeks after her arrival, stolen by a next-door neighbor who had once studied Portuguese at Berlitz.

Once come by, the idea began to smolder. Albert at first resisted. It seemed bizarre. He was simply not the sort of person. It was not the sort of thing he would do, and perhaps not the sort of thing *anybody* would do.

And yet, sitting in the cafeteria where he habitually ate lunch, he found himself forming with his lips the word *non-ownership*, whispering it lovingly and with longing. And if that be a communist notion, he thought, glancing about the cafeteria with a shrug, then let J. Edgar Hoover make the most of it.

Still and all . . . could this really be Albert Miller, a man who once had so gloried in his own red-blooded American individual entrepreneurship?

Albert by profession was an industrial consultant, a troubleshooter. With a solid background in accounting, and some knowledge of tax law, personnel management, industrial psychology; with some notion of the harmonics of space-and-bulk, time-and-motion, light-and-air, and noise-and-silence, he made his living by bolstering up infirm companies. Once he had been fond of saying that he, to an ailing business, was what a marriage counselor is to a shaky marriage, but over the years he had grown bored with saying it.

Still, until rather recently, he had continued to take pride in knowing that he was a staunch holdout against a system that was becoming increasingly corporate, increasingly institutionalized. He had considered himself a hardy relic—

the small businessman, naked in the world, naked before his government, refusing even to accept a partner, going it alone with the aid of a couple of secretaries.

And he was proud too of the way he had managed to go it alone at home, without the overpriced help that so many of his friends needed to keep their houses in repair. He saw himself as a man of true versatility, self-taught at all levels, preparing his own income-tax returns, discovering his own Mozart, checking his own points and plugs, forming his own acquaintanceship with Freud and Rousseau, stacking his own storm windows, mowing his own lawn, repairing his own downspouts.

He was of the same hardy breed to which the country owed so very much of its development. But wasn't his breed done for? It was indeed. It grieved him to think so—yet he had no choice. He had only to look about. Everywhere people had taken shelter, more and more each year as employees of the federal, state, county, and municipal governments; more and more each year at educational institutions; others under the comforting testudinal shelters offered by such as IBM, GE, GM, FoMoCo, and other kindly sempiternal giantesses.

What Albert Miller now finally admitted to himself was that he too longed to be institutionalized.

This might be a form of self-betrayal and might even incur some loss of face, but otherwise there seemed little to lose and much to gain. He was weary of going it alone, weary of his business, weary of supporting his many possessions, weary of making ends meet—for the ironic fact was that *his* business, running counter to the surging, bucking trend-line, was at best standing still and perhaps even slipping a little, weakened by the sheer health of the economy. What profit could a doctor expect among the robust? Or a marriage counselor among the sexually compatible?

To sell out . . . to convert all his worldly goods into cash . . . to own nothing, and yet everything . . . to lick the system by finding its loophole and jumping in feet foremost, dragging his wife in with him . . .

His wife, who would take some convincing . . .

Preparing for bed on a night in early March, he glanced at the set of her head as she sat determinedly at her typewriter, an electric portable on which, for some years now, she had been writing the story of her father's life. She could do that *anywhere*, he told himself.

Watching, he saw her place the fingers of both hands to her lips and peer at the page through her onyx-rimmed, harlequin glasses.

"I'm going to bed," he said.

Her fingers went to the keys.

"Okay?" he asked, not expecting an answer.

There was indeed no answer. Her powers of concentration were remarkable in anything she did. When she was at the typewriter, they were truly startling.

Back in the days when Beverly was still at home, she would return from school in the afternoon to find her mother at the typewriter. "Mother . . ."

No reply. Fingers pressed to lips.

"Mother . . . I'm home . . . from school."

A nod. A weak smile.

"Mother, I was just in a horrible auto accident."

"That's nice," Jane replied, fingers moving over the keys.

7

"I was in the hospital."

"Really?"

"*Mother!*"

It was not that Jane was a poor mother. She simply entered a trance when she put on her glasses and sat down at the typewriter. In those days she had barely begun to etch out the story of her father, but after Beverly went off to college she went at it in deadly earnest. Beverly was now a junior.

In bed now, and listening to the keys clattering away down the hall, Albert told himself again that, yes, she could do *that* anywhere. Anywhere at all.

The idea became a fixation, a Jekyll-Hyde thing which began to fret him at all hours of the day. "Yes, mum," he would find himself muttering, and then frown, lost in thought.

From time to time he would scribble lines on the backs of envelopes, indulging his daydream. And then one day, when he could stand it no longer, and even *then* telling himself it would merely be a trial balloon and that he was not really *serious*, he took a cab down to the morning newspaper and inserted a classified ad under Situations Wanted:

Live-in couple, highest references, many talents, seeking position with respectable exurban family. Reply Box No. . . .

2

The ad ran in the morning editions of Tuesday, March 17. By Friday, there were ninety-seven replies.

On Friday evening, lingering in the office after his secretaries left, Albert stood at his tenth-story window and watched the cold March twilight fall over the spires of the nation's capital. Along the sidewalk far below, a wind-tossed newspaper flattened itself hard against the trunk of a tree, sideslipped free, and rushed on down the block, clinging momentarily to a miniskirt and then, free once more, skipped from sight.

Albert turned from the window and moved to his desk. A smile played at his lips. The desk was piled high with letters, and here and there among them the telltale yellow of a telegram. Chuckling, he let them sift through his hands.

What braggarts they were! And how kindly in their self-regard. All, to judge from their replies, lived lives of the most beautiful serenity, in homes which any live-in couple must surely look upon as rainbow's end. Homes never sullied by the presence of children, never marred by a contentious phrase. And how very rich they all sounded! Save for one missing element, their lives were beautifully complete. All they lacked was a live-in couple.

His eye fell upon the signature of a Millicent (Mrs.

Edward A.) Marks. "Saints be praised!" wrote Mrs. Marks, more outgoing than most. "Thinking that live-in couples were a thing of the past, we had all but given up hope! When could you and your good wife begin? I know we would get along splendidly."

Mrs. Marks went on to say that her husband was afflicted with a stomach disorder but possessed of a genial nature and a truly up-to-date attitude toward servants, having served for a number of years on a Big Steel management panel charged with handling labor relations.

The Marks estate, it was easy to surmise from the address, was in the fox-hunt area of Virginia, not far from Warrenton. Albert was predisposed against living among the fox-hunt set. His preference would be for a watering place, if it came to that.

Flipping the toggle switch of his desk lamp, he read on. A Mr. Roger Knox begged for a chance to match or better any offer he might be inclined to accept. At some length, Mr. Knox described a guest house built on his property at great expense, complete with color TV and bomb shelter. "Your privacy would at all times be respected," Mr. Knox wrote. "The guest house will be *de facto* yours and your good wife's."

Some of the replies were addressed to Sir and Madam while others were addressed to Dear Sir. In these when mention was made of his wife, she was never referred to merely as his wife but almost invariably as his good wife. And it was also remarkable to note that fully six of those who answered, six ladies, saw fit to mention the colleges from which they and their husbands had graduated. "I was Sweetbriar and Mr. Hampton was U. Va.," wrote a Mrs. May

Hampton. There were also couplings of Mount Holyoke and Yale; Goucher and Princeton; Goucher and Johns Hopkins; Smith and Rutgers; and Vassar and Tufts.

In all, there were seven telegrams, each addressed simply to Box 8G and handed across the counter to him by the classified clerk along with the rest of the mail. All said in effect: Do nothing till you hear from us.

MOST URGENT, wired a Mr. William A. Gatling, THAT YOU MAKE NO COMMITMENT UNTIL WE CAN MEET. LETTER FOLLOWS.

The letter that followed was near heart-rending.

"Dear Sir & Madam," wrote Mr. Gatling. "Have you ever had a lifelong dream tarnished before your very eyes?"

Choking with self-pity, Mr. Gatling went on to describe the dream—to retire to the country and to live in splendor, to live life as it was meant to be lived, as Washington and Jefferson and Monroe—"the men of Albemarle"—lived it, each to a fiefdom, and what matter if the horse was now a station wagon.

"We found just the house," Mr. Gatling went on. "A splendid thing of pink brick, built with grace and care in the 18th century and restored by my wife with care fully as loving, fully as meticulous. But there was one thing we had not reckoned with—and that is the *virtual disappearance of the servant class in America today.* So we sit here in our splendor, in our great house on its 50 acres—and we drive each morning 20 miles in the station wagon to the nearest village, Girdletree, where we pick up one of the local girls, all we can find in the way of help, and then drive her to our house, where she puts in a listless day, and then in the evening one or the other of us must make the 40-mile round trip involved in getting her back to her home. She refuses to do the sensible thing and live in, although I'm not at all sure, all things considered, that we would even want her. So, in short, our beautiful estate cries out for someone like yourself to make it complete. We hope you may see fit to share it with us. We feel moreover that you would like the little village of Girdletree. It's a place of very little bustle, but it has a great deal of quaint charm."

The others did not lay it on the line with such mawkish self-pity. Many even played it rather cool, fearful perhaps lest they overcommit themselves into a poor bargaining position. But even these permitted their eagerness to show through, and Albert, reading and rereading, had a most unusual feeling. Never in his life had he felt so wanted, never had he felt so important, even though he was, to all intents and purposes, up to this point only a box number—and had no more specific identity than 8G.

There were three replies from Georgetown, chiding him for choosing the exurbs over the manifold pleasures of the city, and another alleging that Georgetown was in fact "an exurb of the intellect and spirit," and suggesting that he would do well to reconsider his locale.

One of the replies which most impressed him—more for its equable tone than for its myopic aim—was from a Mr. J. K. Dutton, who described his home as "an island of sanity against the utter chaos of today.

"We attempt so far as possible," Mr. Dutton wrote, "to pretend that our island is the real world and that the one we read about does not exist. Indeed, we rarely even read of it, since most magazines are debarred from our home. Without ever being ostentatious, we live a good comfortable life, dedicated to such old-fashioned watchwords as courtesy and graciousness and kindliness. We are trying to hold out against the tawdry and the angry. Is there anything wrong with that?

"I'm sure," Mr. Dutton surmised quite accurately, "that you must be swamped with replies, and I suppose our chances are slim, but I hope you will come and at least have a look at 'Rear Guard' before you make your choice. You would, of course, have swimming pool privileges. . . ."

Although the fact had never been lost upon him, Albert, as he read on and on, could not escape a feeling of surprise at the remarkable number of very wealthy people in the United States. Clearly there were vast legions of them, slipping furtively in and out of their estates, happy and eager to remain inconspicuous and silent until something of great import flushed them out. When they wanted something worthwhile, their determination knew no limit.

Three letters seriously discussed the possibility of setting up a pension plan for Albert and his good wife, and there was even one—from a Mr. Ramsay Connaughton of Habnab, Va.—which, in thinly veiled terms, seemed to be offering Albert the services of a mistress. Mr. Connaughton's letter included the lines: ". . . living in the country can sometimes give a man lusty appetites—well, perhaps something could be arranged."

Chuckling at this and at others fully as eager, Albert after a time began to detect a breathless, giggly quality in his own chuckle. The thing smacked of enormous brute power— his own. He knew that of 97 aspirants, 96 must ultimately be disappointed, and his would be the power to say which. Momentarily, it made him feel uncomfortable, for it would, in the end, involve a form of cruelty, however unwitting, however involuntary.

He was reminded inevitably of the radio spot commercials used by the local newspaper to underscore the quick, solid results one could get by placing a classified ad. The spot commercials went as follows:

Wanted: 45 used refrigerators to take care of the 45 people who were disappointed when they called too late to buy the used refrigerator advertised for sale by Mrs. Naomi Hotchkiss of Hyattsville. . . .

Wanted: 69 used air conditioners to accommodate the 69 unsuccessful would-be buyers who called Mr. Holloway Tolliver. . . .

In the end, Albert asked himself, would his cruelty be any greater than that of Mrs. Hotchkiss, who advertised a used refrigerator and drew forty-six buyers—automatically dashing the hopes of forty-five?

The answer had to be yes, for a live-in couple was clearly much harder to come by than a used refrigerator.

By Tuesday, one week from the ad's appearance, the number of replies had grown to 148, a truly remarkable response. The letters now were coming from those who had missed the ad when it ran but who had been told about it by friends.

In bed that night, when he closed his eyes, Albert had a picture of 148 couples, 296 human beings, aquiver with anticipation and hope—and somewhere among them was his benefactor and protector, his socio-economic loophole. Nearly 300 souls, strung out along the Middle Atlantic seaboard, hoping against hope, some perhaps even praying, that their life now would change for the better, knowing that somewhere off in the darkness, somewhere in the far-flung reaches of the night, two jewels existed.

One of the jewels, Albert thought, grinning in his bed, is me. And down the hall, all unknowing, tapping away at the typewriter, was the other.

3

Just as intently as if he were serious about what he was doing, Albert Miller now embarked upon a winnowing process.

Quickly he eliminated 112 whose addresses were clearly inland, near no body of water worth mentioning. Of those that remained, he chose an initial batch of five for investigation. Their appeal was mainly geographic, all being in the so-called tidewater area, four in Maryland, one in Virginia, and so clustered that he could handle all five in a single day's driving. Each listed a swimming pool among its physical assets, all spoke of ample time off. All five had suggested, indeed entreated, that he call collect, which in each case he did, receiving in each case a warm invitation to come ahead, even though, as he was careful to tell them, his good wife would not be along. Mr. J. K. Dutton of "Rear Guard" was among the five. The mawkish Mr. Gatling, of Girdletree, was not.

On the appointed day he dressed with humility and, eschewing both Buick and Thunderbird, he rented a gray Ford from Avis and drove over the Chesapeake Bay Bridge. The day was Monday, March 30, the weather gray and cold, although over the weekend it had been quite warm, promising spring. It might very well be, he told himself, a spring and summer to remember.

He drove directly to the southernmost of his selected quintet and worked his way northward, feeling little enthusiasm for the first four sets of applicants, all of whom impressed him as being given to dyspepsia and existing on Rolaids. Their houses on this gray day occupied murky settings, surrounded by deep forests of virgin pine.

It was late afternoon when he entered the long lane leading to the home of Mr. J. K. Dutton, and it could be prophetic, he thought, that just as he turned in, the sun burst through, sending long shafts of light streaking up the lane ahead of the car.

He was greeted at the door by Mr. Dutton himself, a man slight in stature and no longer young, yet robust-looking and extremely ruddy, perhaps merely out of excitement, or perhaps from the good outdoor life at Rear Guard.

The room into which Dutton now ushered him was remarkable on a number of counts, among them a cathedral ceiling of such enormous height as to provide ample space for a balcony which ran around the room on three sides and which was accessible by a spiral staircase. Lining the walls at balcony level were the mounted heads of big game animals, along with a number of photographs and plaques.

Done in accents of beige and mahogany, the room also boasted a huge, multi-paned picture window looking out upon the river which curved its way about the shoreline of the property.

Dutton, for the occasion, wore a hound's-tooth jacket over a turtleneck sweater. "Please be seated, Mr. Bagby. . . ." He indicated the semicircular sofa with its view of the river.

"Jake," a woman's voice called. "Was that somebody at the door?"

"Yes," Dutton replied. "Come on down. Our visitor is here."

He grinned at Albert, who grinned humbly back, thinking that Dutton was perhaps the last person in the world to be called Jake. With his silver cap of hair and his mild eyes, he didn't look at all like a Jake.

The next surprise was Mrs. Dutton. Albert had been prepared for someone Dutton's own age. Mrs. Dutton was clearly his junior by any number of years and could only be a second wife, or perhaps third, fourth, or fifth. In her tight green capri pants and floppy yellow sweater, and with her heavily made-up dark eyes and her mane of auburn hair, she looked hardly more than thirty.

They sat on the sofa before the picture window. The sun had disappeared once more, and the river had the tone of steel. Willows lining its bank were fresh with green fuzz.

The two of them looked at him appraisingly. Albert, star-

ing at the willows, holding his old gray felt hat tightly by
the brim, cleared his throat nervously.

"I'm sorry Mrs. Bagby was unable to come with you,"
Dutton began.

"I'm sorry too, sir," Albert said. "She had a touch of the
virus, and I thought it best she stay in where it was warm.
Although she is not what you would call a sickly woman,
sir, not by a long shot."

"I'm sure she's not," Dutton said.

"What is your wife's name, Mr. Bagby?"

"Jane, mum."

"What a lovely name."

"Yes, mum."

"Albert and Jane . . ." Mrs. Dutton savored the names
and her eyes seemed to glaze with greed. "Although to us,"
she went on quickly, "you would of course be Mr. and Mrs.
Bagby."

Albert rotated his hat a half-circle. "Whatever you say,
mum, although I think we would prefer Albert and Jane,
mum, if you wouldn't mind. I believe we would both feel
more comfortable that way."

He was aware of Dutton's eyes on his face and then on
his hat. Albert looked down at his hands and found them
pale.

"When could you start?" Dutton asked.

"Well, you see, sir . . ." Albert raised his eyes, looking first
at one and then the other. "In coming here today, I don't
want to create any false impressions. I mean, if you don't
mind, sir, I meant this to be more or less of an exploratory
visit, you might say. I'm not, strictly speaking, applying for
the job, not yet."

18

For a fleeting second, Dutton's eyes seemed to glaze. Briefly they seemed the eyes of a madman, but Albert decided that he must have been mistaken, for the strange look passed as quickly as it had come, and Dutton was nodding soberly that he understood.

"Oh, dear," Mrs. Dutton was saying.

Albert glanced at her and smiled. "To be perfectly truthful, mum, we had an awful lot of answers to our ad, ever so many."

Mrs. Dutton laughed, and he found her appealing when she laughed. "I'm not at *all* surprised," she said. Now she draped one green-sheathed leg over the other knee, toe pointed, torso erect, hands laced behind her neck, and there was, Albert thought, something of the ballet dancer about her. "I'm *sure* you must have been *swamped*," she said. "Who in this day and age could ever expect to be so lucky as to happen upon a genuine live-in *couple*? Especially one so attractive . . . Mr. Dutton could hardly believe his eyes when he saw the ad!"

Albert smiled modestly. "What I did, sir," he said, turning to Dutton, "if I may explain, is to pick out a few of the answers that sounded especially nice—yours included, of course—and decided to see the people and let them see us . . . except that Mrs. Bagby took ill."

"In other words, to accept the best offer?" Dutton asked.

Albert let several moments pass. When he spoke, it was with dignity and pride. "I would have to answer that question yes and no, sir. If I may say so, sir, I've never been one to gouge people. Nor the missus either. We place greater store on other things . . . other aspects of the position. . . ."

"Oh, I'm so glad to hear you say that," Mrs. Dutton said, eyes shining.

"What other aspects?" Dutton asked.

"Well, sir, whether we truly like and respect our employers, sir. Whether they're people of quality, you might say, and by such other things as working conditions. Neither Mrs. Bagby nor myself likes to be driven, mum. We give full value, indeed we do, but we'll give even more if the initiative is allowed to come from *us*, you might say."

"Of course," Mrs. Dutton said, and Albert saw her nudge Dutton with a nudging glance.

Dutton shrugged. "Well, Mr. Bagby," he said, "what would you like to know about *us*? There are no children, although my nevvew Nick is in and about a good deal. By the way, does Mrs. Bagby cook?"

"She is an excellent cook, sir, and she *enjoys* cooking, if I may say so."

Mrs. Dutton gave a little shriek. She seemed about to swoon with delight and topple from the sofa.

"*Except—*" Albert said. "She doesn't cook breakfast."

"Oh?"

"To be perfectly honest, mum, she has the kind of metabolism—I mean she functions poorly in the mornings. She's what you would call a *night* person. Her metabolism. All her energy is at the other end of the day, as it were. Now me, I'm a day person, and *I'll* be happy to get the breakfast. That's the way we've always worked it."

"Oh, Mr. Bagby!" said Mrs. Dutton. "How considerate of you!"

"Actually we're not breakfast eaters," Dutton said. "What else can you do, Mr. Bagby?"

"I can do almost anything, sir."

"Drive, of course . . ."

"Oh, yes, sir," Albert said, nodding vaguely toward his car.

"Gardening . . ."

"Yes, sir."

"One of our main problems is the mowing. . . ."

"You can count on me, sir. And I can also *fix* a mower, should it get cranky. I see you have a pool. . . ."

"You'd have pool privileges, of course," Dutton said.

"I could maintain the pool for you," Albert said. "I'm good at that."

Dutton nodded, clearly pleased.

"Keep your cars waxed and cleaned, of course," Albert went on. "And any chauffeuring you might care for. And I also happen to be a very capable bartender, sir, and enjoy tending bar. And if it happens to be crossing your mind that I may nip here and there, then I'll come right out with the truth of it here and now, sir. I drink. I enjoy a highball or two in the evening as well as anyone, but there's one thing I can promise you. I would never disgrace you or myself. Dignity is a thing I believe in first, last, and always. And moreover, whatever I drink will come from a bottle paid for by myself and kept in my room, and not much of that either."

"Well, that seems candid enough," Dutton said.

"Beautifully candid," Mrs. Dutton said. "Just beautiful."

"That's the fact of it, mum," Albert said.

"Would you object to serving at dinner parties? We'd be expecting to give some dinner parties." Mrs. Dutton gave him another warm smile.

"Not at all, mum. I should tell you also that I'm very handy at fixing things, if I may say so. I can do some carpentry and painting, and I also have a little knowledge of plumbing and electricity. Little things, mind you, but important. Things you'd hate to call a plumber or electrician for."

"Well," Dutton said, and there seemed some evidence that he was about to drool by now. He looked away, as if to compose himself. "What salary would you require?" he asked, trying to get some steel into his voice.

"I think I'd rather leave that up to you and Mrs. Dutton," Albert said. "I do want you to understand that this is all according, of course."

"All according to what?" Dutton asked.

"All according to whether it's you folks we choose or someone else."

"Oh, *dear*," Mrs. Dutton said. "I was *afraid* that's what you were going to say." She cocked her head at Dutton. "Don't open a vein, Jake."

Dutton got to his feet and stood grimly at the picture window, looking out at the river. While he was so engaged, Mrs. Dutton laughed and brought her hand down lightly on Albert's knee, letting it trail off in a caress.

Albert looked humbly at the floor.

Dutton turned. "Mr. Bagby," he said. "I wonder if you would excuse us for a moment. . . ."

They withdrew and he heard the low hum of their voices somewhere off down the hall. Then the telephone rang, and he heard the quick tread of Dutton's step as he moved to answer it. In another second or two, Dutton shouted that

22

it was Hoboken, New Jersey, calling and that he would be a while.

Albert stood at the picture window. The lawn was soaked by the spring rains. It still looked squashy. The drainage obviously was poor.

"Mr. Bagby . . ."

She had moved as silently as a cat. "Mr. Dutton will be on the phone for a while, I'm afraid. Would you like to see where you and Mrs. Bagby would be . . . in case you decide . . . Come on."

She linked her arm through his and steered him toward the front door.

4

What he was shown was hardly the guesthouse complete with bomb shelter promised by Mr. Knox, nor was it the relique smokehouse he might have expected from Mr. Gatling of Girdletree.

It was more what Howard Johnson might have built had he been in the habit of building his motel units over stables.

The stable, of course, after the invariable fate of stables, had been converted to a garage. The servants' quarters were reached by an outside stairway.

Mrs. Dutton, swaying up the stairway ahead of him in her tight green capri pants, suddenly came to an abrupt halt for no very good reason. The brim of his hat bent double under the impact of its collision with the capri pants. "Sorry," Albert muttered.

"See over there, the new pine trees Mr. Dutton planted last fall," she said, and continued to stand just where she was.

"Yes, mum. Very nice." Albert refocused on the pine trees, which stood no more than a foot high and were barely visible to the naked eye.

"They'll be double that size in another year," she said.

"Yes, pine trees do grow very fast indeed," Albert said, feeling a compulsion to stand either a step higher or two steps lower.

"Well, shall we go on up?" she asked.

"Yes, mum," he said. "Whenever you're ready."

She swayed on up to the top and swung open the door. "Voilà, Mr. Bagby!"

Under different circumstances, he might easily have imagined himself in a Holiday Inn. There were the same double beds facing the same maple, or perhaps walnut, dresser unit, which ran on for miles along one vast wall, with a mirror stretching full length above it. But now, doing a double-take, as it were, he saw that midway in the mirror a section had been cut out, and a sizable window inserted. The framing of the window section had been done so skillfully that it was difficult to tell by the seams where the mirror left off and the window began. The effect was startling and not entirely displeasing, although to one, say, who might be lying drunk abed, it could perhaps be very confusing.

The view through the window section was of the water, and the effect was of a river, a very short river, which had its headwaters in one double bed and emptied into the other.

At each end of the counter unit stood a television set. One was a color set.

Mrs. Dutton snapped on a light. "Isn't it charming?"

"Yes, it's certainly very nice, mum. Very . . . compact. Beautiful use of the space, one might say."

"I think it's just charming," she said. "I think in many ways it's really the way to live. You know . . ." She cocked her head, and the long swish of auburn hair went off in the opposite direction. "Sometimes I just like to come up here, you know, by *myself*, and just enjoy it."

Albert nodded, moving close to the mirror, and then side-slipping to the window section.

"See the river?"

"Yes, mum," Albert said.

"Isn't it beautiful?"

"Yes, it certainly is."

"I love it when the sun comes out late in the afternoon after a dreary day, don't you? See how the sunlight falls on the river?"

Albert nodded.

She had moved up very close behind him and now stood there, looking past his shoulder toward the river. "I think sunlight is so beautiful when there's just a little patch of it and all the rest of the sky is gray, don't you, Mr. Bagby?"

"Yes, mum, I do."

"I love the way the gulls tilt their wings when they fly. See that one? So graceful. It's really such a beautiful river.

In the summer, it's just dotted with sailboats. You have no idea."

"I guess it would be," Albert said.

"Mmmmmmm," she said, and then fell silent. He became acutely aware of the sound of her breathing, and of the fragrance she wore.

"I have a *thing* about motel rooms," she said.

"Yes, mum, they're very nice," Albert said.

She turned away finally, and he did the same. She was bending close to the long mirror, frowning at her reflection, touching a delicate finger to her dark lashes.

"That's the bathroom, of course," she murmured, tossing her head, still facing the mirror.

"Yes, mum," he said.

"It has a wonderful shower."

"Really?" Numbly he wandered toward the bathroom and swung open the door. A flimsy pale blue garment fell to the floor and he bent to retrieve it.

"Oh, here, I'll take it," she said. "That's mine. I forgot I left it here."

"Yes, mum."

"I love this shower so much," she said, "that sometimes I just come up here and stand in it for hours."

"Really?"

"Just letting the water flow over my body."

"Yes," Albert said, drawing back the shower curtain. "That can be very nice."

"It's one of the most sensual things a person can do, don't you agree?"

"Indeed so, and that's a very nice shower-head, mum." It

26

was indeed, a very expensive one, of the sort he had always wished he could afford.

"Let me show you the rest," she caroled, slipping her arm through his.

"The rest?"

"You haven't seen the kitchen yet." She led him beyond the dresser unit, off into the dim recesses of the vast room. "Dining alcove," she said softly. "You like?"

"Yes, mum. Very nice."

"And this is the kitchen." She flipped a light switch and turned to face him, gazing into his eyes with a faint smile. "Electric oven," she murmured.

"Yes," he said, bending and peering intently into the dark interior of the oven.

"Electric dishwasher . . ."

"Yes," Albert said. "Where?"

"Right here." Placing her hands on his shoulders, she turned him ninety degrees.

"Oh, yes, of course, very nice," he said.

"A little bar, with its own sink. Seen enough?"

"Yes, mum. I've seen enough to know that these are certainly very attractive quarters and I think they're a credit to the person who devised such a compact layout."

She flicked off the light. In the near-darkness, he could see only the gleaming glass of the oven door. "The oven cooks just beautifully," she said.

"That's nice," he said.

"The heat is so even. . . ."

"Yes, mum, they say that electric ovens give off very even heat."

"They do," she murmured. "They *do*, Mr. Bagby."

"Very even distribution, so to say."

"Very even," she said. "You see, I've been up here and tried it."

"I see."

"Well . . ." With lingering step, she moved back into the more brightly lit part of the room and stood once more before the mirror. Giving her eyelash a final caress, she turned. "Well! Shall we see what's on television?" She flicked on one of the sets and seated herself on the edge of the bed. "Oh, dear. Cartoons. But you see, the beauty of it . . ." She stretched full length on the bed. "You can watch it from here, and there's one of those remote-control things you can punch to change the channel. You don't ever have to get up. Of course, Jake just hates television and refuses to watch it."

With the remote-control selector panel now in her palm, she pressed it languorously to her cheek, looking at him with a smile. "And look!" Dropping the selector panel, she wriggled toward the other side of the bed. "From here you can lie in bed and see right through the window. You can see the river, the willows, the sunrise, the full moon when it rises . . . everything! Try it!" She patted the bed.

Albert gave her a weak smile. "Yes, mum," he said. "I can tell."

Elevating one long leg, she pointed the ballet slipper at the ceiling. "Oh, darn! Is that Jake calling?" She wriggled her way to the bedside phone and picked it up, then put it down. "Yes. He's off."

She swung open the door and went out to the small landing. "Coming," she called. "I was just showing Mr. Bagby the room."

She came back inside. "Ready?"

"Yes, mum," Albert said.

"There's only one thing wrong with your taking this room, Mr. Bagby," she murmured, moving much closer than seemed necessary for him to hear what she was saying.

"What's that, mum?"

"It means I wouldn't be able to come up here any more, and I just love coming up here. There's nothing I love better than to steal up here in the late afternoons."

"I can see that it would be very peaceful, mum."

"Do you suppose," she murmured, "that you would let me steal up here occasionally . . . or would Mrs. Bagby object?"

"No, mum," Albert said, edging toward the door. "No, mum, I don't really think she'd object at all."

"She wouldn't?" Her eyes widened with delight. "How wonderful! I do think people become more understanding as they grow older, don't you, Mr. Bagby? Are you sure she wouldn't object?"

"To your coming up here, mum?"

"Yes."

"No. Uh . . ." With a weak smile, he waved to Dutton, who stood at the foot of the stairway. Nodding vigorously, he called down, "Very attractive quarters, sir, most attractive."

"Anything else you'd like to see?" Dutton asked.

"No, sir," Albert said, reaching the bottom of the stairway. "No, I think I've seen quite enough for the time being, sir. I think under the circumstances I'd better be getting back now."

"How shall we leave it, then?" Dutton asked. "Will you contact me, or shall I contact you?"

"I'll contact you, sir."

"We didn't get around to salary," Dutton said. "I think I could see my way clear to offering you a thousand a month plus your room and board."

"Plus extras, of course," Mrs. Dutton called from the top of the landing.

"Yes, of course," Dutton said. "One other thing. This is only a formality, so far as I'm concerned, but I want to be businesslike about this. I'd need a reference."

"Yes," Albert said. "Naturally you'd want a reference, sir."

"Where did you last work?"

"In England, sir. We came direct from England. We're Americans, but English-trained, you might say."

"Have you ever worked in this country?"

"Oh, yes sir, for a number of years, sir . . . before we went to England."

"For whom?"

Albert was fully prepared. "For a Mr. Miller, sir. Would you like his address?" He waited while Dutton took a pencil and envelope from his jacket pocket. "That would be Mr. A. W. Miller, sir, and his business address is Suite 902, Monumental Building, Washington, D.C., zip 20005."

"Very good." Dutton put pencil and envelope back into his pocket. He offered his hand, which, after a moment's hesitation, Albert took and clasped firmly. "We hope you'll keep us in mind, then. That thousand a month, by the way . . . you understand, of course, that's the *total*, for the two of you. Five hundred each."

"Oh, of course, sir. I understood that perfectly. Very good."

"I hope we'll see you again then," Dutton said. "I honestly think you would like it here at Rear Guard."

30

"Thank you, sir." Albert looked toward the head of the landing. "Goodbye, mum," he called.

She reared back her head, arching her back. "Until we meet again, Mr. Bagby . . ." she called.

Albert turned then and strode resolutely to his Avis Ford.

5

From his interview with the Duttons, from his day in the misty exurbs, Albert Miller returned home badly shaken on a number of counts.

Most disconcerting of all was Mrs. Dutton. Having given little thought to the human element, he had fully expected to assess his socio-economic loophole in purely socio-economic terms. With Mrs. Dutton representing the human element, he could admit that life would not be dull. She was certainly a live wire and could be counted upon to keep things popping. And that very long dresser unit in the motel room would be an ideal place for Jane to do her typing, with plenty of good light and plenty of counter space to spread out her papers.

On the other hand, there *was* Mrs. Dutton, and Mrs. Dutton was not exactly what he had had in mind when first seized by his *idée fixe*. He was flattered, of course (he! at *his* age!), but he didn't want that kind of trouble, *her* kind of trouble. She, with her habit of standing for hours in the warm shower and letting the water course and flow over her naked body; she with her tight green capri pants and her predilection for pointing one foot at the ceiling. All in all, he felt he would be well advised to look further.

He had, after all, no end of applicants to choose from. He had barely begun to cull. So thinking, he picked another cluster of five, but for the nonce did nothing about them.

Meanwhile at the office, he received the following letter:

Dear Mr. Miller:

Your name has been given as a reference by Mr. Albert Bagby, who has contacted me about the possibility of accepting employment in my home. Under the terms of our discussion, Mr. Bagby and his wife, if all goes well, would serve as a "live-in" couple. It is my understanding that Mr. and Mrs. Bagby once served you in a similar capacity and I would very much appreciate it if you would be good enough to drop me a line letting me know your opinion of them. I am particularly interested, of course, in their honesty and general moral rectitude, as well as some indication of their capacities and efficiency, also their health. May I hear from you at your convenience? I would be most grateful.

Yours sincerely,

J. K. Dutton

The following day, Albert replied as follows:

Dear Mr. Dutton:

I am happy to comply with your request of March 30th concerning the Bagbys. There is perhaps no better way to express it than to say that we always regarded Mr. and Mrs. Bagby as members of the family. We have for them only the very highest regard. Their honesty we found always beyond question and their moral rectitude of the highest order. Mr. Bagby is a man of many and diverse skills and of bulldog pertinacity. He is conscientious almost to a fault and mixes, moreover, an outstanding martini. If I were to harbor any reservations whatever, it might be to note that Mrs. Bagby, for all her many attractive qualities, is not at her best in the morning hours. On the other hand, once started, she performs with efficiency and speed, albeit occasionally with an air of distraction. She is, moreover, healthy as a horse, as is her husband. We feel they would serve you competently and conscientiously, and in these days of shortage, who could ask more? I might add in closing that both Bagbys have charming manners, derived doubtless from their years of service in England.

If further information is desired, I would be happy to hear from you.

Very truly yours,
A. W. *Miller*

Albert typed the letter himself and dropped it into the mailbox with something very close to a shudder. He realized that he might very well be going too far.

33

The following morning, he received a telephone call from the manager of the classified-ad section of the morning newspaper, who began the conversation by saying:

"Mr. Miller? Congratulations!"

"What for?" Albert asked warily.

"You've been selected as one of the three classified-ad users we'd like to mention on the radio in one of our spot commercials, Mr. Miller. We understand that at last count you received something over two hundred replies to your ad in Situations Wanted for a job as a live-in couple. Have you made your choice yet, sir?"

"No. I haven't."

"What we'd like to do, Mr. Miller, with your permission, of course, is to run a spot something to the effect of: Wanted —two hundred and three live-in couples to take care of the two hundred and three unsuccessful homeowners who—"

"No," Albert said firmly. "Absolutely not."

"But, sir—"

"Actually, I didn't even place that ad for myself. I placed it for an Hungarian friend of the family who doesn't speak very good English—a Mr. Bagbeiyvich. He's very sensitive. I'm sure he wouldn't want the publicity."

"Do you mind if I approach Mr.—what was his name again?"

"Bagbeiyvich."

"Do you mind if I approach him personally? Do you have a number where he can be reached?"

"No. No number. Just between you and me, he doesn't want the Russians to know he's even in this country. Some trouble in Hungary involving one of his relatives." Albert took a deep breath. His voice increased in resonance. "You'd be doing him a disservice. You might even be responsible for getting somebody shot."

"In that case—"

"That's one of the reasons we have such a bad reputation with Europeans. Everything for the almighty dollar."

"All right, sir. I'll let it drop. I understand perfectly. Very sorry."

Albert hung up, badly shaken, ready to give it all up before he reached a point from which there might be no turning back.

But in no time at all, he was asking himself why. Wasn't that exactly the point that he had wanted to reach?

In his mind's eye, he kept thinking of Rear Guard, collecting all his many visual impressions and seeing, even though in blurred detail, an emerald isle, mint-green, spring-fresh, a veritable Camelot, with its willows lining the banks, dipping their barely fuzzed-out fronds into the river; the freshly painted white house and the white outbuildings; the swimming pool, still covered for winter, but ready, all of it, a huge pleasure-dome, ready and waiting, bursting to break the fetters of winter, bursting to meet the spring, for in warm weather it would come into its own.

He could not easily forget the way the streaks of sunlight had raced ahead of him up the lane, skimming along the honeysuckle, already leafing out along the fence; lighting the way like so many darting arrows pointing to the graceful white house at the head of the lane, and to the water flowing in disparate trickles and confluent gleaming rivulets over her naked body as she stood hour upon hour in the shower.

Nor could he forget the way the river had looked through

35

the inserted window when the sun came out again, the beautiful combination of light and shadow created by the pool of sunlight on the river, and the heavily banked clouds which covered the rest of the sky, giving off a deep purple backdrop for the one spot the sun had found. It was as though even the sun had singled out Rear Guard. It was very much like an omen.

Never, moreover, would he forget the infamous day a little more than two months ago, the day in mid-January, when, under the chilling impact of near-zero weather, one of his hot-water pipes froze and burst. At the moment of rupture, he had just finished spreading out a fantastic array of bills on the desk he used at home, Christmas bills and other bills, along with reminders from attentive federal and state governments that on January 15 he would owe both state and nation a payment on his income tax. The pipe had frozen during the night and he was warming it with a portable heater, hoping that it would thaw before it burst. Hearing the telltale trickle of water splattering on linoleum, he had, in a moment of rare rage and frustration, swept all the bills and tax reminders to the floor and jumped up and down on them.

He had been both alarmed and ashamed. Was he to spend his remaining years becoming increasingly vituperative and rancid? Was he to become, in the end, little better than a churlish old son of a bitch?

Now, more than two months later, he asked himself again: Was not the point of no return exactly the point to be wished for?

Up the stairs he climbed. Jane was wearing her glasses, tapping away at the keys.

"Jane, listen . . ."

No reply.

"I've decided to sell the house."

The fingers of both hands went to her mouth, and she stared at the page in her typewriter.

"The house, the business, sell everything . . ."

She looked at him blankly and then at the ceiling.

"Okay?"

She nodded.

"I've decided you and I are going to work as a live-in couple."

Her hands went to the keys and began to move swiftly.

"Okay?"

"Fine," she said. "I'll be through in a little while."

He looked over her shoulder and read:

His heavy-lidded eyes drooped. The long finger of gray ash fell from the end of his cigar and spilled over the vest of his best blue suit, but he dozed on, a man emasculated by fate, by circumstance, by family. It was Sunday afternoon in Queens. Somnolent Sunday.

"A live-in couple," Albert said. "Okay?"

"Yes," Jane said.

"I'd have somebody take the cigar out of his hand. He'll burn himself up, for God's sake."

Jane's fingers were fairly flying.

It was, of course, not quite ethical, and not yet conclusive. He would have to await one of her lucid moments, when she was ready to re-compartmentalize.

37

Toward eleven o'clock, ready to re-compartmentalize, she came downstairs and staggered into the kitchen for the nip of Scotch that would allow her to sleep, that would break the spell of Sunday in Queens and return her to Thursday night in Bethesda.

She was groping for an ice cube when he entered the kitchen and told her how glad he was that they had decided to give up their home and take jobs as a live-in couple at a place called Rear Guard.

6

"Now wait a minute," he said.

With her glasses now off, her trance was gone. She was living the moment, the here and now, dark eyes flashing, lips moving with a wonderful muscular swiftness.

"Hold on," Albert said, marveling at the way her words ran together. "Come on. Bring your drink into the living room. There's no need to get excited."

"Idhdoois andoidle odidhgl-tahexcited. *Excited?*"

"Calm down. Let's talk it over."

Giving him a malignant, sidelong glance, she allowed herself to be led into the living room, where she sat down, clutching her Scotch. "Honestly, Albert," she said. "I do think you've lost your mind."

He smiled.

"*Have* you?"

"No," he said.

"If you think for a minute I'm going to be somebody's *maid*, you must have lost your mind. Do I look like somebody's maid?"

Sadly he shook his head.

"Jane, Jane," he chided. "That's really one of the most snobbish things I've ever heard you say. I don't like to hear you talk that way. There are people in this country who've spent their entire lives working as maids, decent people doing an honest day's work, doing their best to support their families. Really, are you that much of a snob? I *mean*. To say you don't *want* to be a maid, that's *one* thing. But to ask in that haughty, superior voice whether you look like somebody's maid—that disappoints me."

"Hah!" she said bitterly.

"Is that all you have to say for yourself?"

"I have plenty to say for myself . . . or I would have if I thought for a minute you were serious. Sell the house? You, give up your business? To go work as somebody's *handyman*?"

Albert grinned.

Perched on the black velvet sofa, Jane pouted. She wore her customary writing outfit—black slacks and white cardigan. Her face was winter-pallid, and with her dark eyebrows and thick dark lashes and her loosely fashioned helmet of dark hair, she made a glum study in black and white.

She sipped her Scotch and continued to pout. There was no sound in the room now but the stately, measured tick of the grandfather clock which once, because of faulty underpinning, had fallen flat on its face and shattered. Skilled cabinetmakers had restored it for $165.50.

"I'm going to bed," she said. "I'm tired."

"You don't want to hear me out?"

"I've already heard you out. I've heard enough to know you can't possibly be serious."

"The surprising thing," he said, "is that I *am* serious. I've thought about it very carefully. I've considered it from every angle. If you'll look at it with an open mind and stop yelling and screaming, you'll see that it makes a great deal of sense. Actually, it's sort of a discovery, and I'm rather proud of myself for thinking of it."

"Somebody already thought of it," she said. "In *Tovarich*."

"The compartments of your life are mainly three—writing, housework and recreation. The compartments of *my* life—"

She wasn't listening. "We'd *live*—on a maid's salary, a handyman's salary?"

"We'd get a thousand bucks a month."

"Who in their right mind would pay us a thousand dollars a month?"

"A man named Jake Dutton would."

For the first time, she seemed to be giving him her serious attention. "Albert," she said, tilting her head, "do you honestly mean that you've talked to somebody about this?"

"Yes, a man named Jake Dutton. And—Mrs. Dutton."

"You *applied*? For a *job*?"

"I haven't committed myself yet. I didn't think it was fair to commit myself until I talked it over with you. Look, Jane. Let me tell you something. Nothing is in such short

40

supply as live-in couples. And among the rich, nothing is so highly prized. It's a matter of basic economics. Why shouldn't we be important if we have the chance?"

"You'd give up your life's work?"

"Gladly."

"And the house we've loved?"

"The house is killing me. Draining me, financially, physically, and spiritually. It's a nice house. So what? You should see the room we'd have."

"Where?"

"At Rear Guard. It's an exact replica of a large motel room. It has a long counter where you could do your writing, plenty of space for your typewriter and your papers—"

"When on earth would I have time if I was somebody's maid?"

"You'd have plenty of time. That would be part of the deal. You don't seem to realize. We can call the *tune.*"

"You mean you've actually *been* there?"

"Yes. If you'll just keep quiet for a couple of seconds, I'll tell you."

While her attitude changed from one of disbelief to one of curiosity and then to outright interest and back once more to scorn, he told her everything, leaving out only the allure of Mrs. Dutton.

"Now then," he said. "Let's take the compartments of *my* life. As presently constituted."

"Why does he call it Rear Guard? It sounds like a deodorant."

"That's his problem. It's because he thinks he's fighting a

rear-guard action against a world he's retreated from, because he doesn't like it."

"That's what you'd be doing too. Retreating."

"So what? Actually, if you want to know the truth, I'm doing all this in kind of a cold fury."

"How would you like to get me a little more Scotch?"

He took her glass. "Think of the thrill of *use* without ownership!" he called back on his way to the kitchen.

"That sounds communistic."

"It does not. It sounds like common sense." Returning, he handed her the glass.

"Albert, Albert," she said.

"I'd feel released," he said. "I'm very tired of the treadmill, Jane. Very very tired. At first, I'll admit I felt the same way you do about it, but then it began to make eminent sense. As I see it, the compartments of my life are actually three—"

"What would Beverly say?"

"For God's sake, will you let me tell you about the compartments?"

"Where would she spend her vacations? In the servants' quarters? Going to an expensive college and coming home to the servants' quarters!"

"So what? Beverly has good values. Besides, she'll be graduating in another year. Listen, kids nowadays don't have the values *we* were raised on. In many ways, they're a lot smarter."

"Decorating our Christmas tree—in the *servants' quarters?*"

"If you could just *see* that place . . ."

"Right Guard?"

"*Rear* Guard, dammit. If you could just see it, you'd realize it would be *no* hardship to live there, believe me. Or for Beverly to come home there. What difference would it make who owned it? Now I run my business at the office, do a handyman's job at home, and my third compartment is the same as yours—recreation. What I'm trying to say is that down there we'd both have the same compartments that we have here. We'd live just as well if not better, and we wouldn't have to *own* anything."

"Well . . ." She finished her drink. "I'm going to bed. The whole thing is just too ridiculous even to talk about."

He walked over to the sofa and put his hand on her head. "I realize it's not easy to absorb something so radical as this in one night, Jane. What I'd like you to do is think it over for a few days and see what happens. If you refuse, then of course I'll give it up. I'll do my best to keep going . . . but . . ."

"But *what?*"

"I'm afraid you may not have me much longer."

Jane burst out laughing. "Oh, Albert. Don't be ridiculous, Albert. You sound like something out of a bad third act."

"Okay," he said bitterly.

"There's nothing in the world wrong with you."

"How would *you* know?" he demanded. "In a trance at that typewriter. Hell, I could be walking around half-dead and you'd never even notice."

She frowned. He had hit her where her guilt was.

"Of course," he went on sadly, "maybe everybody would be better off. At least you'd have the life-insurance money, and you'd be able to live a very good life, all in all."

"Albert! What are you *talking* about?"

43

"It's nothing definitive," he said. "But I thought it best to talk it over with the doctor."

"The *doctor?*" She clutched his hand.

"I didn't want to bother you with it."

"What did the doctor *say?*"

"He said it was probably nothing more serious than hypertension."

"What *was* it?"

"Sort of a prickling of the scalp."

"Your scalp prickles?"

"A good deal of the time, yes . . . but the doctor said it was a fairly common syndrome. Sort of a treadmill syndrome, he called it. Well . . ." He smiled regretfully. "Maybe on your next book you could write a story about *my* life."

"Albert!"

"It's okay, Jane. I thought I saw a way out. I saw a way of continuing to give you a good life, one where you wouldn't have to work any harder than you work now, one where you could write just as you've always written, and one where you'd live in a home far more beautiful than anything I've ever been able to give you. At the same time trying to ease some of the pressure on myself."

He got to his feet. "It was a nice dream, but I guess it won't work. Okay." He pulled her to her feet and kissed her gently on the brow. "It's okay. Dear."

"Albert, that scalp business *worries* me."

"It's nothing—oooh!" He touched his head lightly.

"Albert! What's wrong?"

He shook his head. "Nothing, really. It's not actual *pain.* It's—different."

"In what way different?"

44

"The doctor—I mean the *medical* doctor—said he didn't think it was exactly organic."

"The *medical* doctor? What other kind did you see?"

"*You* know."

"Psychiatrist?"

He nodded. "Just exploratory. Just a session or two. He said it was not uncommon, in fact that it was getting *more* common all the time. Treadmill syndrome. Caused by a feeling of never getting anywhere. Just barely making ends meet. A sort of perpetual brinksmanship. There's such a feeling of stagnation about it that, according to him, outright failure is often more therapeutic. There at least the bubble ruptures. But—" Albert shrugged.

"What did he say the cure was?"

"All depends. Changing jobs maybe. Or moving to different surroundings. In short, getting out from under. But of course, as the psychiatrist says, many wives don't really want their husbands to get out from under. The C.I., this guy called it."

"What's C.I.?"

"Castration Impulse. A wife can castrate her husband just as effectively with a heavy mortgage, liens on the cars, chairs that need gluing, as she can . . . in some other way. I told him you weren't that kind of person. And that you couldn't *possibly* be. Because you had seen it happen to your own father."

Tenderly he touched his head and then yawned. "I'm sleepy," he said. "Coming up?"

7

It was on the last Thursday of April that Albert and Jane Bagby crossed the Chesapeake Bay Bridge and headed off in a southeasterly direction to begin their new life at Rear Guard.

They traveled in a newly acquired secondhand Ford station wagon, its back piled high with such chattels as they had decided to retain, among them Jane's portable typewriter, a carton filled with her manuscript, their clothing, and various other personalty too trivial to mention.

Albert's preparations had been simple, direct, in some cases sketchy, in others downright slovenly. Yet such was his air of abandon that he didn't really care. What would happen would happen, he assured himself.

When he telephoned Dutton to accept the job, he drove what he considered to be a hard bargain, mostly for the benefit of Jane. Jane would have her mornings free (to sleep) and her evenings free (to write). Jane would be responsible for only one meal a day—the evening meal. During the afternoons, she would do some light housework.

All this was perfectly acceptable to Dutton.

"Would you like to meet Jane before we close the deal, sir?" Albert asked. "Would you like me to drive her over?"

46

"That won't be necessary," Dutton said. "We received a very glowing recommendation from your former employer."

"Thank you, sir," Albert said. "That's always nice to know."

With single-minded determination that at times seemed hysterical, Albert set about the task of winding up his affairs. First off, he traded both Buick and Thunderbird on the more self-effacing Ford, clearing both liens and coming out of the deal with a lien-free station wagon plus $247.25. Abruptly, for the first time since 1946, he no longer had car notes to pay each month. Even though the titles had borne his name, he realized that he had never really owned his cars. In company with most other Americans, he had merely rented them from various banks.

Most of their furniture was sold through an auction house, although a few pieces which Beverly might want someday were put in storage. From the sale of the furniture, he realized a cash return of $1,701.33, a pittance, but the house more than made up for it.

The house—to think of the house was to feel a glad song bubbling at one's lips. He had bought the house in 1952 for $40,000, of which he still owed the bank roughly $17,000. It was a good solid house of brick, painted white, splendidly maintained, and over the years he was well aware that its value had increased. Yet he was totally unprepared for the asking price suggested by the real-estate broker, namely $125,000. Albert was skeptical. "No problem," the broker assured him. "*Brick?* In *this* neighborhood? Pure gold." The house was first listed on a Sunday and sold two days later for the full asking price. Settlement was set for May 29, still a long way off, but by dusk of May 29 he would, after paying off the mortgage and commission, have in his willing hands somewhere in the magnificent neighborhood of $100,000 cash, more than he had ever dreamed of possessing.

With a reckless confidence inspired by the house deal, he tossed away his business for a trifling sum, glad to be rid of it. The senior of his secretaries, a Mrs. Jarboe, self-styled office backbone and wife of a haberdasher, had been with him almost fifteen years and knew his customers better than he did himself. She seldom lost an opportunity, particularly when asking for raises, to claim that she could, if necessary, handle the business alone. Now she had her opportunity. With Mrs. Jarboe and her husband, Albert signed an agreement to sell them the business in return for a share of the profits made during their first year of operation.

After a cocktail party given in their honor, Jane and Albert had a brief discussion, hardly an argument, concerning whether there were ten people they would miss, as Jane maintained, or merely four. More to be missed in Albert's view were the large number of movie houses which city living afforded, and as the time for departure drew near, he took himself off to a movie almost every night, in the manner of a man for whom, cinematically, there would be no tomorrow.

The story they told was that they were about to embark

upon extensive travels, first to Madagascar to permit Albert to indulge a lifelong interest in the lemur and the unique "crossroads" position it occupied in the animal kingdom.

Telling Beverly was a problem that he approached with some delicacy. "We have made a huge decision," he wrote. "One you may think rather strange, but on the other hand maybe the message of *your* generation is finally getting through to us. House-pride, we realize now, is false pride. We saw ourselves in the end as a pair of money-grubbing pawns, living for *things*, chained to possessions, getting more neurotic with each passing year. Isn't the younger generation right after all? I asked myself the question and the answer was yes. The important things are things of the spirit— freedom and love and so forth. In our new life we will own nothing except your mother's typewriter and a few clothes and an old car. We will be employed, more or less, as a live-in couple on a beautiful estate. Does this bother you, Bev? Will it worry you to think of your mother as a maid and your father as a handyman? I have great faith in your sense of values. And it may be of interest for you to know that as maid and handyman we will be far better off than ever before. In fact, thanks to the house sale, we'll be downright wealthy.

"Rear Guard is truly beautiful," he went on, "and we want you to see it. Maybe some weekend you could come up to visit us—if it wouldn't embarrass you. For that matter, you may want to spend part of your summer with us. One final thing. Taking a new life, we decided to take on a new identity as well, at least while we have our new job. We decided

49

to be called Mr. and Mrs. Bagby, because Bagby is your mother's maiden name, of course, and Jane Bagby is the name under which she will someday, God willing, publish her novel about your grandfather. So when you begin to write us at Rear Guard, please don't forget to address your letters to Mr. and Mrs. Albert Bagby. And if you come see us, you, of course, will be Beverly Bagby. . . ."

The next evening there was a collect phone call.

"Beverly Bagby! *Beverly Bagby?* That's one of the most horrible-sounding names I've ever heard in my life! Couldn't you have picked something else?"

"Is that all you have to say?" Albert asked.

"I think you're both crazy," Beverly said. "What do you think you are—a couple of flower children?"

"Flower children . . ." Albert chuckled as they sped down the dual highway into the twilight. In spite of her protests, he felt that Beverly rather admired what they were doing, although she would not admit it. Such was the perversity of youth, as Jane had observed earlier in the week, when she was still communicating. Now she drooped against the door, riding in silence, with the attitude of one nursing grave doubts. "Do you feel like a flower child?" Albert asked.

"I don't know *what* I feel like," Jane said sourly.

"Come on now, Jane. Chin up."

She slumped lower and then sat abruptly bolt upright. "Oh, *Albert*," she said, wincing. "What are we *doing?* What in the name of God are we *doing?*"

"It's perfectly simple," he said. "We're driving down to Rear Guard. We're going to spend tomorrow and Saturday and Sunday getting settled, and then on Monday we're going to begin work as a live-in couple. If it doesn't work out, we'll quit."

"Where will we go? We won't have any house or furniture or *anything*."

"We can buy another house. Anywhere. In another month, we'll be loaded. One hundred thousand bucks."

"I *liked* the Thunderbird. I *loved* it. I don't see why you had to sell it. With all the money we're going to have."

"Because it wasn't appropriate to our station in life," he replied. "How would it look—driving up in a *Thunderbird?*"

"Oh, the hell with how it would look. If you think I'm going to go around kowtowing to these people you're crazy, Albert. If they so much as look at me crooked, I'm warning you—I'll quit and expose you."

He chuckled. "Repeat after me . . . 'Good morning, Mrs. Dutton, mum, and how would you like your eggs this morning, mum?'"

"*No!*" Jane flounced about in the seat, stamping her heels rapidly against the floorboard. "Not one egg! Not one breakfast! I thought that was agreed!"

"Of course it is. They understand that." He patted her hand. "Just wait until you see the place, you'll love it. And on Sunday, Daylight Saving Time starts. Only three days to go."

"Oh, God!" she said wearily. "I don't understand about you and Daylight Saving Time. You'd think it was the first Sunday of Advent!"

"You'll love Rear Guard," he said. "Just wait till you see it."

When they arrived, it was far too dark, as Jane was quick to point out, to see much of anything at all. As they moved slowly up the driveway, he inhaled deeply. "Ummmmm," he said. "Smell the honeysuckle. . . ."

"I don't smell a thing," Jane said. "It's too early for honeysuckle. Honeysuckle doesn't come out until June."

The house, for some reason looked rather bleak, perhaps merely because it was dark. A single light burned downstairs. The parking lot was empty.

"Welcome," Jane said bitterly.

Albert approached the front door and knocked lightly.

"There's *obviously* nobody home," Jane called.

He turned away and climbed back into the car. "Well, there's no law that says they have to stay home at night, is there? What's gotten into you? You agreed. You made a bargain."

"Okay, so I made a bargain. So now I'm bitter."

"I don't quite understand why both cars should be gone though," he mused.

"What kind of cars do they have?"

"A Bentley and a . . ."

"And a what?"

"Thunderbird."

"Damn!"

Starting the engine, Albert drove slowly over to the garage area and got out. "Oh," he said. "The Thunderbird's in the garage."

"Wonderful," Jane said. "Now that that's settled—this! Is where we're going to *live?*"

"Up there," he said, pointing.

"God, Albert!"

"Come on, we'll unload later." He paused. "I wonder if they left it unlocked."

"You'll soon know."

He led the way up the flight of steps on which Mrs. Dutton had paused so fetchingly.

A note was thumbtacked to the door. He lit a match. "Walk in," it said.

He shoved open the door and switched on a light.

On the counter, before the mirror, stood a vase of flowers, with another note:

"Hi! Welcome! We're out for the evening! See you tomorrow! Make yourselves at home!"

It was signed, "The Duttons."

"Isn't that nice?" Albert asked.

"Peachy. I wonder why they didn't put an exclamation mark after their name. They must have run out." Hands on hips, Jane swept the room with a jaundiced eye.

"How do you like it?"

She shrugged. "What's our number?"

"You've never objected to motel rooms."

"I think they're fine for spending the night in."

"Look in here." He led the way to the dining alcove and the kitchenette. "Look, they even bought us a can of coffee."

"You say it so lovingly." Jane strayed back into the bedroom.

"It's not bad, you've gotta admit."

"It's clean. That's all I'll admit."

"Furniture's not bad, do you think?"

"Not bad if you like Howard Johnson Modern. If you happen to be hooked on HoJoMo."

He laughed.

"Don't laugh," Jane said.

"Here's the bathroom," he said, giving the shower a quick, covert glance, as if half expecting to see her there, yielding her body to the warm spray. "Well," he said, "I'll unpack the car. You rest. Watch TV or something."

In the first load he brought her typewriter, which he opened and set upon the dressing counter, even plugging it in for her, while she glowered from the edge of one of the huge double beds.

"What's wrong?" he asked.

"I think I feel a castration impulse coming on."

Laughing, he went out again, returning this time with her box of manuscript. "You could even write a little, Jane. Just to get the feel of the place."

"At this hour? Are you crazy, Albert?"

When he returned with the first suitcase, she was standing at the counter, reading a page of manuscript which she had taken from the box.

Two suitcases and one umbrella later, she had pulled up a chair and put on her glasses.

"Not too tired?" he asked pleasantly.

"I'm not going to write. I just want to see something."

The last thing to come out of the car was her wig box. Wearily carrying it up the stairway, he heard the chatter of keys.

"Where do you want this wig?" he asked.

"Okay," she replied.

"I'm tired," he said. "I'm going to bed."

There was no reply.

Albert awoke early. The sun was barely up, just high enough to send first rays over the ledge of the inserted picture window. In the adjoining mirror, he could see the reflection of Jane's dark head, burrowed between two pillows in the other double bed. The sun's rays probed at the back of her neck.

There was a yellow page curled in her typewriter. Next to the typewriter were her glasses and an ashtray filled with half-smoked butts, a familiar enough still-life.

Rising on one elbow, he looked through the window and felt a touch of glory. Behind a distant rim of trees, the horizon was a blaze of red. I own no house, he thought and bounded from bed, dressing quickly and hurrying outside.

The air rushed into his nostrils, sweet and liquid. A mist overhung the river, and the willows standing along the bank were graceful, drooping silhouettes, nearly black against the sun, and totally without motion in the still morning air. He followed the shoreline, tracing its indentations and curves, pausing now and then to take a deep breath of the pure air, stopping to sniff and to listen. The water lapped the shore in a steady, gentle rhythm. Listening intently, he thought that he could even hear the steam, the moisture, being sucked by the sun from the mud along the shore. Now he could hear the tiny hum of invisible insects and wondered if the daffodils gave sound as they opened their petals and turned to the sun. A gull wheeled and soared high above the mist. Not ten feet from where he stood, a heron rose with its peculiar rasping croak—and went croaking low over the water, disappearing into the sun.

Albert breathed deeply and grinned with exultation. He found a white bench near the bank of the river and sat there for a long while, until the sun had burned away the mist.

Heading back to his room, he passed close to the main house, and although he kept his eyes discreetly cast down, he could not help catching a glimpse of a first-floor bedroom with a tiger-skin rug. I suppose, he thought acidly, that in her idle moments she lies there on the tiger skin—naked, likely as not.

Noticing that the Bentley was now in the garage, he went on with his tour of the property. The swimming pool was still covered with a huge green plastic netting, but there were signs of preparation nonetheless. Peering through the window of the poolhouse, he saw that it had been cleaned. Furniture was scattered about and there was even a bottle of whiskey on the bar. A ping-pong table stood against one wall, and two large studio couches were set at right angles, ready to double as sleeping accommodations if the occasion arose.

Finally he climbed back up to his room. Jane still slept. Remembering the coffee the Duttons had so thoughtfully provided, he started a pot brewing and was about to turn back to the bedroom when he heard footsteps on the stairway and then a gentle knock.

Jane's eyes popped open. "Oh, my God!" she whispered.

"They're here!" he whispered in reply. "Get up!"

Lunging from bed, she grabbed her robe and staggered into the bathroom.

After glancing quickly at himself in the mirror and pushing back the hair at his temples, Albert flung open the door.

There on the landing, facing him, was a middle-aged woman with white hair and sharp patrician features. At her elbow stood a smiling J. K. Dutton.

"Good morning, good morning," Dutton said jovially.

"Come in," Albert said, trying not to feel mystified.

"We don't want to disturb you," the woman said. "We just wanted to say welcome and good morning." She sniffed. "I see you found the coffee."

"Yes," Albert said. "Thank you. Uh . . ." He turned. "Jane . . ."

"Coming," Jane trilled.

The bathroom door opened, and there stood Jane, simpering with good will.

"My wife, Jane," Albert said.

"Good morning, good morning," Dutton said.

"So nice to meet you," Jane said.

"And *my* wife, Mrs. Dutton," said Dutton.

"Frances Dutton," said the white-haired lady, offering her hand.

Albert moved back a step and set about the job of composing himself. For the briefest of moments, Dutton's eyes met his. Was it a twinkle he saw in Dutton's pale blue eyes? He stared down at the parking lot, at the hood of his humble secondhand, lien-free station wagon. The chrome twinkled in the early-morning sunlight.

8

Albert spent the next hour with his thoughts, reliving the occasion of his first visit to Rear Guard on a cloudy day in March.

"What?"

Jane was looking at him curiously across the dinette table. "I asked if you'd like some more coffee."

He shook his head. "No, thanks. I think I'll walk around outside a little."

Wandering along the shoreline, he was forced to concede that never once during his visit in March had the girl with auburn hair been introduced as Mrs. Dutton, nor even *addressed* as Mrs. Dutton. She had called Dutton *Jake*, that much Albert clearly remembered ("Don't open a vein, Jake . . ."), but Dutton had not called *her* anything.

Even so, he was sure it had been planned. It was a vast deceit of some kind, and he had been its willing victim, gulled by his own sense of importance. Dutton had played it smart. Relying on the frailty of middle-aged man, he had schemed well and won.

Obviously there was no limit to what some people would do to get domestic help.

Albert grinned. Irritated though he was to have been

duped, he could not avoid feeling some admiration for the old bastard. It had been a good scheme. Dutton knew, or at least could gamble, that Albert must keep his mouth shut. It was hardly something he could complain about—not to Dutton and certainly not to Jane.

Maybe it was all for the best. *He*—at *his* age. In the end, it could only have led to trouble.

Sitting on the white bench in the sunlight, he reminded himself that his original plan had been to find a socio-economic gimmick, not an escapade with his employer's wife. He must not let it spoil things. He must carry on as if nothing had happened. Above all, he must not mention it to Dutton. He could not give Dutton the satisfaction of flinching.

Yet a certain element of mystery remained. What, for example, had been the *real* Mrs. Dutton's role? Had she been in on it? Perhaps with a few guarded questions . . .

His opportunity to probe was not long in coming, for, as he sat there on the bench, staring over the brilliant, rippled blue of the river, he saw Mrs. Dutton approaching over the lawn.

She joined him on the bench and said with a sigh of contentment, "I just love to sit here and watch the gulls floating on the water, and the boats passing. I've often told myself, Mr. Bagby, that if a person can't be happy here, surely it would be impossible to be happy anywhere. I do hope that you and Mrs. Bagby will be very happy with us."

"Yes mum, I'm sure we will be. . . . You know the day I came down in March—the very first day I ever came to Rear Guard . . ."

"Yes?"

"I liked it from the very first," he said, watching her eyes.

She nodded, looking out over the water. "Yes," she said, and her reply was easy and natural. "I wasn't here, of course. I was in New York that week, doing some shopping and seeing some shows. I can never get Mr. Dutton to go with me."

"I see."

"*Actually*," she went on, "I didn't even *know* about you until I got home and Jake told me about seeing your ad in the paper and how he had written you and you'd come down to interview him. Then we were both so afraid you would choose someone else. I'm so very glad you chose us." She smiled warmly.

"I am too, mum."

He found himself believing her. She didn't seem the sort of woman who would stoop to such a trick. She was clearly a woman of grace and charm and he liked her immediately. At the same time that he might glance at her thinning, carefully coiffed white hair and wish it might be a long auburn fall, at the same time that he noticed her sparsely lashed blue eyes and her rather angular body, he could still warm to her dignity. As a young girl, she could not have been very alluring, yet age had given her a softness and serenity, a patrician thoroughbred bearing, that made her pleasant to look at.

She was telling him again how glad she was that he and Jane had come, and how very much it meant to her husband, who had worked so very hard all his life and was determined to enjoy his retirement which, so far, he had not enjoyed at all, not in the entire seven months.

60

"You and Mr. Dutton have only been here seven months?" Albert asked.

"Yes," she said. "We moved in last October. You see, Mr. Dutton did not retire from his plastics business until November, and the first month we were down here he had to spend going back and forth to New Jersey. For a while there, before we found you and Mrs. Bagby, we were almost ready to call it quits—which would have broken my heart and Mr. Dutton's too, and might even have had a bad effect upon him psychologically, because he feels he *deserves* a happy retirement."

She was looking out over the river with an extremely wistful expression. "I feel he deserves one too," she said. "And that's another thing about having you, Mr. Bagby. My husband has never been a man to have a great number of friends, and I feel you will be not only a helper but a companion to him."

"Yes, mum." Albert turned. A car had just driven up.

Mrs. Dutton looked over her shoulder. "Oh, there's Nicky."

"Nicky?"

"Our nephew. He works in Washington for the government and often comes down for the weekend. He'll be around a great deal, an awfully nice young man. If you'll excuse me, please, I'll go say hello."

Albert slumped lower, closing his eyes and letting the late April sun caress his face. The morning passed. Presently he heard a rustling sound. Dutton was advancing toward the bench, pausing to scuff the ground and then coming on once more. He had rather small feet, shod in blue sneakers, a shade lighter than his blue blazer. "Well!" he said. "Taking the sun?"

"Yep." Albert nodded. Once more he was aware of the twinkle in Dutton's eye, the faint smirk of victory, and was amused by it. Dutton jerked his head toward the parking lot. "My nevvew. Nick. Nice boy, except for his crazy ideas."

Albert said nothing.

"Lots of damn-fool doctrinaire liberal ideas he picked up somewhere, certainly not from me or his father."

Albert nodded.

"There's a boy who'll be worth millions someday and all he cares about are causes—some of the craziest things you ever heard of."

"I see," Albert said.

"Underdogs and so forth. Do you know how to work a chain saw?"

"I've used one, yes."

"Come on over to the toolhouse a second."

Dutton started off and Albert, after a second or two, followed, muttering to himself.

The toolhouse was a small white outbuilding next to the poolhouse. On the way, they crossed the parking lot, where a small black sports car, a Triumph, glittered in the sunlight, side by side with Albert's humble tan station wagon.

The toolhouse was well equipped but sloppily kept, with expensive tools strewn over a workbench and even on the cement floor. What Dutton wanted to show him was a chain saw, obviously brand-new, with its chain dangling and long jagged scars in the shiny red paint of its motor housing.

62

"See if you can get that chain back on, would you mind?" Dutton said, and left.

Albert glared after him, acutely aware that he did not begin work officially until Monday. Then, challenged, he spent fifteen happy minutes getting the chain back on and properly tightened. After lunch, humming to himself, he spent another hour and a half rearranging the tools. The toolhouse had a lovely smell of dampness, lubricating oil, and steel.

When he went outside again, he saw a tall, slim young man in khaki work pants and a blue denim shirt, hosing down the sports car. Hearing Albert, he looked up and smiled warmly. "You must be Mr. Bagby," he said. "How do you do, sir? I'm Nick Dutton."

His handclasp was overpowering, his eyes small, dark, and friendly, his nose thin, and his dark hair parted on the side and molded close to his head, giving the impression of a cap, just as Dutton's did. His face was already deeply tanned, although it was not yet May, and his forearms, beneath the short sleeves of the blue shirt, looked surprisingly muscular. He was actually, Albert thought, not a bad-looking boy, considering he was Dutton's nephew.

Albert acknowledged the introduction, spoke a few words of admiration for the sports car, and strayed off toward the stairway that led up to his room—from which now he could hear the sound of rapid typing.

"Nice to meet you, sir."

Albert turned and nodded and then, for a brief second, stared, hardly willing to believe what he saw.

Nick was looking at him with what was unmistakably a look of sympathy—and even of deep compassion.

63

Frowning, he went on up to his room, tried unsuccessfully to engage Jane in conversation and then, looking from the window, saw that Nick had trained the hose on the station wagon and was washing it for him.

"Thanks," Albert called from the window.

Nick grinned, squinting up at the window. "Glad to do it, sir. You know, this is actually a very nice-looking wagon. It looks to be in wonderful condition. Terrific paint job."

With a rag in one hand and the hose in the other, Nick crouched and began scrubbing at the wheels.

Albert withdrew from the window, shaking his head. "Do you realize something?" he said to Jane. "That little son of a bitch *pities* me. He actually pities me and I think he also pities our car."

"Yes. All right." Briefly Jane stopped typing. "Oh . . . Beverly called."

"What? When?"

There was no answer. The typing resumed. Gently but firmly, he removed her glasses. She looked up at him with a blank stare, indicating, no doubt, her great surprise to find that he was not an ice-cream parlor in Queens.

Then she got up from the typewriter. "She's coming to see us tomorrow. She got a ride and— What's wrong?"

"Are you serious?"

"Yes. She's getting a ride as far as Paxton. I told her to call us when she got there and we'd come pick her up. What's wrong, Albert? Who's that nice young man and why is he washing our car?"

"Why is she coming so soon?"

"She said she was dying of curiosity and she got a chance for a ride, so she's coming. Are you embarrassed?"

64

"Did you tell the Duttons?"

"No. I thought it would be better if *you* did. This *is* our place up here, isn't it? Is there any law that says our daughter can't visit us?"

"Of course not."

"I think I'll have some coffee." Jane moved toward the kitchen. "Would you like some?"

She returned with the coffee and they sat next to the window that overlooked the parking lot.

"Who is that down there?" Jane asked.

"The Duttons' nephew. Nick."

"Why is he washing our car?"

Albert shrugged. "I don't know. I think because he feels sorry for us."

"*Sorry* for us? Why?"

"Either for a reason I know nothing about—or else because we're the servant class. I'm inclined to think the latter."

Jane looked at him quizzically and then burst out laughing. Albert, after a moment, permitted himself to grin. "God Almighty," he said. "I'm not sure about all this. I think maybe we picked the wrong place."

"I think it's perfectly lovely," Jane said.

Toward five o'clock, Albert went over to the house. He found the Duttons and their nephew in the large room where he had first been interviewed, the room with the balcony and the heads of the big game animals.

"Mr. Dutton . . ." Albert tapped discreetly at the molding.

"Come in, come in," Dutton said.

"Please come in, Mr. Bagby," Mrs. Dutton said.

They were seated before the picture window, sipping martinis. Nick, on the floor, was having a can of beer. He got to his feet as Albert entered.

"Something we can do for you?" Dutton asked.

"How about something to drink, Mr. Bagby?" Nick asked, already poised for a sprint to the kitchen.

Dutton's faint frown was not lost upon Albert. "No, I don't believe so, thanks just the same," he said. "Mr. Dutton, I just thought I should let you know, sir . . . my daughter is coming in tomorrow afternoon and will be spending tomorrow night with us."

For a bare second, Dutton seemed taken aback. Before he could say anything, Mrs. Dutton said, "Oh, how nice. We'd love to meet her, Mr. Bagby."

"Will it be all right?" Albert asked.

"Oh, of course," Mrs. Dutton said.

Dutton nodded. "Yes," he said. "I don't see any reason why it won't be all right."

"Thank you very much, sir," Albert said, jaw set.

9

Paxton was a town of roughly ten thousand souls, located some fifteen miles from the village of Brightwater, whose brightest waters flowed past the shores of Rear Guard, which was just outside the village limits.

Beverly telephoned from Paxton at 4:30 on Saturday afternoon. Albert drove up to get her and they were back by five. Of the approximately twenty-four hours she spent at Rear Guard, he and Jane saw her perhaps forty minutes. The rest of her waking moments were spent with Nick.

When Albert and Beverly drove up in the station wagon, Nick, having thoroughly washed his Triumph only the day before, was washing it again.

Albert introduced them, and he could tell almost immediately that Nick's reaction to Beverly was much more than mere compassion for the daughter of servant people.

One indication was that Nick, momentarily rattled, lost control of the hose and squirted him in the leg—and then almost licked the fine white pea-gravel of the parking lot in mortification and profuse apology.

Albert, gingerly patting at the front of his trousers, assured him there was no harm done, while Beverly ran upstairs to meet Jane, who had emerged onto the landing and who, in fairness, had not passed up the trip to Paxton because she was typing, but because she was cooking a humble supper in the humble kitchen for their family of three.

Albert noticed Nick's eye on Beverly's slim, tanned legs, which seemed to rise endlessly before reaching the hem of her short yellow dress, and once again Albert felt for certain that what Nick was experiencing was more than mere right-thinking on the subject of the underprivileged.

"I'm really sorry about your pants, Mr. Bagby," Nick said again as Beverly and Jane embraced and disappeared inside. "Are you sure I can't—uh—I'll be *glad* to pay for having them cleaned, sir."

Once more Albert assured him that it was nothing and then climbed the stairway, feeling more comfortable when he walked spread-legged.

Dinner was most pleasant, eaten in candlelight in the dinette, while Beverly talked about school and Albert twice remarked that it was the last day of Eastern Standard Time, eliciting only casual responses.

In the candlelight, he was struck by the resemblance between mother and daughter, a resemblance most pronounced in their large dark eyes and their coloring, although Beverly's hair was much longer and perhaps a shade lighter than Jane's, more brown than black. Noticing the resemblance had always given him a feeling of pride and satisfaction, for no logical reason that he could determine.

Several times during the meal, he had to remind himself that they were where they were. It was just as if they had never left home. Finally he asked Beverly, "Well, what do you think?"

"Did you really sell *everything?*"

"Just about."

"Hmmmm." She had been fooling with a pellet of wax from the candles and now was scraping a layer of it from her thumbnail. "That class in economics I took last year," she said. "It's very communistic, the whole thing. Mr. Dutton, I suppose, is the State. Right? Karl Marx said that eventually the State is supposed to wither away. What do you think?"

Smiling, Albert sipped his coffee. "I doubt it," he said. "He's not the type."

There was the scrape of a footstep and then a knock at the door. Albert frowned. "Yes?" he called.

"Nick, sir. Excuse me, I hope I'm not interrupting. I wonder if I could speak to your daughter a second."

Beverly's eyes widened. Her eyebrows went up, as did Jane's. Smiling, Beverly left the table.

"Hi," Albert heard Nick say.

"Hi . . ."

Nick's voice dropped to a mumble. The door opened and closed. They were out on the landing. In a few minutes, Beverly returned. "He asked me for a date."

"What did you tell him?" Jane asked.

"I really didn't know *what* to say. So I said yes." She looked from one to the other. "Was that all right?"

"Yes, I guess so," Albert said.

"Well, *was* it? I told him not until around nine o'clock because I wanted to spend some time with you and mother and help with the dishes. But what *should* I have told him,

Daddy? I couldn't turn him *down*, could I? He's the nephew of your employer. After all."

Albert nodded.

"I didn't really know how to act. Ah! A ride in your sports car, sirrrrah? Ooh? Me? Faith! Should I wear my hair in a neat bun, or what?"

She was in the next room, and he could see her piling her dark hair on top of her head and peering at herself in the mirror. "Hmmmm, not bad," she said, and let it fall again over her shoulders. "Why the window right smack in the middle of the mirror, by the way? It's nerve-racking."

Returning to the dinette, she stood there, looking from one to the other. A glazed expression transformed her face. Her body went slack. "Hey, man!" she said. "You Nick Dutton? How you?" Her head seemed to wobble. "Oh, man, *you* know. Just barely making it, like." She sat down at the table again and sipped her coffee. "I could ruin you."

"I doubt it," Albert said.

"Do you say yes, sir, and yes, ma'am?"

Albert grunted. Jane laughed. "Your father does. He says 'yes, mum,' in fact."

"You're really a couple of phoneys," Beverly said.

While Beverly and Jane did the dishes, Albert strolled outdoors, ending up on what had so quickly become his favorite spot, the white bench at the crook of the land. He sat there watching a lopsided pink moon rise above the distant cove.

After a while he saw Beverly crossing the lawn to join him. "It really is gorgeous here, Daddy," she said, sitting next to him. "Just beautiful." She let her head rest on his shoulder. "You haven't actually started work yet, is that right?"

"We don't start officially until Monday morning. Day after tomorrow."

"You're on the eve of a great adventure, aren't you?"

"Do you miss the house, Bev? Knowing it's not ours?"

"Yes, of course. But I'll get over it. Anyway, it's not good for somebody my age to have a nice warm secure childhood home to come back to after college. After I graduate, I guess I'll go to New York and take my chances."

In her sophomore year, she had had the prize role of Adelaide in a spring production of *Guys and Dolls*. Proudly Albert and Jane had driven down for the occasion, reveling in the applause and even "bravos" she had received for the sheer precision of her Brooklyn or perhaps Bronx accent. In the current year, when the production had been *Oklahoma!* she had lost the lead to someone else, a misfortune which she attributed to the fact that she was ten pounds overweight during the tryouts. But now she had slimmed down nicely again.

"What a fantastic moon," she said. "Well . . . you deserve a little eccentricity in your life. Actually, I guess I'm rather proud of you for doing it. But you won't be doing it for long, will you?"

"Who knows? We're a very flexible, floating commodity. We could get our next job in Hollywood . . . or the Riviera. Anywhere."

"I think you're right about Mr. Dutton not withering away. He strikes me actually as more fascist than communist."

"Why? Did you meet him?"

71

"Sort of a clown fascist."

"Did you meet him?"

"Yes, just now."

"Was he nice to you?"

"Yes, he was all right."

"Are you sure?" Albert asked, his gorge rising.

"Yes. He was very polite. He asked if I'd seen Nick—seen his *nevvew*. *Nevvew!* Nick's car was gone." She looked over her shoulder as the arc of headlights bounced over the lawn. "Here comes a car now. I guess that must be his nevvew. I'll go and get ready. Good night, Daddy." She kissed him on the top of his head and left.

With Beverly gone and Jane typing, Albert brought out a chair from the room and sat on his landing. The night was warm, and the moon was doing strange things to the landscape. The parking lot below was suddenly a Spanish courtyard. Albert sat there, admiring the effect of light and shadow, and occasionally finding himself about to drowse. There were only a few hours now until midnight, when the clocks would be moved forward. Back home, it had always given him great pleasure to go about the house, setting the clocks forward, all five or six of them. Now he had only a wrist watch and an alarm clock to reset.

It was true what Jane had said—the change of time affected him profoundly, perhaps in some strange, atavistic way that was beyond his comprehension. Perhaps it was truly allied to a feeling of sun-worship, or perhaps it satisfied a craving of man to tamper with the conditions of his life. There was something powerful about moving the hands of a clock and, Godlike, announcing that it was no longer twelve o'clock but one.

He was stirred from his reverie by an abrupt snatch of song, and a male voice bellowing, *"There ought to be—"*

It stopped, and was followed by the haphazard notes of a piano. The piano was being played by Mrs. Dutton. He could see her through an open window, seated at the piano. Dutton stood beside her, reaching in front of her now to turn the pages of her music.

Standing back then, he bellowed a few more warm-up notes. Finally, with a preliminary bob of her head, Mrs. Dutton started playing, while Dutton sang in a surprisingly deep, resonant voice that was not at all bad.

"There ought to be a moonlight saving time . . ."

The coincidence of their selection was rather startling, Albert thought, but then he realized that perhaps it had been prompted on their part by very much the same thoughts he himself had been having. Daylight Time prompted a feeling of festival, perhaps akin to Midsummer's Night—yet it was neither midsummer nor vernal equinox but somewhere between the two, and more meaningful than either.

"There ought *to be a moonlight saving time,"* Dutton was singing, *"so I can love that girl of mine, until the birdies wake and chime, good mornin'. . . ."*

To hear such lyrics coming from Jake Dutton was an arresting experience, almost an absurd experience, and yet Albert somehow was touched. He recalled the song vaguely from the dim past. At the time of its popularity, the Duttons must have been in the courting stage.

73

"There ought to be a law in clover time, to keep that moon out overtime . . ."

On and on they went, from one ancient song to another. *"I'm flyin' high, but I've gotta feelin' I'm fallin' . . . fallin' for nobody else but you. . . ."*

Occasionally, Mrs. Dutton's rather shrill soprano would blend with Dutton's firm baritone, and gradually Albert realized that they were thrilled by what they were singing and even by the way they were singing it.

Albert dozed off. When he awoke, Beverly stood beside him, touching his shoulder. The singing had stopped.

"Daddy . . ."

"What time is it?"

"Midnight."

"New time or old?" he asked warily.

Beverly laughed. "Daddy, are you awake?"

Albert yawned. "How was your date?"

"Fine. He's really a strange boy. He's the most idealistic person I think I've ever known. He's so *good* that he worries me. Not sissified. Just good. *Nice.*"

Just before he fell asleep, Albert remembered the dream he had had while drowsing outside on the landing. The Duttons were in the dream, and he and Jane, and Beverly and Nick, but also a lot of others that he didn't know. They had all been dancing, joining hands in a large circle, and dancing in the light of a pink moon, with circlets of flowers on their heads, all singing for joy.

74

The next morning, Nick took Beverly out in Dutton's power boat, and they were gone most of the day. Toward four o'clock, Albert began to scan the river, looking for them, concerned by now that she would miss the bus that left Paxton at 5:05.

It was 4:30 before they returned. Beverly came running up the yard from the dock. "It's all right," she said. "He's going to drive me to Washington and I can get a bus from there." Panting, she took a deep breath. Her shoulders rose and fell. "In fact, what he wants to do is drive me all the way back to school."

By five, Beverly and Nick were in the car, surrounded by Jane and Albert and Mr. and Mrs. Dutton, waving goodbye. Mrs. Dutton, Albert and Jane continued to wave as the car moved rapidly down the driveway.

"What a lovely girl," Mrs. Dutton said when they were gone from sight. "You must be terribly proud of her."

"Yes, mum," Albert said, addressing her but watching her husband, whose wave had been perfunctory and who now was moving with short, determined steps toward his front door. His lips were moving and, briefly, before he turned away, his eyes had seemed clouded with the same look of dementia that Albert had noticed and so quickly forgotten the first day he had ever seen Rear Guard.

10

The next morning, Dutton put him to work, clearly relieved that the time at last had come, after three days of idleness and the visit of a freeloading daughter, for his hired man to earn his keep.

Carrying the chain saw and a sickle, Albert was led by his employer down to a dense clutch of underbrush, vast in scope and containing no end of honeysuckle, briar patches, slanting stunted saplings, and deeply rooted plants which Dutton identified as "stinkweed."

"What I'd like you to do is get to work and clean up this thicket for me," Dutton said. "Then let me know when you're finished."

"Is that the remains of a wire fence I see in there?" Albert asked.

"Yes," Dutton said. "It's fallen down and it's gotten itself all intertwined with honeysuckle. See?"

"Yes," Albert said. "I see."

"It won't be an easy job. Honeysuckle can be very tenacious."

Putting Albert to work had done much for Dutton's spirits. Eyes twinkling, he turned away.

Albert looked at Dutton's receding figure, then at the

76

maze of wire and honeysuckle, and then again at Dutton.

Finally he set to work and worked steadily all through the morning and again, after a brief lunch period, throughout the afternoon. Several times he returned to the toolhouse, once for a crowbar, once for a pair of pruning shears, and last for a hammer and screwdriver with which to loosen the pronged fasteners binding the wire to a fallen iron post which he had dug up from the mud.

Occasionally he stopped to rest, sitting at the foot of a pine tree and looking up at the cloud formations, brooding upon Jake Dutton—upon Dutton's snobbish attitude toward Beverly, and upon the nasty trick Dutton had pulled with the fake wife. He no longer felt deprivation. He had already lived past that. What infuriated him was the sheer deceit of it.

By late afternoon, the thicket was only three-quarters of a thicket, so vigorously and so angrily had he attacked it. Sawing the sapling stobs off level with the ground, so a lawnmower might pass over them, he spotted the white Thunderbird moving rapidly down the lane, Dutton at the wheel. In a few minutes, he saw the car return and stop at a point in the driveway abreast of where he was working.

Dutton, in his blue blazer and yellow ascot, got out of the car and sauntered over. "How's it coming?" he called cheerily.

Albert killed the chain saw and set it on the ground. "Okay," he said.

"Good. Oh, *good*. Yes. You're really going to town on it, aren't you? Mmmmm, boy." Dutton looked at the cleared ground with admiration. "Maybe you'd better ease up a little. After all, it's the first day." He glanced at his watch. "Knock off. Come on up and join me in a Fresca."

Albert rode beside him in the Thunderbird, balancing the chain saw on his knee and leaving the other tools at the job site.

"Just leave the saw here by the front door and come on in," Dutton said.

Albert wiped his feet on the doormat and brushed wisps of weed from his trousers, then was angry that he had done so. He followed Dutton into the large room with the cathedral ceiling, the trophy room, the *Safari* Room, he thought sardonically, being by now very much in the mood for sardonicism.

"You like Fresca?" Dutton asked.

Albert hesitated.

"Can or bottle?" Dutton asked.

"Either one," Albert said.

Dutton disappeared, and Albert sat looking moodily through the picture window at a lone melancholy gull which stood in an attitude of despair on top of a red channel marker.

The old son of a bitch.

Looking up at the balcony, at the heads lining the wall, he squinted, blurring his vision. It was easy to imagine that each of the mounted heads was human. It was easy to see a man's anguished face superimposed over the face of the zebra; the stuffed head of a plastics company shop foreman in place of the stuffed head of the lion. He opened his eyes and the heads became animal once more.

Somewhere off in another part of the house, there was

the sound of voices, and then a delighted peal of laughter—Jane's! And then the hum of a vacuum cleaner.

"Here we are." Dutton sat on the window seat, back to the picture window, and raised his can of Fresca. "Here's long life to our association, Mr. Bagby."

Nodding, Albert sipped gingerly at his Fresca.

"I haven't really told you what I have in mind for this place, I suppose. . . ."

Dutton placed his can of Fresca on the floor and wiped his mouth. "Doing what we were doing down in the thicket today, for example—it may seem like unnecessary work, but it's all part of a plan . . . you might say part of a dream. And the dream in short is this. If one doesn't live in a perfect world, then *create* one, however small. Am I making myself understood?"

Albert, realizing that he was expected to react, nodded. Glancing at the dark stain on his dirty trousers where he had knelt on the damp ground, he felt every inch the sullen caretaker and for these moments rather relished it.

"I have a theory," Dutton was saying pompously. "What is reality?"

Albert frowned. "I beg your pardon?"

"I say, what *is* reality? Reality is what we make it, am I right?"

"Yes, I suppose it is," Albert said, taking a large gulp of Fresca and regretting it.

"A group of people on a desert island with no means of communication would assume that all the world was just like their island, wouldn't they? I think you get what I'm driving at. It's an angry, nasty world out there, Mr. Bagby. You know it and I know it, but frankly I don't feel I deserve that kind of world. I've worked very hard all my life, dammit, Mr. Bagby!"

He fixed his pale blue eyes unwaveringly upon Albert's. Albert looked on the floor for his Fresca.

"Eventually," Dutton said, "I hope to have these grounds, these ten acres, an absolute bower of beauty . . . just plain old-fashioned beauty. I want it to be a place where people—a very *few* people, *invited* people—will come and say, yes, there is beauty in the world after all, at Jake Dutton's house. It will be a place where people live in harmony, where people feel something steal over them when they enter the grounds. There is no one else to share it with us except occasionally my nevvew, and that's why I'm so glad to have you and your wife to share it with us."

"Thank you," Albert said. "Sir."

"Now I can well understand that you're not a man who likes a great deal of responsibility, else you would not have chosen the line of work you did. But that's perfectly all right. I happen to believe there are two classes of people in the world. Those willing to accept responsibility and those unwilling to accept it. Leaders and followers. We need both, I suppose. I'm willing to be one of the leaders because I've always been. And Mrs. Dutton, too, in a quiet way. Some of the *very oldest blood in America* flows in Mrs. Dutton's veins. I don't know whether you know that or not, but it's true. Anyway, what was I saying? Oh. Yes. Leaders and followers. The point is, there's room here at Rear Guard for us both."

He smiled.

Albert felt himself bridling.

"And now . . ." Dutton looked at his watch. "Nearly

five-thirty, eh? Why don't you knock off until supper. And oh, yes, speaking of supper . . . you'll be serving it, eh?"

Albert nodded. "Yes . . . sir."

"What were you planning to wear? What have you *normally* worn?"

"Well . . . what would you suggest?"

"I'd suggest a white mess jacket and dark trousers, isn't that usual?"

Albert nodded. "Unfortunately," he said, "I don't have a white mess jacket."

"You can't be serious!"

Albert looked at him tight-lipped and then out at the river. "I had one, but it got lost when we moved down."

"Well, in that event, it so happens that I have one. I'll get it for you. What's your size? Forty-two about right? Mine's a forty but it won't miss by much."

In a few minutes, Dutton returned with a white mess jacket of soft linen. "Okay?"

"Fine. Thank you. Well, I'll get over to the room and clean up some."

"Good day's work," Dutton said. "And don't forget to put away the chain saw."

Back in his room, Albert flopped on the bed to wait for Jane. When, by ten of six, she still had not come, he could only conclude that she had moved direct from light housework to kitchen.

Hauling himself from bed, he took a shower, found the darkest pair of trousers that he owned, and with them put on the white mess jacket, noting with irritation that the short pointed tabs of the jacket did not quite cover the beltline of his trousers.

Having no necktie of solid black, he put on one of black and white polka dots.

Thus attired, he stood before the mirror. Staring back at him was the image of a thoroughly miserable man.

The telephone rang and he jerked it to his ear.

"Albert . . ." It was Jane. "What are you doing? It's time for you to get over here." Her voice was guarded, and at the same time taunting.

"I'm coming," he growled.

"Well, shake a leg. The master wants his martini served in the drawing room promptly at six and you're the one doing the serving, old buddy."

11

Back in the dear distant days at home, Jane, while waiting for dinner to cook, would sit in a rocker in the kitchen, sipping a martini. To sit thus, to pick up the martini and take the first sip, was instant release, she always said. Immediately, almost automatically, her brain would detach itself and become creative, directing her toward the next turn and twist of her narrative, resurrecting some long-forgotten childhood episode which would illumine some facet of her father's uniquely cantankerous nature. Frequently, although by no means always, she would burn something.

Now, as Albert entered the Dutton kitchen for the first time, he was greeted by a sight which was in some respects quite familiar, and in others not familiar at all.

In the enormous, whitewashed room, seated in a pine rocker before the huge maw of a rough-hewn fireplace, was Jane, rocking gently, sipping a martini, staring fixedly into infinity.

Had she been wearing a longer skirt, she might have very much resembled a hostess out of Colonial Williamsburg. Her dress was black, undeniably a uniform. And about her neck she wore a sort of silken kerchief, its two ends dropping into and secured by what looked like a silver napkin ring.

On a highly polished butcher's block next to her rocker were the uncapped gin bottle and a bottle of vermouth.

Reluctantly she focused upon him. "They're waiting." Getting to her feet, she set the martini on the butcher's block and stirred something on the stove.

"Whadda they want?" Albert growled.

"Martinis, I guess, but don't you think it would be appropriate to *ask* them?"

"Where are they?"

"In the drawing room, I suppose."

"You mean the safari room," he said.

"I suppose." Turning from the stove, she looked closely at his get-up. "Couldn't you either pull that jacket down over your belt . . . or else pull your pants up? There's sort of a no-man's-land . . ." Jane giggled.

83

"You should talk," he muttered. "With that damned thing around your neck, you look like your name should be Prudence Godspeed or somebody."

"I love it." She fingered the scarf. "Mrs. Dutton gave it to me. She's adorable, she really is. We had such a nice time this afternoon."

"Great," he said, and shoved open the swinging door.

He found the Duttons in the trophy room. As he entered, Mrs. Dutton glanced up and smiled, but Dutton kept right on talking, totally ignoring his presence until he had finished his thought.

His thought, as it happened, proved to be: ". . . so I'm not at all sure that camellias would thrive without some protection from the wind, but on the other hand they don't do well in full sunlight either."

Only then did he acknowledge Albert's presence. His eyes went first to Albert's midriff, then up to rest briefly on his polka-dot tie, and finally to his face. "Good evening," he said.

"Good evening, Mr. Bagby," said Mrs. Dutton.

"Good evening mum . . . sir. . . ." Albert said gamely. "May I serve you something?"

"Two martinis if you please," Dutton said. "Mrs. Dutton likes hers plain and unadorned. I'd like mine with a twist of lemon and one ice cube. Both very dry."

Albert nodded, stood there a moment longer, and then withdrew.

Jane once again was in the rocker, glass in hand, lips parted.

Albert began opening cabinet doors, looking for glasses.

84

Finding them, he mixed the martinis as directed, while Jane, all unaware, continued to stare at the wall.

"Where's a tray?"

Jane didn't answer.

Placing both hands on her shoulders, he looked deep into her eyes. "Can you tell me where I might find a tray in this damned place?"

"A tray? Oh. There's one over behind the breadbox. See it? Propped against the wall."

"Thank you, Jane."

Gingerly, he carried the martinis in. Mrs. Dutton accepted hers, sipped it, looked up gratefully, and said, "Perfect, Mr. Bagby. Just perfect."

Dutton took a sip. "Good," he said. "Very good! He was absolutely right."

"Sir?"

"Your former employer, whatever his name was. In his letter of recommendation, he told me you mixed a mean martini. He was right."

"Oh," Albert said. "Thank you."

"I walked down in the fields to see what you did today, Mr. Bagby," Mrs. Dutton said. "It's already such a wonderful improvement. And you got so much done in such a short time!"

"Thank you, mum." Mollified now, and even pleased, Albert sat down on the window seat and hugged his knee with clasped hands. "What's on the schedule for tomorrow?" he asked.

There was a brief silence. Dutton looked at him, and then into his glass. "We'll see," he said, glancing again at the seated Albert.

"Mr. Bagby . . ." Mrs. Dutton said. "Do you suppose I could have a paper napkin?"

"Two," Dutton said curtly.

Albert by now was on his feet, feeling burned about the rear.

"And you can tell Mrs. Bagby," Mrs. Dutton said, "that we'll be ready in fifteen minutes."

Returning with the napkins, he made, this time, an immediate withdrawal. Pointing a finger at Jane's clavicle, he said, "Fifteen minutes."

"Oh, dear," Jane said and began to scurry.

"Does that mean fifteen minutes for me too?" he asked. "I'm hungry as hell."

"You'll just have to wait," Jane said. "Do you know how you're going to do this, by the way?"

"Do what?"

"*Serve.* Serve from the left. Remove from the right. Remember."

"Wait a minute. Do I take in everything at once, or what?"

"Of course not. Take in one dish at a time. First the meat loaf, then the potatoes, then the peas. Here. You can put these salads on now, and light the candles."

"I'm hungry."

"Too bad. Here. Finish my martini."

He drained it at a gulp.

"And get a grip on yourself. You're being a bad sport. Whose idea was this, anyway?"

"Yes, mum." He moved up behind her as she stood at the stove.

"Albert!" She gave a small shriek.

86

"That's what butlers always do to cooks," he said. "It's classic."

"I think I hear them."

"Where's the damned meat loaf?"

"Take the tomato juice first. No. Wait a minute. Go in and ask them first if they're *ready* to be served."

"Yes, mum," he said.

He swung open the doors. Seated at either end of the long mahogany table were Mr. and Mrs. Dutton. Candles flickered near the fifty-yard line.

"Are you ready to be served, mum?" he asked.

"Yes, Mr. Bagby, thank you," said Mrs. Dutton. He saw a look of approval on Dutton's face.

Having served tomato juice, meat loaf, mashed potatoes and peas, he withdrew to the kitchen, where, in a strangled voice, he announced once more that he was starved.

"Well, here . . ." Jane set a full platter on the butcher's block and shoved up a short stepladder for him to sit on. Frowning, he perched himself on the top step and began eating.

In a very few seconds there was, from the next room, the unmistakable sound of a bell. Jane pointed a forefinger at his chest. "That's *you*," she whispered.

Grimacing, he got to his feet and reported.

Dutton's eyes gleamed in the candlelight. "Please tell Mrs. Bagby that this meat loaf is absolutely superb," he said.

Albert nodded. "Would you like some more, sir?"

"No, but it's just fine."

"Wonderful," said Mrs. Dutton.

Nodding, Albert withdrew. "They like your meat loaf," he said, resuming his evening meal.

87

"I know. I heard." Jane looked pleased.

The bell tinkled.

Albert threw his napkin to the floor.

"You should have waited," Jane whispered. "*I'm* waiting."

"I was *hungry*, damn it. I've been working in the fields all day."

Composing his features, he reported.

"Think maybe I've changed my mind," Dutton said. "I think I'll have some more meat loaf after all, if you don't mind."

"Very well," Albert said, leaving, and returning with the meat loaf platter.

Dutton helped himself to another slice. "Good. Thanks . . . Albert," he said.

Albert said nothing.

"Now what?" Jane asked.

"Son of a bitch called me by my first name. Called me Albert."

"Oh, what difference does it make? She called me Jane this afternoon. Who cares? Finish your dinner before they start ringing for dessert."

Albert swung open the doors. "Anything else you'd like while I'm up?" he asked.

"I think not, thank you," said Mrs. Dutton. Dutton said nothing. He simply sat there looking as if he'd just heard a question he found incredible.

Albert returned to his stepladder. Glowering at his food, he began to shovel it in rapidly.

While he finished, Jane stood at the window. "The river looks so gorgeous in the twilight," she said. "I love it when the buoy lights come on and start to blink. Mrs. Dutton says it's simply heavenly here in summer, when all the boats are on the water and the swimming pool is open."

"Ummmmm," Albert said.

Turning from the window, she placed a hand on his shoulder. "You know, I think I'm going to like it. Very much. And you're right about Daylight Saving Time. It's so much nicer."

The bell rang.

The Duttons had finished dessert and were lingering over their coffee when he was summoned for the final time.

"Very nice, Albert," Dutton said. "There's only one thing . . ." He now assumed what one might suppose was an attitude of joshing, of benevolent, chiding solicitude. His eyes danced. "Do you always wear your pants that low?"

Albert looked down at the rampant expanse of shirt front.

"Do you suppose a pair of suspenders might do the trick?" Dutton asked.

"They might," Albert said.

"And how about a plain black tie? What would you say to that?"

"Oh, Jake," Mrs. Dutton remonstrated lightly.

"Albert knows I'm not finding fault, don't you, Albert?"

"It's just his way, Mr. Bagby," Mrs. Dutton explained.

"But seriously," Dutton said. "I *do* think a black tie might be better with that outfit. If you don't have one, why not take off long enough tomorrow to run up to Paxton and pick one up?"

"All right," Albert said.

"Good," Dutton said. "Well, everything was simply

wonderful, Albert. I think we're off to a very good start, don't you?"

"And we'd like to tell you again," Mrs. Dutton said, "how very charming we both think your daughter is."

"Thank you, mum."

"She certainly is, certainly is," Dutton said. "Uh—except a word of caution is perhaps in order, Albert. . . . Uh, we certainly wouldn't want to see her hurt. . . ."

For a brief moment, something peculiar was happening to Dutton's face. His nose twitched and his upper lip rose from his front teeth. It was as if he were waging some struggle with himself.

He gave Albert a smile which he may have meant to be benign. "You being her father and all . . . and I say this, of course, for her own good. I mean, Albert, in cases like this the clock always has to strike twelve at *some* point."

"Jake!" said Mrs. Dutton.

That evening, while Jane sat at her typewriter, Albert, already in his pajamas, lay prostrate in one of the double beds. For the most part his face was without expression, his glance a dull stare. From time to time, however, his eyes would move from left to right, and from right to left, and then come to rest on the ceiling. Occasionally his mouth would twitch and his nostrils dilate. For the most part, however, he stared at the ceiling with a fixed expression.

Finally, even while the typewriter keys continued to clatter, he dropped off to sleep, weary in flesh and spirit.

Part Two

12

In the days immediately following, Albert toyed with the thought of quitting.

He had found a gimmick, dreamed a dream, yes, and in so many respects the dream was intact. The outdoor work was giving new tone to his body, and there were other pleasures as well. To lie up in his room resting after lunch, thinking of the $100,000 cash he would have in another month; gazing through the window-insert, gazing beyond the gabled roof toward the river; to hear the cry of a gull and then to be aware that it was the gull's shadow that had just passed over the slope of the roof; to watch the changes of coloration and mood in the face of the river as the hours passed and the shadows moved; to touch the back of his hand lightly against the fresh green willow fronds—these things could not be discounted.

In so many respects the situation was ideal, just as he had imagined it would be. It seemed cruel irony that it should be spoiled by Jake Dutton. The clock sooner or later must strike midnight, eh? And Beverly must return, streaked with ashes, to the kitchen hearth, eh?

Dutton seemed to have no conception of the realities involved. It was, after all, a sellers' market and Albert was a man of some importance. He had, in the end, received no less than 297 replies to his ad. Of all this, Dutton seemed totally if not willfully unmindful.

It was very easy to find the man's behavior infuriating, yet Albert refused to quit. He liked the place far too much to quit. All he really had to do, he decided, was to restore things to their rightful balance, to put Jake Dutton in his place.

During the next few days, working with the chain saw down in the thicket, or painting patio furniture and setting it in the sun to dry, he mulled over ways to establish the upper hand.

One morning, as Dutton bent to inspect a rocker he had just finished painting, Albert offered a preliminary sally. Knowing Dutton's aversion to the outside world, he dropped a chance remark. "By the way, sir," he said, "I was listening to the radio this morning and I heard they were going to increase welfare payments by as much as fifty percent in some cases."

Dutton flushed. Above the yellow ascot, his face darkened. His forefinger came away smeared with white paint. "I don't want to hear about it," he said, wiping his finger angrily on the grass.

That evening, Albert deliberately put an olive in Dutton's martini.

94

Mrs. Dutton had not yet arrived for the cocktail hour, and the two men were alone. Dutton looked at the olive and then at Albert. He cleared his throat and set the glass on the windowseat.

For a few seconds, he seemed to be studying the river, and when he turned his face was composed, his voice icy.

"Take this back and replace the olive with a *twist of lemon,* if you don't mind, Albert."

"Oh, that's right," Albert said. "You do prefer a twist of lemon, don't you? Of course."

The welfare payments and the olive, of course, were merely for openers. If he was going to make his day-to-day relationship with Dutton bearable, he must transform Dutton into the fawning, abject employer that he should be in a sellers' market.

About Dutton, there was nothing abject. Happy, dominant, exuding confidence, loaded with money, master of a beautiful estate, possessed of a live-in couple, he gave the impression of a man ready now to know real happiness. He too had his commitment to life—he was determined to taste the true sweetness of retirement. No obstacle stood in his way.

Against such a man, talk of welfare payments could have little impact. Albert decided that he must take a calculated risk, which he was positive would be no risk at all. He decided that he must *threaten* to quit without ever in the least intending to do so.

While he was awaiting the right opportunity, a far better thing was handed him on a silver platter, a gift, as it were, from the posh waters of the Peacepipe River, an old Indian name.

It all began with the first of what Dutton described as "a series of intimate dinner parties," which he and Mrs. Dutton had long planned and which the arrival of Albert and Jane had finally made possible.

First on the list were the Merritts—Clinker and Doris—who lived on an estate of their own, some twenty miles away in a quiet cove of the Peacepipe.

From bits and scraps of information, Albert learned that the Merritts and Duttons had bonds which reached deep into time. Clinker Merritt and Jake Dutton had been together in college, where Clinker was a flying-wedge fullback of national repute. Mrs Dutton had said that Jake was a man of few friends. The surprise to Albert was that he had any at all. Yet Clinker apparently was the exception. The two couples had kept up with one another over the years, and it was the Merritts who had persuaded the Duttons to spend their retirement in the area in which they now found themselves. Clinker himself had known the area since boyhood, or at least early young manhood. His family, wealthy steel people, had bought an estate back in the very early 1930's, envisioning the area not merely as a pleasant place to live but indeed as a sanctuary where they might flee and hide out in case the then-hordes of unemployed became unruly, in case the Great Depression should give rise to something approximating the French Revolution.

The dinner party was scheduled for a Monday night, one week following the day Albert and Jane began work. As the big night approached, there was an atmosphere of excitement that Albert could not fully understand.

"Well," Jane said, "if you were spending this much money on a place to live, wouldn't it make you feel better to know you were using it? She's talked to me four times about the menu. We're having roast beef. I get an impression that somebody is on the defensive. . . ."

"What? Why?"

"I think they're slightly miffed—or at least Mr. Dutton is—that these people have sort of ignored them after persuading them to come down here and live. They haven't been quite as thick as the Duttons expected they would be. But Mr. Dutton thinks it's because they haven't been in a position to entertain until now. So this dinner is important, very important, in Mr. Dutton's scheme of things."

On Sunday evening, as Albert appeared in the Safari Room with the martinis, Dutton stopped him as he was about to withdraw.

"Oh, by the way, Albert, as you know, we're having company for dinner tomorrow night."

"Yes, sir," Albert said.

"The Merritts—from over Peacepipe River way. Mr. Merritt is the best friend I've ever had, or ever hope to have, so naturally . . ." Dutton's voice seemed to thicken with emotion. "I'd like to put our best foot forward, so to speak."

"I've already gone into it thoroughly with Mrs. Bagby," Mrs. Dutton said. "We're all set."

"I'd just like to have things go well," Dutton said. "I'm sure you'll like the Merritts, Albert. Wonderful people. I don't know any man in the world I admire more. I wouldn't take anything for his friendship. Oh, by the way . . ."

"Sir?"

"Mrs. Dutton and I are going up to Annapolis to a lacrosse game on Saturday, so you and Jane will have the place to yourselves."

"Yes, sir."

On the following night, Dutton entered the kitchen dressed in a dinner jacket with which he wore a white turtleneck shirt.

"My, sir!" Jane exclaimed. "You look very handsome tonight!"

Dutton seemed pleased. He did indeed look well pomaded and he smelled of lime. Smiling, he turned to inspect Albert, who by now had both his black tie and his suspenders. With an approving glance at Albert's midsection, Dutton placed a hand on his shoulder. "Mr. Merritt takes a martini before dinner," he said. "Not exactly sure what he takes in it."

"I'll ask him, sir," Albert said.

"Good," Dutton said. "His wife, Mrs. Merritt, I think drinks nothing but sherry usually, but do we have some vodka, just in case? There should be some here."

"Yes, sir, we have vodka."

"Good. She may want vodka. Or sherry. I'm just not sure. Sometimes she goes one way and sometimes another."

"Yes, sir."

"Good. Oh, and Albert . . . I know I can count on you to

be tactful. I know you won't drop any pleasantries about welfare payments, or *Bonnie and Clyde*, or anything of that sort, will you?"

"Of course not, sir."

Dutton looked gravely into his eyes and then, giving him a clap on the shoulder, withdrew.

The dinner itself was a thing of no particular moment. Clinker Merritt had a thick shock of white hair. He was as ruddy and well-groomed in his dinner jacket as Jake Dutton was in his, although considerably larger.

With his ear pressed now and then to the swinging door, Albert heard himself and Jane praised as jewels. There were remarks about the state of the world, there was banter about waistlines, and finally there was a lengthy conversation involving the lacrosse game. Dutton tried to talk the Merritts into going along but Clinker seemed unenthusiastic.

"Damnedest man I ever saw," Dutton said with great affection.

On Saturday morning, the Duttons took off in the black Bentley shortly after eleven o'clock.

Jane, not unexpectedly, retired to the typewriter.

Albert sat on the white bench at the crook of the river, determined to dog it.

A letter had arrived that morning from Beverly, their first word from her since she had gone back to school. She said that Nick Dutton had insisted upon driving her all the way and could not, she was certain, have gotten back to Washington until three in the morning.

Albert read the letter and then sat in the sunlight, watching the boating traffic, which this morning was very heavy.

After lunch, he went back to the bench to sit some more, and around two o'clock he noticed a small, speedy outboard motorboat make a pass at the Dutton dock and then veer off, showering spray and nearly colliding with a small sailboat. The man at the controls of the outboard looked familiar, although at the distance Albert was unable to see him clearly.

He lost track of the boat until, perhaps fifteen minutes later, he saw, striding toward him over the lawn, none other than Clinker Merritt.

"Hey-o there," Merritt boomed. "Mr. Dutton around?"

"No, sir," Albert said, rising from the bench. "They're away for the day. They've gone up to the lacrosse game."

Clinker's ruddy face creased with bafflement. "What *is* today?"

"Saturday, sir."

"Of course." The heel of Clinker's right hand found his brow. "I must be getting old or something." He shook his head, chiding his memory. "Well . . . I see *you're* taking it easy."

"Yes, sir . . . for the moment."

Clinker laughed heartily. "For the moment, eh?" Again he laughed. "Well, tell Jake and Frances I was by."

"I sure will."

Clinker started off. He looked, Albert thought, rather overdressed for a small outboard motorboat, what with his nautical blazer and white trousers.

"Hey." Clinker had turned. "Could you help shove me off?"

"Certainly," Albert replied.

The bow of the small boat had been pulled ashore and the motor was tilted up out of the water.

Instead of getting into the boat, Clinker sat on the bow. "Care for a ride?" he asked carelessly.

"No, thanks, I guess I've got some work to do, thanks just the same."

Clinker made a disapproving noise with his lips. "You sound too conscientious."

Albert smiled.

Clinker squinted at the bright sun and then squinted at Albert. "Jake treating you right?"

"Very well."

Clinker nodded. "Would it be impertinent for me to ask how much he's paying you, uh, Albert?"

"A thousand a month, sir."

"Thousand apiece?"

"No. Five hundred apiece. A thousand in all."

Clinker smiled. "Good old Jake," he said softly.

"Sir?"

"Nothing. Nothing at all."

"I'm not sure I heard you, Mr. Merritt."

"The hell with that Mr. Merritt stuff. Call me Clinker. By the way, how do you like your quarters?"

"Very nice indeed."

"Where does he have you—above the stable there?"

"Yes, sir. Above the garage."

Clinker nodded. Inspecting the bottom of his white canvas shoe, he asked, "Was he ever able to get rid of the smell?"

"Smell?"

"I guess he must have gotten rid of it."

"I wasn't aware of any smell," Albert said.

"Well, I guess that means he must have finally licked it. I'm not even sure what it was exactly. Something left over from the days when it was still a stable. Horses. Cows. Sheep. I was never sure what he meant. Something about the smell seeping up through the floorboards."

"Well," Albert said, "we haven't smelled it. At least I don't think we have."

"It's funny sometimes about smells," Clinker said. "Sometimes you smell them and sometimes you don't."

Albert looked dubious.

"Well, anyway . . ." Clinker rose and stepped into the boat. "I guess he must have licked it. I mean, if you and your wife don't think you smell anything, then he *must* have licked it. Listen, Albert . . . come on out with me for just a second or two. Jake tells me you're good with motors. I don't like the way this thing is sounding. Would you give a listen?"

"Well, okay . . . sure."

"Just give a shove and step in."

Albert did as directed and when they had drifted far enough from shore, Merritt dropped the motor into place and touched an electric starter. In a matter of seconds, the boat was roaring down the river at high speed, weaving in and out among small sailboats and making of itself a clear-cut menace to navigation.

"Whaddya think?" Clinker shouted.

Albert shook his head. "Sounds fine to me."

Clinker nodded and shrugged. Letting go the wheel, he spread his hands and grinned. He said something.

Albert leaned toward him, hand cupped to ear.

"I said it never acts up when you *want* it to!" Clinker roared.

As they zoomed around the bend of the river, Albert saw, riding at anchor perhaps a quarter-mile distant, what seemed to be the largest yacht on the river, perhaps in the world. It faced them stern-to, a gleaming turquoise and white monstrosity, with flying bridges on top of flying bridges, and as they zipped closer he read the name on the transom, painted in large gold block letters: *Peacepipe Hilton*.

A boarding ladder was in readiness. Clinker cut the speed of the outboard, and his wife appeared at the rail far above. "Come on aboard a second," Clinker said.

"Good afternoon, Mr. Bagby," Mrs. Merritt called down.

"Call him Al," Merritt bellowed. "He's Al. You're Doris. I'm Clinker, what the hell."

Dubiously Albert climbed the ladder, while Clinker, after tying the outboard, climbed after him. "How about a beer, Al?"

He produced three and led the way to the afterdeck, where reclining chairs were set in the sun. Clinker pointed to a chair and Albert reclined, holding the beer can on his stomach.

Mrs. Merritt's turquoise slacks and white blouse exactly matched the blue and white of the boat, as did her white hair with its blue rinse. "We were out cruising around," she said, "and I said to Mr. Merritt—to Clinker—why not drop by and see if Jake and Frances want to go out with us. So he got in the outboard and off he went. You see, we can't take the big boat very close to their house. It has too much draft, except on a high tide. They couldn't come?"

"They went to the lacrosse game," Clinker said. "Remember?"

"Oh, of course," Mrs. Merritt said. "Of *course*. I'd completely forgotten."

Sipping his beer and placing the can carefully on his chest, Albert sighed with contentment. "It's certainly a beautiful boat," he said.

Clinker nodded, tossing his empty beer can overboard and watching it float off with the tide. "Yeah," he said matter-of-factly. "We take her out and cruise around a lot in the summer. Lie out overnight . . . fish . . . lie in the sun . . . Easy livin' . . . *You* know . . ."

Albert nodded. From somewhere, Clinker had produced a braided yachting cap which rode very high on his head, pushed up by his thick, bouncy white hair.

"How about another beer, Al?"

"No thanks," Albert said.

"Not much of a beer drinker?"

"Not too much."

Clinker laughed. "That's a switch," he said. "Now Millard —Millard Beckley—we used to have a live-in couple, Millard and Annie Beckley—well, my God, let me tell you that Millard could really polish off beer, remember, honey?"

Mrs. Merritt's eyes were closed against the sun. "Mmmm, couldn't he, though!"

Clinker nodded. "Yep. They'd go out cruising with us, you see . . . whenever we went, that is, which was pretty often, and still is, for that matter. Anyway, there was nothing much for them to do aboard except lie here in the sun and draw their salary. Twelve hundred bucks a month, we paid them, and that, of course, was almost four years ago."

Clinker brought his big fist down on the arm of his reclining chair and guffawed. "Old Jake," he said. "He's really a shrewd old devil if ever there was one. A real shrewd old son of a bitch . . . but I love him. We both do."

"He's a lovely man," Mrs. Merritt said.

"But old Jake didn't get to be a multimillionaire by *giving* money away, that's for certain. But . . ." Clinker was getting to his feet, opening another beer. "But nobody does. So you can't blame *that* on him."

Whatever else one said about him, Albert decided, Clinker Merritt could drink a can of beer faster than any man who ever lived.

"Clinker," Mrs. Merritt said. "Please. I've asked you. Please don't throw the cans overboard."

"Sorry about that," Clinker said. His hand went up as a boat passed. "Hi, Cap'n . . . There's Bob Underwood, Doris. Hey, Skipper, whaddya *say?*"

He turned from the rail. "If there's anything more relaxed than getting out on the river on a day like this, boy, I'm telling you . . ."

"I think maybe I'd better be getting back now, sir," Albert said.

Briefly Clinker's lips compressed. "Right," he said. "Never one to keep a man from his work."

"It was wonderful to have you aboard, Albert," said Mrs. Merritt as they debarked.

The outboard roared and in a very few minutes the smaller boat was nosing up on the Dutton shoreline. Clinker cut the motor and tilted it up out of the water.

He came forward to the bow, offering his arm to help as Albert stepped from the boat. "Well, Al, it was good to have you aboard," he said.

"Many thanks to you, Mr. Merritt."

"Clinker! Clinker!" Clinker roared. "Cut out that Mr. Merritt stuff, will you, Al?"

He extended a huge hand which Albert took, shook briefly, and was held by. Clinker wouldn't let go. "Well . . ." he said jovially, "if you and your wife ever get tired of living at Right Guard—say!" Finally Clinker turned loose his hand. "It just occurred to me! I wonder if they decided to name it Right Guard on account of the smell that seeps up from the stable. . . ."

"It's Rear Guard," Albert reminded him.

"I know." Clinker guffawed. "I know it is. I just kid him about it now and then. Well, anyway, Al, as I say, if you ever decide to pull out . . ."

Clinker leaned forward and his voice became tense and conspiratorial. "Of course, you understood it would have to come from *you*, not me, because after all Jake and I are good friends, the very best. But if you ever *should*—I mean, I think we could go up to fifteen hundred without any trouble at all."

"Do I understand you correctly, sir?" Albert asked. "You're offering us a job?"

"No, no, no, don't get me wrong," Clinker said quickly. "Like I say, it would have to come from *you*. Not me. Well . . . see ya, Al."

Once more the motorboat roared off. Clinker turned once and waved. Albert waved back and stood there on the bank, smiling in the bright, early-May sunlight.

13

For a day or so, Albert felt spasms of sympathy for Jake Dutton, as he might have felt sympathy for any man who was knifed in the bowel by his best friend.

However, such was Dutton's nature that it was impossible to pity him for long. At dinner, Dutton, indicating his full coffee cup, said, "Would you mind pouring this out, Albert, and filling it again. Make sure there are no grounds."

It was spoken civilly enough, and yet there was about it an air of hauteur that Albert found intolerable, along with the implication that he had always been in the boorish habit of serving his employers coffee with plenty of grounds.

Returning to the kitchen, he stood at the back door and watched the green flasher buoy blinking in the twilight. How infuriating it was to think that this place he had come so quickly to love should be spoiled for him by the personality of its owner.

It was clearly time to make his move.

Waiting until Jane had finished the dishes and gone to her quarters, he went looking for the Duttons and found them, as usual, in the Safari Room.

"Yes, Albert?" Dutton said.

Albert shuffled his feet and cleared his throat.

"Is there something on your mind?" Dutton asked.

Mrs. Dutton's eyes darted about in a way that seemed to indicate a recognition of danger.

"Sorry, sir . . . mum . . ." Albert began. "I really don't like to do this but—well, I've come to give you our notice."

"What was that you said, Albert?" Dutton demanded.

"I say, I've come to give you notice, sir."

From Mrs. Dutton there was a little moan of despair. "Oh, *Albert* . . ."

The struggle that Dutton himself was going through was quite visible. Albert saw the lip-twitch, the cloud of anger that passed over his eyes, and he knew that Dutton burned with the desire to tell him to get out and stay out. He saw the effort Dutton now made at composure, and the deliberate way he placed his brandy glass on the window seat. "What's wrong, Albert?" he asked evenly. "Things not to your liking?"

"It's not *that*, exactly, sir."

"Then perhaps you will do me the courtesy of saying what it *is* exactly. Is it Mrs. Bagby?"

"Mrs. Bagby is quite satisfied, sir."

"I thought as much," Dutton said. "Well, then?"

"It's simply that we've been offered a better position, sir."

"Oh, dear . . ." Mrs. Dutton said.

"May I ask who *offered* you this better position, Albert?"

"I'm not at liberty to say, sir. I mean, I think it would be untactful . . . under the circumstances."

Dutton frowned. He glanced at his wife, who looked as one might who had just suffered a compound fracture.

"You say a *better* position?" Dutton said. "Better in what respect? More money?"

"That would be an inconsequential part of it, sir," Albert said. "More money, yes . . . but . . ."

"How much money do you want?"

Albert shuffled his feet, not replying.

"Eleven hundred a month? Twelve hundred?" Abruptly Dutton lost control. "Is *that* what you're doing? Holding me up for more *money?*"

With a sorrowful glance at Mrs. Dutton and making it clear that his dignity was badly damaged, Albert withdrew from the room. As he walked down the hall toward the kitchen, he heard Mrs. Dutton exclaim: "Jake, you're so boorish. You're dealing with a human *being.*" Her voice became more stern than he had ever heard it. "When will you ever *learn?*"

Well pleased with himself, Albert was perched on the short stepladder when the swinging door creaked open.

"Mr. Bagby . . ." Mrs. Dutton touched him gently on the shoulder. "Mr. Dutton is terribly sorry if he's offended you. Could we discuss this further?"

"I'd do almost anything for you, mum," Albert said. "But . . ." He looked sadly at the floor.

"Mr. Dutton has had a very difficult day," she said. "He heard something on the radio that upset him dreadfully. I know he's very sorry for being rude."

Albert continued to stare at the floor.

"Why don't you mix yourself a drink and—join us? Please."

"All right, mum." Looking up, he gave her a brave smile. "For you, I will."

"Please do, then."

She left. Albert, grinning, poured some Scotch into a short glass, added an ice cube and a little water.

It was with an air of surrender that Dutton glanced at the drink in Albert's hand. "Sit down . . . Mr. Bagby. Make yourself comfortable."

"Thank you," Albert said. "Mr. Dutton," he went on with great dignity. "There's one thing we should straighten out before we go any further, sir. I'm not the type, you see, to take advantage of people for the sake of a few extra dollars. I'm just not that sort of person."

"Suppose," Dutton said, "I were to offer you, say, twelve hundred. Would that be enough to meet this other offer?"

"No sir, it really wouldn't *meet* it, but I'd consider it quite adequate."

"*Adequate!*" Dutton's chemistry again had gotten the better of him. "Holy God!" he wailed and, leaving his brandy behind, walked over to the circular iron staircase by which one ascended to the trophy balcony.

"Jake!" Mrs. Dutton remonstrated.

Dutton was up on the balcony, walking aimlessly past the heads of the animals. "Frankly, Albert," he shouted, "you've got me over a barrel. I suppose you *know* that. And frankly, I don't *like* being over a barrel."

"I'd never be one to want to put anyone over a barrel," Albert replied.

"Oh, I know you wouldn't, Mr. Bagby," Mrs. Dutton said.

"I had no intention of anything like that," Albert said. "And I don't really think you *are* over a barrel, sir. It's not as though we're all that important, Jane and I. Because I'm sure there are plenty of live-in couples you could find to replace us."

Dutton was standing eyeball to eyeball with a zebra. "If it's not money, then what is it?" he asked in a strained voice.

Albert hesitated.

"Your living quarters?"

"We find them admirable," Albert said.

"Is the work too hard?"

"Not at all, sir. I love the work."

Dutton was leaning over the balcony rail. "Then what *is* it?"

"Well, sir . . ." Albert sipped his Scotch. "A certain dignity, sir, that's the only way I can express it."

Dutton snorted and withdrew from the rail.

"I know exactly what Mr. Bagby is talking about," Mrs. Dutton said softly.

Dutton was coming slowly down the spiral staircase.

"The fact is, sir," Albert said, "that I'm just not accustomed to being treated like an employee, shall we say."

"I know what Mr. Bagby means," Mrs. Dutton said. "You're referring, I would imagine, to—to certain ways that Mr. Dutton has of saying things, and asking certain things, for instance the polka-dot tie, but you see, Mr. Bagby, he's really only joking, I do want you to know that."

"That's just my way!" Dutton howled. "Don't you understand, Albert? It's just my *way*."

"Well, sir," Albert replied stiffly. "I can only repeat what I said before—that I'm not used to being treated as an employee."

Dutton slumped to the windowseat and picked up his

empty brandy glass. He looked helplessly across the room at his wife. "Surely you realize I'm just kidding, Albert, and that it's just my *way*."

"That may very well be, sir . . . but, well, you see we give respect and we . . ." He smiled sadly.

"Expect respect in return," Mrs. Dutton finished. "I can understand that perfectly."

"Well, just tell me, Albert," Dutton said. "In what respect do I fail to give you—respect?"

"Oh, just small things, sir, now that we have it out in the open, so to say." Albert shook his head as if he were very rueful about the entire interview. "Certain mannerisms."

From Dutton, there came a very brief laugh, but in the laugh there was surrender. "Okay, Albert, okay. All I can say is that it was not intentional. I apologize. I'll change my ways."

Getting to his feet, he clapped Albert heartily on the shoulder. "For a starter, what would you like to do? Sleep in my bed?"

Albert laughed. Dutton laughed. And Mrs. Dutton, after a second's uneasiness, laughed uneasily.

"You see, sir," Albert said humbly, "I—"

"Yes, Albert?"

"I *love* this place, sir. We both do. That's the fact of it."

Mrs. Dutton's eyes seemed to mist. "So do we, Albert," she said huskily.

"Well, we're agreed on that much." Dutton was pacing again. He came to a halt and turned. "There's only one thing that still sticks in my craw. I'd just like to know who made you that offer."

Albert was silent.

"You haven't been away from here, haven't even had any phone calls except from your daughter—unless you got one on Saturday while we were at the lacrosse game. Did you get a phone call on Saturday, Albert?"

"No, sir," Albert said promptly.

"Did you leave here on Saturday?"

"I'd rather not say, sir."

"Albert, I'm not worried about whether you *worked* all day or not. You don't have to punch a time-clock around here. You know that."

"Yes, sir," Albert said. "I'd never accuse you of such a thing, Mr. Dutton."

"But I'm still interested in knowing what—"

"Don't make him tell if he doesn't want to, Jake."

"You see, sir," Albert said. "I'm a very honest man. Sometimes to my disadvantage. I find it very difficult to lie."

"I can understand that, Albert," Dutton said. "I'm the same way myself. But I'd still like to know one thing. Was anybody here while we were away on Saturday?"

Albert remained stubbornly silent.

"Just answer me yes or no, and I won't ask you anything else."

"Yes," Albert said softly.

"Somebody you'd met? Somebody who knew you? It must have been. Somebody you'd been in *touch* with before?"

Albert's face went through contortions of agony.

"You don't even *know* anybody around here," Dutton said, pacing again. "You've not even *met* anybody, at least that I know of."

"Jake, don't. What difference does it make?"

Dutton turned. "Have you?" He paced and halted. "Except

for Mr. and Mrs. Merritt, and I know it couldn't have been the Merritts because they happen to be our very best— Was it the *Merritts?*"

The last four words were a roar.

Albert stared steadfastly into his empty glass.

"Was it Clinker Merritt who tried to steal you away from us?"

Albert twitched.

"Was it? Yes or no?"

Albert raised his eyes to the cathedral ceiling.

Mrs. Dutton's face was twisted with concern. She was clearly as eager to know as her husband. "You may as well tell us, Mr. Bagby," she said. "It's better to know than not to know."

"*Was it Clinker Merritt?*" Dutton demanded.

"Yes, sir." Albert hung his head.

"It *was?*"

"Yes, sir," Albert whispered. "It was him."

Although he would have eavesdropped happily if it had been necessary, it was not at all necessary. Even with the swinging door closed, he could hear Dutton loud and clear, bellowing over the telephone. He heard Dutton call Clinker several different kinds of son of a bitch as well as a "scut-bastard," whatever that might have been, and the conversation came to a close with Dutton's suggestion that Clinker take the *Peacepipe Hilton* and do the obvious with it followed by the rather illogical companion threat that if he ever saw the *Peacepipe Hilton* anywhere near his dock he would personally sink it.

114

Returning to his room, Albert told Jane that Dutton had just raised their salary to $1200 a month.

"Oh, how very nice," Jane said.

14

Whatever hostility Jake Dutton felt for the world—and it was certainly a great deal—was now focused upon his old friend Clinker Merritt. His behavior toward Albert was eminently satisfactory and even for a time rather deferential.

Pressing his advantage, Albert demanded and got an umbrella attachment for the sulky of the ride-on lawnmower. The mowing season was now upon him, and during the second week of May he became a familiar sight to passing boatmen, riding along under his blue-and-orange umbrella with a look of bemused concentration. What he was doing was mental arithmetic, calculating how much the extra $200 per month would help him in saving enough to pay the capital-gains tax on the huge profit he was making on the sale of his house. How nice it would be, he thought as he bounced along, to save enough from his salary so that, even after paying the tax, he would still have the $100,000 intact. There was something so neat and fully rounded about $100,000 that it would seem a shame to lop at it.

Things then were going nicely apace. A certain equilibrium

had been reached. Jane seemed quite content, certainly at least as content as she had ever been at home. She was aware of her surroundings only during a modest fraction of the twenty-four hours in any given day—subtracting the hours she slept, the hours she worked on her book in the morning and the hours she worked on it in the evening, and also subtracting the hour she sipped at her martini while waiting for the dinner to be cooked.

During her hours of light housework, however, she was apparently alert enough to get by, for Mrs. Dutton seemed well pleased with her, and often, from down in the field or from his seat on the mower, he would look up to see the two of them in the afternoon, walking about the house, inspecting flower beds and the like, and once he even saw them standing arm in arm.

"Yes," Jane said. "I'm quite fond of her. She really is a lovely person and essentially a very lonely person. She is not what you would call brilliant, not by any means, but she has a kindliness and refinement that I like, and she's terribly sincere about her beautification projects."

The Duttons meanwhile pursued their perfectly natural desire to make use of their beautiful home, to make use of their wonderful live-in couple, and do the sort of entertaining they had always expected to do.

Next on their list of dinner guests were the Beckfords, Tom and Marcia, rather younger than the Duttons and even rather richer. However, as Albert learned from Jane, who had been told it by Mrs. Dutton, all the wealth was Mrs. Beckford's, who had inherited it from her father's nuts-and-bolts business and multiplied it many times over. Tom Beckford, Jane said, spent his days almost exclusively in polishing the fittings on the sixty-foot sailing yacht which his wife had given him several Valentine's Days ago.

Once again there was a long discussion of the menu, once again roast beef was chosen, once again the table was set with the best Meissen china and the gleaming silver appointments which Mrs. Dutton had so long dreamed of using in the setting for which they were intended.

Dressed in his freshly laundered mess jacket and his black tie, Albert served smoothly and well, moving with consummate ease and grace about the long polished table, in and out of the shadows, aware almost immediately that he was the target of admiring and even covetous glances on the part of the Beckfords, particularly Mrs. Beckford, who could have been, he judged, no more than forty-five, and was already beautifully and impressively tanned in her white sleeveless dress. Her husband was of about the same age, looking stalwart and rugged and equally tanned in his dinner jacket. His face, Albert noted, was curiously free of lines.

Having served the roast beef, Albert, as was his habit, stood near the swinging door, ear close to the crack, while Jane read over the yellow pages she had written that day.

Through the crack, Albert could see that Mr. Beckford was still gorging himself on roast beef. The others had finished. The bell would be summoning him at any second now, unless Mr. Beckford decided upon another helping.

"How about some more beef, Tom?" Dutton asked. "There's plenty."

"Do you have a piece there that's overcooked, Jake? Almost burned?"

"Sure, here's one. Crisp enough?"

"Great, Jake. Is everybody waiting for me?"

"Take your time, take your time," Dutton said.

"*Really,*" Mrs. Beckford said. "You're absolutely the most fortunate people in the world. We've advertised and *advertised* and it's done us no good. How on earth did you *find* them?"

"We just—found them, that's all," Dutton said.

"Would it be sticking my nose in to ask how much you're paying them?" Mrs. Beckford asked in the tone of one who was accustomed to sticking her nose in wheresoever she chose.

"Fifteen hundred a month," Dutton said.

"Lying bastard," Albert whispered.

"Hmmmm," Mrs. Beckford said. "Fifteen hundred?"

"Yes. Now, *listen!*" Dutton said with forced joviality but undeniable suspicion. "Don't go getting any *ideas* now, Marcia. . . ."

From the others there was a ripple of laughter. "I know the rules, I know the rules," Marcia said. "Don't worry."

"Do not covet thy neighbor's live-in help," said Tom Beckford, his mouth full of crisp roast beef.

"But after *all,*" Marcia said. "A cat can look at a king. Can't she?"

"Sure," Dutton said. "Look but don't touch. And just don't look too long or too hard." Again he laughed, joined, tentatively, by Mrs. Dutton but not by Mrs. Beckford, who apparently not only had a low boiling point but was accustomed, what with her nuts-and-bolts wealth, to deferential treatment.

"Jake," she said icily. "I *assure* you, I'm *not* the sort of *person* who goes around *stealing* other people's *help.*" She

118

lifted her fork and put it down again. "I wasn't raised that way."

"Marcia," Jake said. "I didn't say you were."

Mrs. Beckford, after attempting without success to say nothing, said in spite of herself, "Well, I think you *implied* it, though, didn't you?"

"Oh, Marcia, let it drop," her husband said.

She glared at him.

"Jake, dear, please," Mrs. Dutton said.

"I didn't say anything," Dutton protested. "What did *I* do?"

Hoping to smooth things over, he reached out and placed his hand over Mrs. Beckford's, who immediately withdrew her own hand and placed it in her lap.

There was now a silence, broken finally by Mr. Beckford, who ponderously cleared his throat and began to speak in measured, eminently reasonable tones. "I think that what Marcia objected to was not so much the implication—but the simple fact that stealing your people was what she had in mind all along." He exploded with laughter, and the Duttons laughed too. "I think she was mad because you caught her out, Jake," Beckford said slyly.

Mrs. Beckford, finding none of it funny, sat with lips compressed, agitatedly sliding a silver bracelet up and down her deeply tanned forearm. "I assure you that was not the case," she said. "What I truly object to is the *paranoia* of it all. Excuse me, please . . ."

Albert saw her sweep from the room, while the others sat in uncomfortable silence. The silence continued until her husband said, "Maybe I'd better go see what's sticking in her craw." He got up and left the table.

"God Almighty!" Dutton said.

"Well, Jake," Mrs. Dutton said. "You *did* imply . . ."

"Hell."

"Oh, dear."

"Oh dear, hell."

"If you hadn't been so snake-bitten by Clinker . . . You should apologize to her, Jake."

"She's got a rich-bitch attitude, that's what's wrong with *her*, by God."

They were both silent, nursing their private and common gloom.

"What in the hell are they doing?" Dutton asked finally.

"You don't suppose they left . . . ?"

"I didn't hear any car start. Here they come. Shhh."

Albert, still at the crack, saw the Beckfords enter the room. Dutton got to his feet. "Marcia," he said, "perhaps I owe you an apology."

"Not at all," she said. "But . . ." She turned to Mrs. Dutton. "Will you forgive me, Frances? I have a simply dreadful headache."

"Oh, *dear* . . ." Mrs. Dutton was on her feet. "Let me get you a headache tablet. I have some that work like a charm."

"No. No, thanks. I know from experience. When they hit, they *really hit*. I simply have to surrender and go to bed."

"Oh, Marcia, how simply dreadful. I'm *so* sorry."

"I hope it wasn't what I said," Dutton said.

"What you said? What did you say? Oh. That. Of course not, Jake."

"Because I had no intention of implying—"

"She knows that, Jake," Mr. Beckford said.

"Won't you have some dessert?" Mrs. Dutton pleaded.

120

"I'd love to, Frances, but I simply must get home to bed. Will you get my sweater for me, Tom?"

"Let *me* get it," Mrs. Dutton said.

The three of them moved out, leaving Dutton sitting alone, moodily sipping his water. Then, muttering to himself, he threw his napkin angrily to the floor and stalked after them, turning back almost immediately and heading for the door to the kitchen.

Albert stepped back just in time.

"Albert," Dutton said. "Would you bring our dessert and coffee into the living room, please?"

"Very good, sir. Four?"

"No. Just two. Wait about five minutes and then bring it."

"Yes, sir."

In a few minutes, Albert heard a car start. He saw headlights come on, and then the car went swiftly down the lane.

When he took the tray into the Safari Room, the Duttons were sitting in moody silence.

Albert distributed dessert and coffee.

"Thanks, Albert," Dutton said sadly.

"Thanks so very much, Albert," said Mrs. Dutton.

As he departed, both sat staring sadly at their lemon mousse with the attitude of two people who lacked both energy and heart to lift their spoons.

The next evening, as Albert served their martinis and turned away, Dutton stopped him.

"I've been doing some thinking, Albert," he said. "Something happened last night—well, there's no need to go into details but the fact is—I haven't even discussed this with *you*, yet, dear," he said to Mrs. Dutton. "But I've got an idea."

Albert waited respectfully.

"It seems," Dutton said with a rueful grin, "that every son of a bitch and his brother around here would like to have you and Jane working for them."

Dutton looked at him closely. "Yes," he said finally. "And if everybody we have to dinner is going to go gunning for you, then by God we're not going to have anybody else to the house . . . which of course defeats the whole purpose."

"Not the *entire* purpose, Jake," Mrs. Dutton said. "I'm delighted that we have Mr. and Mrs. Bagby regardless."

"Okay," Dutton snapped. "I've got an idea. Shall we discuss it or not?"

"Of course," Mrs. Dutton said. "Go ahead, dear."

"Well," Dutton said. "This is what we'll do. We'll say that Albert is my cousin."

"I'm to be your cousin, sir?" Albert asked.

"Yes. Nobody would think they could steal a man's *cousin*."

"But, Jake," Mrs. Dutton said sadly, "I don't think it would *work*. Surely you wouldn't have your own cousin serving us dinner while we sat there eating. What would people think? What kind of cousin would *that* be?"

Dutton frowned. "All right," he said. "How about this, then? On the nights we have company, Albert and Jane can eat with us. I don't think there'd be any harm in that."

"Well . . ." Mrs. Dutton said. "Yes. *That* might work."

"I mean, Albert," Dutton went on enthusiastically, "you could prepare everything in the usual way and Mrs. Bagby of

122

course would cook the dinner and set the table, you know, get everything all set up—but then you just sort of casually bring in your drink and Mrs. Bagby joins us too. Then we introduce you. What do you think?"

Both Albert and Mrs. Dutton were silent.

"Well, *hell!*" Dutton snapped. "We've got to do *something!*"

Albert nodded. "Would I continue to wear this?" he asked, indicating his mess jacket.

"No, of course not. Do you have a dinner jacket? Black tie?"

"Yes, sir."

"Well, wear it. And Mrs. Bagby can wear something suitable. A dress. How would that be?"

Albert nodded.

"Both of you can join in the conversation like a cousin would, and then, after we've all finished eating, you can just go into the living room with us for a while, but then excuse yourselves and go out and wash the dishes." He turned to Mrs. Dutton. "How does that sound?"

"I just don't know, Jake. Maybe it would be all right."

"Well, hell," Dutton said. "It's true, we can say to ourselves that *all* the friends we've made down here can't *all* be sons of bitches, but we can't count on it. We've got to do *something*. We can't lose every friend we've made."

15

It seemed, at least superficially, to be a workable idea. Jane had no objection. In fact, she said, it would give her an opportunity to wear something decent for a change and perhaps even meet some interesting people.

The night chosen was a Thursday, which, as it happened, was what Albert described to himself as Settlement Eve. Friday would be a very big day, and long since he had asked for and been granted the day off. He and Jane were due in Washington by late morning to sign the papers necessary to complete the sale of their house—and to receive the long-awaited money. Beverly was coming up from school to meet them for dinner and to discuss how she was to spend her summer.

For this third in the series of Dutton dinner parties, the guests chosen were Rob and Billie Wilson, to whom the Duttons were in debt for two cocktail invitations. They had met the Wilsons just after moving to Rear Guard and did not really know them very well, but it was said that they enjoyed a reputation for popularity and for a broad range of interests.

"We've always wanted to get to know them better and this is our chance," Dutton said. "They've lived around here for a long time, so they're undoubtedly steeped in local lore. I think we can count on some interesting conversation."

Jane cooked dinner, Albert had the ice bucket filled with cubes, the liquor bottles were all lined up, and everything was in readiness.

When he heard the guests arrive, he waited a suitable interval and then joined the group in the Safari Room, where he was introduced as Jake's cousin, Albert Bagby.

"*Well!*" Albert said, rubbing his hands briskly. "Who'd like what to drink?"

He saw Dutton give him a quick glance but could not say for certain whether it was a glance of approval.

"Mrs. Wilson?" Albert asked.

"Bourbon," said Mrs. Wilson hoarsely. "I never drink anything but bourbon. What was it—Al?"

"Al," Albert confirmed. "And Mrs.—uh—Frances? A martini for you? Good. Mr. Wilson?"

"Rob," said Mr. Wilson. "I'll have some bourbon too, Al, please, and easy on the water."

"Gotcha," Albert said. "Jake—I *know* what old Jake wants." Dutton turned away.

"How about your wife?" Mrs. Wilson croaked. "Will she be with us?"

"She'll be along. Well, back in a flash," Albert said, and left.

Jane, wearing a black cocktail dress and looking quite lovely, was seated in her rocker before the stove, sipping at her martini, lost in thought. She had washed her hair and it had a sheen. She had even applied some eye make-up.

"Save some of that," Albert said.

She looked at him vaguely.

"Bring it in with you when you come," he said. "Is dinner ready?"

"What?"

"I said save some of that martini and bring it in when you come. Is dinner far enough along so you can leave it?"

"Oh. Yes. Just about." She went back to sipping her martini while he fixed drinks for the others. Dropping in the ice cubes, he gave her a look of misgiving, knowing her cocktail-hour habits.

"Concentrate," he said.

She smiled at him.

Returning with the tray to the Safari Room, Albert distributed the drinks and then sat on the windowseat, listening to the conversation, which, at the moment, concerned the many disadvantages of urban living.

As he sipped his drink, he saw Dutton making a circular motion with his hand, which he took to mean that he was to talk it up, join in. He nodded and cleared his throat.

Rob Wilson, whose drink was already down to roughly the quarter-inch level, turned to him and asked politely, "Are you here for a while, Al?"

Albert nodded. "For as long as our welcome holds out, I guess," he said, and chuckled as a cousin might.

"Al is here on a kind of a sabbatical," Jake said, frowning at Albert now and ducking his head in the direction of Wilson's glass.

"Here," Albert said, "let me fix that for you, Rob."

Wilson did not demur.

"Tell Jane to join us," Dutton said.

When Albert reached the kitchen, Jane had not moved.

126

"Come on in," he said. "It's time." He patted her cheek. Obediently she rose and headed from the room. Splashing in the bourbon, he overtook her as she reached the Safari Room, martini in hand.

Dutton and Wilson were on their feet. "May I present Mrs. Bagby," Dutton said. "Jane . . . Billie Wilson . . . Rob Wilson . . ."

Albert watched with approval as Jane acknowledged the introductions. Dutton, seeing there was no chair for her, gave her his, joining Albert on the windowseat.

Quickly Rob Wilson tossed off his bourbon, and Mrs. Wilson's glass too was empty. "Mrs. Wilson . . ." Albert said.

"Billie," she rasped.

"Can I freshen that for you?"

"Sit still, Al," Dutton said. "My turn."

Wilson's voice was distinctly louder, Albert thought, than it had been only ten minutes ago. "Frances," he said, pointing to the balcony. "What's that one up there . . . the one next to the zebra?"

"Heavens, I don't know," said Mrs. Dutton. "You'll have to ask Jake."

When Dutton returned with the Wilsons' drinks, Rob pointed to the balcony. "What's that one next to the zebra, Jake? Is that a gnu?" Laughing, he drank generously.

"That? No, that's no gnu. That's a wildebeest."

"The *hell* it is," Wilson said. "That's a gnu. It looks like every gnu *I* ever knew." Wilson laughed in his raucous way.

Watching Mrs. Wilson, Albert noticed a curious thing. Even though she had had only her first drink and perhaps a third of her second, her head seemed to wobble and roll

127

about on her neck, and every few minutes she seemed to be making a determined effort to hold it erect.

Clearly, both Wilsons had been drinking before their arrival.

"Jake," Wilson was saying, "I defy you to prove to me that that's not a gnu."

"Nope," Dutton said. "Wildebeest."

"What's the difference, then?"

"Actually," Albert said, "there isn't any."

"Isn't any what?" Dutton demanded.

"Any difference between a gnu and a wildebeest. A gnu *is* a wildebeest, if you want to look at it that way."

"Now . . ." Wilson laughed. "There's the man who knows what he's talking about. Cousin Al."

"Are you sure?" Dutton asked, frowning.

"Positive, Jake," Albert said.

Dutton looked dubious, and then disgusted. His mouth moved as he brought his glass close to his eyes.

Albert watched as Jane sipped her martini and saw the familiar glaze steal into her eyes.

"Jane, I admire that dress," Mrs. Wilson said, head moving.

Jane looked at her without comprehension.

"Did you buy it around here?" Mrs. Wilson asked.

Jane gave her a vague smile.

"I've looked everywhere this spring and can't find a thing I like," Mrs. Wilson said. "It's the first spring I can ever remember when I have absolutely nothing to wear. Nothing. Can you believe it?"

"Yes, oh, how very nice," Jane said politely.

128

There was a brief silence, which Albert felt it was his duty to smooth over. "Jane, dear . . ." he said.

"Yes, Jane, dear," croaked Mrs. Wilson. "What's so damned *nice* about it?"

"About what?" Jane asked.

"Skip it," said Mrs. Wilson.

"Why don't you give the potatoes a look-see, honey?" Albert suggested.

"Yes," Jane said. "Will you excuse me?"

There was another moment's silence after she had left the room. "You'll have to forgive Jane," Albert said. "She had some rather unfortunate news. Her father died."

"Oh, how sad," Mrs. Wilson said, blinking.

"For God's sake!" Wilson said accusingly. "You make her cook when she's just lost her *father*?" He looked at Dutton and shrugged. "Well, what can you expect from a man who doesn't know the difference between a gnu and a wildebeest?"

"Oh, she doesn't mind cooking," Albert said. "She loves to cook. It's good therapy. It's better that she has something to do."

"Was she close to her father?" Mrs. Wilson asked.

"Oh, my God!" Albert exclaimed. "*Was* she!"

"Well, I'm going out and give her a hand," Wilson said, moving unsteadily over the Oriental rug. "Nothing scatological intended," he called back over his shoulder. "*Wait* a minute. Now, just *wait* a minute. First I'm going up to this goddam jungle up here and make certain . . ."

Carrying his glass, he ascended the circular iron stairway and walked along the balcony. "*Gun-bearer!*" he bellowed, then walked up close to the head of the animal in question. He patted its head and backed away. "Yeah," he said. "Al's

129

right. It's both a gnu *and* a wildebeest. I can tell by the skull conformation."

Laughing at some length, he came down the circular stairway and headed carefully from the room.

"Frances," Dutton said, "maybe you should look in on Jane and see if you can give her a—help her."

"Yes, I will. Excuse me please, Billie . . ."

Mrs. Wilson, holding her neck stiff, focused on Albert long enough to ask: "What business are *you* in, Al?"

"Me? I'm in real estate. Or was. I'm just about to get out of it." Albert chuckled. "Another martini, Jake?"

"No, thanks," Dutton gritted.

Mrs. Wilson held her glass aloft. "I'll have some more of that perfectly lovely bourbon, Al, if you're doing it."

After a second's pause, Albert got up and took her glass.

When he reached the kitchen, he found his wife backed against the wall by Rob Wilson, who had his palm pressed to the wall near her right ear. Mrs. Dutton, on the other hand, was nowhere to be seen.

Ducking under his arm, Jane reached for a platter. "Here," Wilson said, "let *me* do that, dear."

Behind Wilson's back, Jane gave Albert a fierce grimace. "I think you can call everybody for dinner now, Albert."

"Oh, the hell with dinner," Wilson said.

Albert, having had rather more to drink than was his habit, could not quite believe in retrospect that dinner was really as it was, although at the time all his impressions seemed sharp and reliable enough.

There was Mrs. Dutton's intensely game effort to keep the conversation in reasonable channels.

There was Jake Dutton's glassy grin and, when no one was looking, his tight-lipped melancholy.

There was Jane, whose sole interest was in hurrying things along so she could get to her writing, and who kept asking brightly, "Who's ready for some dessert?"

There was Wilson, sweating, the ends of his black tie dangling, asking Dutton if he knew the plural of mongoose.

Finally there was Mrs. Wilson. From the very beginning, Mrs. Wilson had paid her food little heed. She simply sat there, wobbling, swaying, blinking gravely, and focusing on each speaker in turn.

Finally she simply fell off her chair.

Wilson at the moment was telling an involved anecdote concerning, so far as Albert could make out, hybrid corn.

When Mrs. Wilson fell, Dutton made as if to go to her aid, but something in Wilson's voice stopped him. What Wilson did was to continue with his anecdote, fixing Dutton with his eye.

Although Mrs. Wilson had fallen off her chair, Mr. Wilson was determined to pretend that she hadn't. Dutton, Albert, and the others were unable to pretend that Mrs. Wilson had not fallen from her chair because they could see her lying on the floor.

Dutton glanced at the floor, then at Wilson, again at the floor, and finally at Wilson again, apparently reasoning, Albert thought, that if a man was determined to pretend that his wife had not fallen out of her chair it was only decent to honor the pretense.

"Who's ready for some dessert?" Wilson asked brightly.

16

After helping Jane clean up the kitchen, Albert found Dutton on the screened porch, standing in the dark against one of the posts, head buried in his arms, sobbing, one might have thought, as if his heart would break.

But, hearing Albert, he raised his head, and he had been coughing, not crying, Albert was happy to see, thinking that he would have liked Dutton less if he had been so unmanly as to sob—or pitied him more than he wanted to.

"Hello, Albert," Dutton said forlornly, although with surprising fondness.

Albert saw the uncapped bottle of bourbon standing on a marble-top table, along with a small glass.

"Join me in a nightcap, Albert," Dutton said, falling harder than seemed necessary into a glider.

"Thank you, sir," Albert said, intending to sit next to him in the glider, but missing and sitting heavily on Dutton's leg.

"For *God's* sake, Albert," Dutton said.

"Sorry, Jake," Albert said.

"You can leave off that Jake stuff now," Dutton said. He still wore his dinner jacket, but his tie was gone and his shirt was open at the neck.

Albert removed his own tie and tossed it to the floor.

"You'd think a man . . ." Dutton's voice faded.

"It was a lousy party," Albert said.

"If I'd wanted to have a dinner party with pigs, I'd have invited pigs," Dutton said, finishing his drink and handing Albert his empty glass.

Albert filled the glass and began drinking from it. Dutton didn't notice. "Wouldn't I?" he asked.

"Wouldn't you what?"

"I'd have invited pigs," Dutton said.

"Hmmmm," Albert agreed.

"The elephants . . ." Dutton said reminiscently. "They were really wonderful, they really were."

"Hmmmm," Albert agreed. "What?"

"The elephants," Dutton said.

"I thought you were talking about pigs," Albert said. "And now it's elephants."

"Yes." Dutton took the glass from Albert and sipped at it. "A man works hard and comes to the twilight of his life and wants to enjoy some of the fruits of his labor . . ."

"What do you mean, elephants, exactly?" Albert asked.

"Has a nice dinner party, invites respectable people, and then what happens? What *happens*? He finds one of the guests chasing around the kitchen after the maid! The *maid!*"

With a wail of anguish, Dutton got to his feet. Groping for the handle of the screen door and not finding it, he elbowed his way outside.

The implication of Dutton's use of the word *maid* was not lost upon Albert. He attempted to bridle but was too drunk. Instead he stood there on the porch, staring with intense concentration at the blinking red light of the channel marker just off the end of the Dutton dock.

Then, thinking that Dutton might be about to do himself harm, he went outside. "Mr. Dutton," he called, circling the house. There was no sign of him. Albert stood in the yard, thinking it over. Across the lawn and beyond the parking lot, he could see the light on in his own room. He could see the shadow of Jane's head on the ceiling.

"Mr. Dutton . . ."

"Here I am, Albert."

"Where?"

"Up here."

Above his head, Albert heard a rustling sound. He looked up. Dutton was high in the tree. "You're up in the tree?" Albert asked.

"Yes." Dutton shifted his weight, trying to get comfortable. A clutch of leaves fell at Albert's feet.

"Don't you think it would be a good idea to come down?" Albert asked.

"No," Dutton said. "I'm not coming down."

"You're not?"

"No. I'm not. I had a poverty-stricken boyhood, Albert, that's what everybody seems to forget. When the circus came to our little town, we boys would carry water from the lake to the elephants at a penny a bucket. That's what I meant about the elephants. Never since, Albert, have I experienced the same thrill . . . to be so near the elephants and the pulse of the circus, and sometimes make as much as nine cents in a single day. It was a long long way to the lake and we couldn't move too fast on the return trip because we might slop water. The elephant keepers were very strict.

You had to come back with a full bucket if you wanted your penny."

"I see," Albert said. "Well . . ." Pulling himself together, he went into the house. "Mrs. Dutton," he called from the foot of the stairway.

She appeared on the landing in a dark robe. "Yes, Albert?"

"Uh . . . Mrs. Dutton . . . I thought I ought to tell you this. Mr. Dutton is up in a tree."

"Oh, dear," she said, hurrying down. "Which one?"

"I can show you." He led her outside to the tree.

"Jake!" Mrs. Dutton clapped her hands sharply. "Are you up in that tree? Come right down this minute."

"No, Frances," Dutton said sadly. "I'm up here now. I'm going to stay up here."

Although Albert had not noticed him take it from the porch, he saw now that Dutton had the bottle of bourbon with him. Holding firm to a limb with one hand, he tilted the bottle to his mouth with the other.

"Jake, you're *drunk!*" Mrs. Dutton said. "Is that bourbon you've got up there? You know very well what bourbon does to you. . . . It gives him diarrhea," she explained to Albert.

"Oh," Albert said.

"Jake, you'll fall. *Come. Down.* This instant. Come down before I call the Volunteer Fire Department."

"No," Dutton said. Doing a juggling act involving bottle and tree limb, he freed a hand, with which he wiped his mouth. "I'm fed up, Frances. I can't take it any more."

"Jake, that's utter nonsense, you come right down. Just because one silly little dinner party didn't work out, that's no reason why you have to go up in a tree. Now come down. You promised."

"I'm fed up," Dutton said.

"I'm ashamed of you, Jake. Do you hear me? I'm ashamed."
Dutton tilted the bottle.

"Is this the Jake Dutton I know?" she demanded sternly.

Albert looked at Mrs. Dutton in awe. Never had he seen
her so formidable.

Her voice crackled. "Is this the Jake Dutton who started
at the bottom of the ladder and fought his way to the
top, rung by rung, until he got to be the president of one of
the biggest plastic companies in the United States? Is it?"

She turned away from the tree and headed for the house.
Then she came back. "No," she said. "I think I must have
the wrong Jake Dutton. This isn't the one that I knew. I'm
sorry. I must have the wrong Jake Dutton. Do I?" She moved
closer to the trunk. "Do I, Jake? Because if it's the wrong
Jake Dutton, there's no reason for me to stay here any
longer."

From high in the tree there came a sound that might
have been a grunt of contempt, or might, on the other
hand, have been a groan of self-pity.

"Because the Jake Dutton *I* used to know wouldn't let a
little thing like this get the better of him. The Jake Dutton
I once knew wouldn't go up a tree with a liquor bottle just
because he happened to have some boorish dinner guests.
He'd be able to see the woods for the trees. He'd put his
keen analytical mind to work and he'd figure out the answer. *That's* what *my* Jake Dutton would do."

The bottle fell to the ground with a soft thud. Looking
up, Albert saw Dutton leaning over precariously, putting
his keen analytical mind to work to see what had become
of his bottle.

Mrs. Dutton thumped the trunk with her fist. "Come on down now, Jake, and we'll sing some of the old songs. *That's* what my Jake Dutton would do. He'd come inside with me now and we'd sing 'Button Up Your Overcoat' and 'Life Is Just a Bowl of Cherries' and all the nice old songs. . . ."

Gingerly, and yet now and again with a trace of extreme carelessness, Dutton had started down. "Slowly now," Mrs. Dutton said. "Be careful . . . careful . . . Help him, Albert, please."

Albert leaned hard against the trunk, stretching his arms aloft. He grabbed Dutton's ankle.

"Leggo my ankle, Albert!" Dutton protested. "I can't move!"

"Sorry," Albert said.

"Here. Put your shoulder over here."

"Put your shoulder up against the trunk, Albert," Mrs. Dutton said.

"All right," Albert said.

Dutton leaned heavily on his shoulder and they fell to the ground together. "Here it is!" Dutton said, picking up the bottle.

"No you don't," Mrs. Dutton said, grabbing the bottle and upending it. A few drops trickled out. She tossed the bottle away and helped Dutton to his feet. With her arm firmly about his waist, they headed for the front door of the house. "Now, *this* is the Jake Dutton I know," Albert heard her say as they disappeared inside.

Unsteadily, Albert started weaving his way across the parking lot and slowly climbed the stairway. The sound of the typewriter drifted down to meet him. He lurched inside and closed the door heavily behind him. Jane didn't look up.

"Old Jake," he said. "You should have seen him. He got drunk and climbed up in that big maple tree and wouldn't come down."

"How lovely," Jane said.

Fully clothed, Albert fell face down across the bed just as the sound of piano notes began to reach him from across the way.

The last thing he remembered hearing was Dutton's voice, singing with surprising resonance:

"*Is it a sin? Is it a crime? Boo-boo-boo-boo-boo-boo-*BOO*-boo . . . If it's a sin then I'm guil-teeeee, guilt-y of lov-ing you. . . .*"

17

For all the fact that he had a slight hangover, the next day was one of the most beautiful days in Albert's life.

He and Jane set out in early morning in their used station wagon, and a beautiful May morning it was, with soft, fleecy clouds and a lilting warmth that still was more spring than summer. The water was a gorgeous deep blue as they crossed the Chesapeake Bay Bridge and went on up the road to their eleven-o'clock appointment.

The lawyer's office had a splendid, reassuring dignity, with its polished dark paneling and its framed watercolors of such landmarks as the Washington Monument, the White House, Natural Bridge, and Harpers Ferry.

The buyers were young folks, in their mid-thirties, Albert guessed, and a most charming couple in every respect. Mr. Cranston was tall and dark and tweedy, with a slightly receding hairline and kindly intelligent eyes. His wife was a delightfully outgoing girl, whose flaxen hair and high color reminded Albert, as he was later to remark to Jane, of a lass from the Scottish highlands.

The lawyer had been retained by the Cranstons. Albert and Jane were represented only by their real-estate broker, a Mrs. Untermeyer. After everyone had shaken hands all around, the small group gathered about a gleaming walnut conference table, whereupon the lawyer expressed the opinion that there was really very little to do except to sign some papers and—with a twinkle—to sign some checks.

Mr. Cranston, Albert noticed, had his checkbook before him, a handsome thing bound in a magenta plastic that was reminiscent of the finest morocco leather.

Recorded music, Sibelius' *Finlandia* at the moment, seeped through the impressive leather-bound volumes that lined the walls.

Mr. Cranston opened his checkbook and uncapped his fountain pen. "There's one thing I'd like to say to Mr. Miller before we proceed. . . ."

Albert felt a small twinge of heat touch his scalp.

"And that is that I've never seen a house so beautifully taken care of. Right down to the last detail."

Albert grinned. "Thanks very much," he said. "We tried to keep it nice."

"I wish," said Mrs. Untermeyer, "that I had forty houses just like it to sell. You folks were really very very fortunate."

"Don't we *know* it!" exclaimed Mrs. Cranston, eyes dancing merrily and high spots of color flaming over her smooth cheeks.

"We do hope you'll be happy there," Jane said. "*We* certainly were."

"Actually," Albert said, "it's rather an easy house to maintain. So long as you don't let it get away from you."

The lawyer now shoved a copy of the settlement sheet to all parties. "Now, according to my figures," he said, "let's see—Mr. Cranston will have three checks to make out. One to the bank for the outstanding amount of Mr. Miller's mortgage, $17,497."

"Right," said Mr. Cranston. "That's $17,497." He wrote it and flipped it toward the lawyer.

"Now one to Mrs. Untermeyer for her commission, $7,500."

"*Thank* you," said Mrs. Untermeyer.

"Seven thousand, five hundred . . ." This check too was flipped toward the lawyer, who in turn passed it to Mrs. Untermeyer.

"And now one to Albert Miller and Jane B. Miller for exactly $100,003." The lawyer looked up at Albert. "Is that according to your figures, sir?"

Albert nodded. "That is correct," he said.

The check slid across the polished surface of the table, coming to rest upside down. Casually Albert turned it right side up.

Somebody was tinkering with the music system. The volume grew louder and louder, swelling, bursting, threatening to lift the law books right off their shelves. The tune now was a waltz, "Tales from the Vienna Woods," unless he was mistaken.

With the check in his wallet, Albert waltzed from the office, out into the glorious sunlight of late morning.

"I'm starved," Jane said. "Can we have some lunch?"

"Not sure we can afford it," Albert said and then laughed very loud, pounding his wife between the shoulderblades.

"Ouch!" Jane said. "Stop it, Albert. You're making a fool of yourself. People are looking. You *miser*."

But nothing she said could really get to him, such was his inner strength.

They ate at a modest restaurant, where he kept adjuring her to speed it up, pointing out that their day's work was far from done.

Once they had eaten, it was out into the sunlight again, first to the bank where for years they had maintained their checking account, a venerable structure of weathered brick, festooned with gargoyles and giving off an air of solid, rugged dependability.

Albert's heart thudded as he filled out the deposit slip and then, seeking composure, he slouched up to the teller's window and slid check and deposit slip across the counter.

"Why, Mr. Miller! It's been a long time." The teller was a young lady whose window he had been in the habit of frequenting for years. "Where have you been keeping yourself?"

"We've been away," Albert said, wishing she'd hurry up and notice the amount of the check.

She looked at it finally, then up at him with a slight frown, then down at the check again. "Wow!" she said.

"Thanks very much," Albert said as she slid his receipt to him.

"Thank *you* very much, Mr. Miller. Don't stay away so long next time."

There was more to come. Hurrying now to make the two-o'clock bank closing observed by some, but confident in the knowledge that others stayed open until three, and savings-and-loan associations until four, Albert steered Jane along through the beautiful amber light, through parks filled with azaleas and tinkling fountains, where pleasant-looking people sat on benches and looked at him with admiration.

"What's that song?" Albert asked.

"*What* song?" Jane looked at him closely.

"Oh," he said.

The seven banks they now visited were similar in many respects, he thought, although there were differences of nuance and detail which would be quite apparent to a close observer such as himself, just as there were differences in the passbooks and jackets.

At six banks, they opened joint savings accounts of $15,000 and at the seventh, an account of $10,000.

"Actually," Albert remarked as they left the last bank and he slid the seventh passbook into his pocket, "the government did us a big favor when they raised the FDIC insurance limit from $10,000 up to $15,000, do you realize that?"

"Can we get some coffee or something?" Jane asked. "I'm exhausted."

"Well you might be," Albert said. "And if they hadn't raised the insurance limit you'd be even more exhausted. If they hadn't raised the limit, we'd have had to go hauling around to *ten* banks instead of just seven. We never would have gotten through."

"Can we have some coffee, Albert?"

"Of course, dear. Oh, Jane, I love you. I really do, you know. All things considered, I think we've had a wonderful marriage."

"Albert!"

At 5:10, they picked up Beverly at the Greyhound terminal and drove to what in the old days had been their favorite restaurant.

Sitting opposite the two of them, he thought once again how very much alike they looked.

"Daddy!" Beverly was laughing. "What's *wrong?* You're so *happy.*"

"Of course," he said. "Why shouldn't I be?"

"How is the State? Is he withering?"

"He's withering," Albert said. "Unless I'm mistaken, the State has spent most of the day in the bathroom with a bad case of diarrhea."

"Poor State," Jane murmured.

"Poor State, hell," Albert said.

"Shall we talk about my plans for the summer?" Beverly asked.

She went on to say that she had been invited by one of

her classmates to spend June and July on an island in Lake Michigan, where the classmate's family had a summer home.

"Would that hurt your feelings?" Beverly asked.

"Not at all," Albert said. "You could come down to Rear Guard in August if you feel like it."

"That's what I told Nick I would do."

"Have you been seeing Nick?" Jane asked.

"Yes. A lot. He's very much against my going to Lake Michigan. He thinks I should get a summer job—so I can take some of the burden off *you*. He's very much concerned over you."

"Over me?" Albert asked.

"Over you both."

"Why?" Jane asked.

"Because you're members of the servant class. So, just to shut him up, I told him I'd be working up there. And I may be, part of the time."

"Doing what?" Albert asked.

"They bring some slum children up for a week at a time, in shifts."

"Thank God for *somebody* in this family," Jane said.

"What do you mean by *that*?" Albert demanded.

"Nothing," Jane said, looking pensively at the far wall.

Beverly caught an eight-o'clock bus and it was dark by the time they left the city.

"Sorry to be going back?" Albert asked.

"No," Jane said. "Strangely enough, I'm not sorry at all. Are you?"

144

"Nope. I don't miss the city. I enjoy visiting it. I certainly enjoyed visiting it today."

"Yes," she said. "I could tell."

Taking first one hand and then the other from the steering wheel, he patted the pockets containing the seven passbooks.

Back in the servants' quarters at Rear Guard, he spread all seven on the bed and smiled at them.

Aside from a used car and few articles of clothing, he owned nothing in all the world. He had licked the system. He had even licked Jake Dutton.

The next morning he was adding oil to the crankcase of the mower, ready to begin the day's mowing, when Dutton approached.

"Good morning, sir," Albert said.

"Good morning, good morning." Dutton's face was pale and had a washed-out look. "Did you and Mrs. Bagby have a nice day off?"

Albert straightened from the mower and looked him in the eye. "Yes sir, we did. Very nice, thank you."

"Good. Good." Absently, Dutton fingered the fringe of the blue-and-orange umbrella that was attached to the sulky. "What did you do?"

"Do?" Albert said. "Oh—nothing very much. I just took the missus for a tour of some of the public buildings. I thought it would be good for us both to see something of our nation's capital."

18

Early June became mid-June. The swimming pool was now open, the trees and lawn were lush, the estate was a tapestry of dark and lighter greens. The pleasure-dome was in full operation, yet there were no guests to share its pleasures, and one evening Jane, filled with compassion, told Albert that she felt the reason was not solely the failure of the dinner parties. It was, she said, because the Duttons didn't know anybody else to invite.

"And look at this," she said. "Look what came in the mail today."

The envelope, which she had already slit open, was addressed to Mr. and Mrs. Albert Bagby. Inside there was an invitation:

COCKTAILS

June 24th
"Land's End"
Billie and Rob Wilson

Regrets only   5-7 P.M.

"I've already turned it down," Jane said. "I'm sure the Duttons didn't get one. It would break their hearts."

Taking it from him, she sailed it over the bank into the river.

Whatever the reason, the Duttons were giving no more parties. Instead, Jake Dutton had become increasingly arboreal, taking to his tree when the shadows lengthened, and Albert often would keep him company, standing at the trunk and sometimes even joining him in the tree, albeit on a lower branch, where he would listen with respect as Dutton remarked upon the beautiful view he had from his higher perch. He would inform Albert that the sun was about to set, whereas for Albert it had, to all intents and purposes, already set. "That's because I'm higher," Jake explained. Loath to leave the tree once he was in it, he would, once or twice during the evening, stand on his branch, hang on with one hand, unzip his fly with the other, shout, "Look out below!" and relieve himself, often with a whoop of gaiety. "Didn't get you, did it?" he would ask politely, and then settle himself once more into his bower, where he might comment on the view as twilight fell, or perhaps herald the appearance of a boat long before it might have been visible to anyone on the flat.

Mention of boats often stirred him to a bitter denunciation of the *Peacepipe Hilton*, for it was increasingly apparent that his anger had become concentrated now upon his old friend Clinker Merritt. Although it was true in large measure that the Wilsons were responsible for bringing the shambles of his social life to a rasping climax, he felt Clinker had forged the first and most devastating link in the horrible chain of events that had now led him to spending most of his evenings in a maple tree.

Yet, being in the tree seemed to give him solace of a sort, and the knowledge that Albert was with him gave comfort to Mrs. Dutton, who, after her initial cajoling, had given up, apparently feeling that his arboreal phase simply had to run its course.

For Albert, the memory of Dutton's deceit was too fresh, the taste of his snobbishness too bitter, to permit sympathy, but there were times when even he could not resist a stab of pity, to see a man so intent upon enjoying his wealth and his retirement and yet frustrated at every turn. Even the solace of liquor was denied him. No longer did he take the bottle up the tree, obviously reasoning that the pleasures of the moment were not enough to offset the discomfiture of the day after. A one-martini man he was and must always remain.

Nor could he find pleasure in boating, as Clinker did and as so many others in the area did. Day after day, Dutton's small cabin cruiser bobbed at the dock, ignored and unused. Albert was not even sure that Dutton knew how to run it.

The tree, of course, was by no means the sole focus of the day. As always, there was grass to mow, borders to clip, the swimming pool to vacuum, errands to run in the village, and there were the heads of the big game animals to dust and brush.

And for Albert there was the splendid point in each day when he would sit on the bench by the river and watch the boats pass. The river was filled with boat traffic now, and more often than not Jane would join him, bringing her martini along while the evening meal simmered. Being outdoors seemed to provide a stimulus for Jane that was lacking indoors, and very often he had her attention.

At such times he would tell her how each and every payday he was socking away the entirety of their salary and that, since it cost them virtually nothing to live, he was quite sure that before the year was out he would have saved enough to pay the tax on their profit.

"That means the whole hundred thousand will be ours?"

"Right," he said happily, gazing out over the river. "Everything's working out fine."

Jane smiled. "I must say that you look positively wonderful. You're so bronzed and you've lost weight."

"I feel fine," he said. "You look good, too. I've given you a good life, Jane, you've gotta admit."

"Yes, you have, Albert. I had no idea."

"I was right, wasn't I?"

"Yes," she said thoughtfully, "except you're the damnedest communist I ever saw. You don't own anything, but you never talk about anything except money."

He chuckled. "I'm interested in other things. A few."

She sighed and sipped her martini. "I'm very worried about the Duttons. They break my heart. Yesterday when I was sunbathing by the pool she brought me up some lemonade. I told her she shouldn't have done it. She said she was *glad* to do it—that we were really the only friends they had, and why *shouldn't* she bring a friend some lemonade."

"Well, if it gives her pleasure . . ."

"I know, but I almost cried. And Mr. Dutton—the way he treats *you*. Do you realize you're his only friend? You're his status symbol, his friend, his crony—everything."

"Including whipping-boy."

149

"Not really."

"Okay, so I'm nice to him."

"He envies that horrible Clinker so, because Clinker has a big boat and is popular. Mr. Dutton simply doesn't know what to do with himself, that's the trouble."

"God knows that's true," Albert agreed. "Do you know what he ordered in the mail? It came yesterday. Did you see it?"

"No. What?"

"It's one of those frogman outfits, one of those black form-fitting suits."

"With aqua-lung?"

"No. It's just a long periscope—I mean a breathing-tube. He showed it to me yesterday. I asked him what he was going to do with it, and he said he was just going to monkey around a little."

"I suppose the thing is that maybe we shouldn't completely discount him."

"What do you mean by that?"

"I don't know," she said. "But after all, he *is* a man of fierce determination and he *was* the president of a large company."

When, ten minutes later, Albert appeared in the Safari Room with the usual martinis, Mrs. Dutton was sitting in her accustomed chair. Dutton, however, was up on the balcony, peering closely at the head of the lion. "Albert," he called down.

"Yes, sir?"

"Did you notice this lion's nostrils?"

150

"No, sir, I didn't."

"They're changing color. They're getting mildewed. They're supposed to be black, aren't they?"

"Yes sir," Albert said, "I should think so. I've never given it a great deal of thought."

"See if you can find something tomorrow and clean them up a little, Albert."

"Yes, sir, I will. Would you like your martini up there, sir? Or down here?"

"No, I'll come down."

Mrs. Dutton sighed.

That evening Dutton did not take to the tree, and in the light of subsequent events it was probable, Albert thought, that he had spent the time in his room, studying his frog-man's costume and the breathing apparatus. For next afternoon, while Albert was riding the mower, he saw Dutton—he could assume it was Dutton—wearing a form-fitting black suit which included a headpiece which entirely obscured his face. In his hand he carried a long tube. Presently he saw Dutton ease himself into the pool and, riding closer on the mower, he saw the end of the breathing-tube moving along through the water.

Later that afternoon, still mowing, he saw Dutton, normally clad, walk to the end of the dock and step aboard the small ungainly cabin cruiser. Over the sound of the mower, he heard a sudden roar, and the cabin cruiser was leaping and straining at its mooring lines. The lines slacked as Dutton succeeded in throwing it into neutral. Several times, again and again, he threw it into gear, first into forward, then into reverse, traveling the foot or so permitted by the lines until they grew taut and threatened to pull down the pilings. Finally he saw Dutton step ashore and head for the house.

"What in God's name is he up to now?" Albert muttered, making a wide turn with the mower and heading off into the vast wasteland of unmowed lawn.

Toward five that evening, as he was putting away the mower, his mystification intensified. He was washing his hands with gasoline when Dutton approached the garage.

"Albert," he said. "No martini for me tonight."

"All right, sir."

"I want you to do something for me," Dutton said. "I want you to meet me down at the dock at ten o'clock."

Albert nodded.

"Wear old clothes. And wear some boating shoes. Do you have any sneakers or anything like that?"

"Yes, sir, I have an old pair of sneakers."

"Wear them," Dutton said. "And don't mention any of this to Mrs. Dutton."

"Right, sir."

He watched as Dutton strode toward the house with the brisk and resolute step of a far younger man.

19

When, shortly before ten that evening, Albert reached the end of the dock, he found Dutton already aboard. "Albert, is that you?"

"Yes, sir," Albert said. In the dim light, he could see that Dutton was wearing his frogman outfit.

"Come on aboard," Dutton said.

Albert stepped aboard, slipping a little on the gunwale and landing heavily with both feet in the cockpit.

"God's sake, Albert," Dutton said. "I thought you were going to wear sneakers."

"I did, sir. They're old and kind of smooth, I guess."

"All right. Look, do you know how to run one of these sons of bitches?"

"I never have, sir."

"Well, just do what I tell you."

"You mean—we're leaving the *dock*, sir?"

"Leaving the dock?" Dutton's laugh was harsh. "I'll tell the world we're leaving the dock!"

"In the dark? At night?"

"Yes. I don't know about *your* eyes, Albert, but I've got the eyes of a cat. All right. Now I'm going to start 'er up. After she starts, you go up there and throw those ropes off. Throw 'em right on the dock. Got it?"

"Yes, sir." Albert started climbing to the raised portion of the deck, headed forward.

"Are you up there?" Dutton called.

"Yes, sir."

"Got hold of the rope?"

"Yes."

"Good. Here she goes!" The motor roared. The boat lurched forward and Albert very nearly fell overboard. "Put it in neutral, Mr. Dutton!" he shouted.

"What? I can't hear you!"

"I say, put it in neutral!"

"Right. That's what I *planned* to do. When I give the signal, I'm going to toss off this back rope and you do the same up there at your end. Okay?"

"Okay."

"Okay! Go!"

Albert hurled his line to the dock and started crawling on all fours toward the cockpit. The boat started in reverse with another pronounced lurch. Once more he grabbed tight. "Slow 'er down," he shouted.

The boat was traveling in reverse at a great rate of speed, threatening, on its present course, to back into a sailing yacht moored in the harbor.

"Throttle 'er down, Mr. Dutton!" Albert shouted.

The boat lost speed. Albert dropped nimbly into the cockpit, brushing against Dutton, whose frogman suit felt very slippery and even rather slimy, as if he had coated it with some substance or another. "This throttle gets stuck," Dutton said. "You've really got to give it a tug. Okay. Now,

154

I think we've got clearance, so we can go frontwards. What do you think?"

"I don't know, sir. I can't see very well."

"Well, I can. I'll take the responsibility."

Dutton jerked at the gear lever and the boat for a moment seemed to be going nowhere, but then it began to make forward speed.

"Where is it we're going, sir?" Albert inquired.

"You'll see. First off, we're heading for the channel. Do you see those red and green lights there?"

"Yes, sir."

"Channel markers," Dutton explained. "Red Right Returning. I've been reading up in the last couple of days. Only we're not returning. We're leaving."

"That's true," Albert said. "Where are we going?"

"You'll see, Albert, I told you. Now what we've got to do is head for that red light and go by it so it's on our left when we pass it, since we're leaving. Doesn't that make sense to you?"

"Yes, sir."

"Red Left Leaving, in other words," Dutton said. The boat shuddered. "What was that?"

"I think we must have bumped something," Albert said. "The ground, I think. Maybe it's not deep enough here. Maybe we're on the wrong side of the red lights."

"Like hell we are. We couldn't be." Dutton spun the wheel, intending apparently to describe a wider arc, but instead the boat started circling back whence it had come. He made an adjustment and headed for the flashing red light.

"May I make a suggestion, sir?" Albert asked.

"What is it, Albert?" Dutton asked curtly.

"Go slower—so then in case we hit something we won't hit it so hard."

"Okay," Dutton said gruffly. He cut the speed. "Except that we haven't got all night, you know."

At the more sedate pace, Albert permitted himself to relax and even toyed with the idea of enjoying the prospect of being on the river at night. The sky was dense with stars. In the very faint light, Dutton, in his frogman outfit, looked like somebody from another planet who had landed and commandeered the ugliest cabin cruiser ever built.

"Now," Dutton said. "Reach down there and you'll find a flashlight. Albert, can you plot a course?"

"Holy God!" Albert said. "Can I do *what?*"

"No matter. I'll do it. I've already got the broad outlines in my mind. Wait until we get past this buoy . . ." There was, in another few seconds, a scraping sound, indicating, Albert decided, that they must have sideswiped the buoy in passing. "God, Albert," Dutton said. "You've got to keep your eyes open."

"I told you, sir. I can't see very well at night."

"Okay, now listen. You take the wheel. Just steer for that next red light. Got it?"

"Yes, sir, I suppose so."

Albert kept one eye on the approaching red light and out of the corner of the other he saw Dutton holding the flashlight close to a large chart which he had spread out on the cockpit cushions. "We're right here," he was muttering. "So if we're right *here* . . ." His voice faded. "What was the number on that last red light we passed, Albert?"

"You've got me, Mr. Dutton. I didn't see it."

156

"Hell, Albert, you can't see *anything*, can you?"

"Not very well, sir."

"Well, here . . . check me out on this. Look here at the map." He held the flashlight close. Albert looked. The boat started to describe an arc. "Don't let go of the wheel!" Dutton shouted. "My God, Albert. Hold a steady course. You're all over the river."

"I'm sorry, sir, I thought you wanted me to look at the book." Mentally he noted that he liked Dutton perhaps better on dry land. The water seemed to change his personality.

"Here," Dutton said. "I'll drive. You look at the map." Albert held the light close, comprehending very little of what met his eye in the cone of light. He saw only a confusing mass of light blue and white streaks, dotted here and there with red and black.

"The way I make it," Dutton said, "that last red buoy must have been Number Fourteen. Find Fourteen. Can you find it?"

"Yes, sir," Albert said triumphantly. "I *see* it."

"Okay, so from there, all we have to do is keep following the red lights, and then—do you see where our river sweeps around a big point of land, curving to the right?"

"Yes, sir."

"And see where it joins that other big river?"

"Yes," Albert said dubiously.

"What's the name of that other river?"

"Don't *you* know?"

"Of course I know," Dutton said angrily. "I just wanna see if *you* know."

"It doesn't seem to be here, sir."

"Don't be preposterous, Albert. Of course it's there. Read the map. Figure it out."

"Whoops!" Albert said.

"Dammit, Albert, you don't have to say whoops just because we hit something. It couldn't have been anything more than a beer can."

"Wait a minute," Albert said. "I've got it. The other one is the Peacepipe."

"Right," Dutton said. "That's using your head."

"Is that where we're going?"

"That's *exactly* where we're going."

Albert stiffened. "Why are we going there, sir?"

"You'll see, Albert." Dutton chuckled.

The boat purred along smoothly now, held to a surprisingly steady course by Dutton.

"You're not going to do anything you'll be sorry for, are you, sir?" Albert asked.

"No, Albert. Not at all. Put the flashlight on this red bastard coming up here. Right. Hold it. Number Ten. Right. Just where it's supposed to be. It's easy once you get the hang of it. No, Albert . . . we're just going to pay a little social call is all." Dutton began whistling a bouncy tune.

One by one, the buoys passed by. One by one, Albert bathed them with the flashlight. Onward the voyagers plowed, making the curve now that would bring them into the broader river that was their destination.

"Whoops!" Albert said.

"Albert! For God's sake, will you stop it!"

"That was the wrong number, sir."

"Not at all," Dutton said. "We have to keep the red lights on our *right* now. Because we're returning."

"We're returning? How do you figure that, sir?"

"If we lived on the Peacepipe, we'd be *returning*."

"I see. . . ." Albert paused. "I don't want to be argumentative, Mr. Dutton, and I'm sure you know what you're doing. But we *don't* live on the Peacepipe, so we *couldn't* be returning."

"That doesn't matter, dammit," Dutton said in rage. "We have to *pretend* that we *do* live on the Peacepipe so far as the map is concerned. Gimme the flash. Right. Number Four. We're heading up the Peacepipe now. See all the lights on shore? Those are houses, Albert. Great big expensive houses, passing by. Look at the map. Do you see a big bulge about halfway up?"

"Yes, sir."

"Is there a Number Ten red buoy next to the bulge, sort of touching against it?"

"Yes, there is."

"That's it, then," Dutton said with satisfaction. "Now. I'm going to ease her down a little." Dutton touched the throttle. The motor roared and the boat lurched nearly out of the water. "Oops, wrong way," Dutton said. He managed to throttle down until the motor was only a low hum. The boat began to lose some of its momentum.

"There it is!" Dutton shouted exultantly. "There's the son of a bitch!"

"There's what, sir?"

"That boat. That obscene floating hotel. See it?"

The familiar skyscraper configuration of the *Peacepipe Hilton* loomed against the darkened sky.

"What are your plans, sir?"

"Never mind, Albert, you just carry out orders."

"Mr. Dutton, sir, there are lots of lights on in the house, people must be still awake. In fact, I think I can see some people sitting on the screened porch, playing cards."

"I see them, Albert." Dutton chuckled with scorn. "The damn thing's so big he can't even get it up to his *own* dock. He has to anchor it out in the middle of the damned river!" Dutton spat overboard. "Look at it! Isn't it the ugliest bastard you ever saw, Albert? Shh! Let's keep our voices down, and don't turn on that flashlight any more."

"But won't our lights be visible?"

"We don't have any lights," Dutton said. "I don't need any lights. I can see just as well without 'em. Okay, I'm cutting the engine."

"Make sure you push the throttle the right way," Albert cautioned.

"Right." Dutton pushed it the right way and then switched off the engine. There was an abrupt and even ominous silence. The boat drifted closer to the monster anchored just ahead. "Drop the anchor now, Albert," Dutton said. "No, wait a minute. I'll do it. You'll make too much noise."

Lifting the lid of a compartment, he withdrew an anchor, which he let gently over the stern, paying out line and then grunting. "I bought a hundred and fifty feet of rope," he said. "I could have bought ten and it would have been plenty." He tied the line to a cleat. "Okay now," he said finally. "You stay aboard, Albert, and be on the alert to haul me back aboard when I tell you to."

"Mr. Dutton, what are you planning to do?"

"Never mind, Albert."

"But, sir, I feel it's my duty to stop you from doing something you may be sorry for later."

Dutton chuckled. "Don't worry, I won't be sorry, not at all. I'll be glad."

He picked up his long breathing-tube and blew through it. "All clear," he announced. "Now then . . ." Once more he was groping in the compartment.

"Mr. Dutton! What are you planning to do with that brace-and-bit!"

"What do you *think* I'm planning to do with it, Albert?" He chuckled. "Bore a hole in something. What does somebody usually do with a brace-and-bit?"

"You mean you're going to *sink* the *Peacepipe Hilton?*"

"Exactly. Look alive now, Albert."

"You can't do this, Mr. Dutton."

"I'm *going* to do it."

"Mr. Dutton, listen. Let me tell you something, sir. Do you know what Montaigne says about revenge? Revenge is *always* more harmful to the perpetrator than it is to the victim. No kidding, Mr. Dutton."

"Nonsense, Albert."

"It's true, sir. It's my duty, Mr. Dutton. You think the *Peacepipe Hilton* will be sunk and that Mr. Merritt will thereby be destroyed, but it's really *you* who will be destroyed, sir. If you'll just read Montaigne . . ."

"Albert, you're out of your mind. What kind of drivel are you talking about? I'm going to sink the *Peacepipe Hilton* and damn the consequences. That's what I came for and that's what I'm going to do. It deserves to be sunk. It's an obscenity. And if you're feeling sorry for Clinker Merritt,

161

don't. He's got enough money to buy a hundred boats just like it. Furthermore, he's got it insured."

"But don't you realize, sir, it's impossible to sink that boat? It's too tall. It may settle a little lower, but that's all. You won't get the satisfaction you'd get out of seeing a boat disappear before your eyes, Mr. Dutton. You'll never be able to get that sucking-down, maelstrom effect."

"Never mind, over we go, matey."

"*We* go?"

"Not you. You stay aboard. Listen, we're making entirely too damned much noise, Albert. Keep your voice down. Shhh!" Dutton was perched on the stern. "You hand down the brace-and-bit after I get in the water—no, on second thought, you might drop it."

Brace-and-bit in hand, Dutton eased himself into the water. "Hand me my breathing-tube," he said.

"Where is it?"

"Right there on the cushion," Dutton said, treading water.

Albert found the tube. It had the texture of light plastic, much like the containers that new toothbrushes come in. "Here it is, sir."

"Thanks, Albert. Wish me luck."

"All right . . . good luck."

Dutton submerged and for a few moments all Albert could see was the top of the tube, moving through the water. Then, with a great splash and commotion, Dutton burst the surface, gurgling and gagging. "It won't work!" he shouted. "I can't get any air out of the damned thing!"

"Blow through it," Albert suggested. "Maybe there's a speck of dirt."

162

Supporting himself by clinging to the anchor line, Dutton blew hard.

"Okay?" Albert asked.

"Seems to be. Here I go again."

In a matter of seconds, Dutton was up again, panting and cursing.

It was then that Albert heard the voice ashore. "Ahoy out there! What's going on?"

"Son of a bitch is clogged up," Dutton panted.

"Shhh . . . Mr. Dutton . . . There's somebody on the dock there." Albert lowered his voice to a hoarse whisper. "It sounds like Mr. Merritt."

"Ahoy, I say!" The voice sounded more stern. "Who's out there fooling around my boat?"

"Shhh," Dutton said. "Don't answer."

"Give an account of yourself!" Merritt shouted, for it was unmistakably Merritt.

"Just lay low, Albert," Dutton whispered up from the anchor line, from which he was once again hanging.

"I know you're out there!" Merritt shouted. "All right, if you don't want a load of buckshot across your bow you'd better sing out."

"Holy God, Albert!" Dutton moaned. "Take me aboard."

"He wouldn't, would he? Actually *shoot?*"

"Take me aboard, I say!"

"Let me have your hand, Mr. Dutton. Come around here to the side, that's it. Gimme your hand now. Okay." Albert leaned far out over the gunwale and Dutton grasped his hand. Albert strained. "Wait a minute, sir. Let me have the brace-and-bit. You need both hands free. Okay. Now." Again Albert strained.

"The side is too high!" Dutton said in panic. "All I do is swing under the boat! Pull, dammit, Albert, *pull!*"

"I'm *pulling!*"

As he pulled even harder, Dutton's hands slipped from his grasp, and Dutton fell back into the water.

"Ahoy! I hear you out there!"

The stillness of the River Peacepipe was shattered by the roar of a shotgun.

"Start the motor!" Dutton shouted, making no attempt now to keep his voice down. "Start it! Get going!"

"But how about the anchor, sir? And how about you?"

"The next one will be closer!" Merritt bellowed. "Unless you identify yourself. What ship is that?"

"The hell with the anchor, Albert," Dutton said fiercely. "*Pull* the anchor. I'll hold on to the anchor. Get going! Pull me!"

"Right," Albert said.

"Make sure it's not in reverse, Albert! You'll run me down!"

"Stand clear of the propeller, sir."

Another shot rang out.

"Albert!" Dutton howled.

With a great roar, the engine started, and since the boat already was in forward gear it started moving even as the engine turned over. Albert shoved up the throttle, heading back in vaguely the direction from which they had come. Looking back, he saw Dutton floundering through the water perhaps twenty feet astern, dragged along like some unique species of fish. Albert saw that he was letting out the line, apparently intent on letting it all out so that he could grab and hold the anchor itself.

164

Although the anchor and Dutton's weight made for a considerable drag, the boat nevertheless was making good speed, churning through the water in the direction of the nearest red light. "Are we returning or leaving, sir?" Albert shouted.

Dutton by now had apparently payed out the entire anchor line and was so far astern as to be out of sight.

"Can't hear you, Albert," he called from a great distance. "Slow down and take me aboard. For God's sake, *take me aboard!*"

Albert touched the throttle and threw the gear into neutral. The boat lost speed, and when the momentum had eased he turned his attention to Dutton, who by now was hauling himself hand over hand toward the stern.

"God Almighty, Albert," he was panting. "Lemme on board."

This time, with much hauling and straining, Albert managed to pull Dutton aboard.

Wet, slippery, and grotesque in his frogman's suit, Dutton sprawled on the floor of the cockpit, panting and cursing and lamenting the fates that had caused his scheme to go awry.

"Take me home, Albert. Take me home."

"Are we leaving or returning, sir?"

"We're leaving for a while and then we're returning. Here, Albert, let me take that wheel. You don't know what you're doing."

An hour later, they bumped the Dutton dock with a crash that must have been heard all up and down the River Swoose. "We made it, Albert," Dutton said. "We're home."

Part Three

20

It was after that night on the Peacepipe River that Jake Dutton's condition took a downward turn, although the change at first was barely perceptible, perhaps because it was psychological rather than physical.

Albert's concern had been with the physical—the long exposure to the water and the night air, not to mention the sheer exertion of being dragged through the water at breakneck speed at the end of 150 feet of anchor line. Dutton after all was in his late sixties and the ordeal could easily have caused a stroke or even a heart seizure. No, Jake said. No such thing. Physically he felt fine. His heart was okay and the exposure hadn't bothered him at all. The night had been quite warm, and the frogman outfit clung to him like a glove. When he peeled it off that night (which he had been thoughtful enough to do in the toolhouse, out of consideration for his wife) he was, he assured Albert, dry as a bone.

Yet it was inconceivable that the failure of his mission should not have left some mark.

Blaming Clinker as he did for the failure of his retirement

and indeed of his life-plan, Dutton had clearly hoped through one explosive act to achieve such total revenge that his misery would be expunged.

And then to have the mission become a fiasco, all because of a clogged breathing-tube, and to be dragged through the water at midnight, an elderly man in a frogman's suit, clutching an anchor line for dear life, with buckshot showering all about him, and with the added danger of striking a piece of driftwood or a stake . . . Albert shook his head in sympathy. Yet he knew that it was not nearly so much the aspect of danger that counted with Jake as the aspect of the inglorious, the utter failure of a mission.

Albert felt reasonably certain that Clinker knew the identity of the midnight marauder, and if Clinker had telephoned to revile or protest, Dutton might have salvaged some measure of respect by calling him a son of a bitch, pointing out that the river was a free river, open to navigation of no matter what sort. But unfortunately Clinker did not call, gave no sign that he even cared.

Jake then was left with very little. Outwardly he seemed untouched, and even blithe. Yet in this very blitheness there was cause for concern and wonder. Albert was undecided whether to look upon him as a man of true indomitability, or a man responding to the encroachment of mental disease.

There were times when he didn't much care, as for example on the following Saturday afternoon. Nick, down for the weekend, was washing his sports car on the parking lot. Dutton, at loose ends as usual, was talking with him, and Albert, upstairs in his room, overheard Jake say:

"Just remember, Nick, what it says in *Poor Richard's Almanack*."

170

"What does it say, Uncle Jake?"

"It says, 'Let thy maid-servant be faithful, strong and homely.'"

Nick's reply was inaudible, drowned out perhaps by the sound of Albert gnashing his teeth.

Presently, listening again, he heard Dutton say, "That's where you make your mistake, my boy."

"But, Uncle Jake, you've got to remember, these are the nineteen-sixties."

"Nonsense."

"They are, Uncle Jake."

"It's your television and your newspapers that make 'em so," Dutton said.

Albert heard no more and when he looked from his window, he saw Dutton reclining in the maple tree.

With so little to occupy him and with the challenges so amorphous, it was perhaps a boon that Jake Dutton should have been introduced to Jolly Dollars, or so it seemed at first.

It began one day when Dutton found one of the Jolly Dollars envelopes on the front seat of the Bentley. The envelope had been left there by Albert, who had just returned from the village after having the Bentley filled with gasoline.

"What's this?" Dutton asked.

"Oh . . ." Albert explained it to him at some length.

"You mean it's a contest?" Dutton asked.

"Not exactly, sir. You see, it comes folded, like this. Then you tear it open and unfold it. You see—this one is a five-dollar Jolly. If we match it with a five-dollar Dollars, then we'd get five dollars. Or *you* would. It's your car, of course."

"But *this* is a five-dollar Jolly . . . ?"

"Yes, sir. They have all different denominations, you see. Up to five thousand dollars."

From Dutton there came a low whistle. "Do we have any more?"

"No, sir. This is the first one I've gotten."

"How about your own car, Albert?"

"I don't normally use Jolloco, sir."

"Wouldn't it perhaps pay you to?"

"Maybe so. But today was the first I'd heard of the contest, you see."

"How about the Thunderbird? Be sure to use Jolloco in the Thunderbird, Albert."

"Yes, sir, I will."

"Hmmmm." Dutton pursed his lips. "Here, let me see. It's a five-dollar Jolly. I wish we had a five-dollar Dollars, then we'd win five dollars, is that what you said?"

"That's it exactly, sir."

"Well, I'm damned. Clever, huh?"

"Yes, sir. I suspect it will drive quite a few people to Jolloco, Mr. Dutton."

"I shouldn't be at all surprised. Well now, Albert . . ."

"Yes, sir?"

"Let me know when you get another one. How often can you get them?"

"Every time you buy Jolloco, I suspect. Although, come to think of it, the sign said no purchase was even necessary."

"Well that, of course, is nonsense," Dutton said. "Likely story, eh? I'm sure you couldn't simply walk into the station—or ride in on a bicycle and say to the attendant, 'Give me Jolly Dollars envelopes.'"

"I guess not, sir."

"Well . . ." Dutton opened the glove compartment. "Suppose we keep them in here?"

"Good idea."

Dutton looked at the gasoline gauge. "Full."

"Yes, sir. I just filled it."

"Hmmmm," Dutton said.

Later that afternoon, Albert, riding the mower, happened to glance toward the parking lot and see Dutton with a length of garden hose, trailing it toward the Bentley. Albert frowned. He saw Dutton removing the gasoline cap and then inserting one end of the hose, after which he seemed to engage himself in some rather spastic maneuver which Albert could not understand. Finally he walked toward Albert, beckoning vigorously.

Albert cut the engine of the mower and dismounted.

"Come here, Albert," Dutton called. "I have something I want you to help me with."

"What are you doing with that garden hose, Mr. Dutton?"

Dutton did not answer.

"You've cut the couplings off, haven't you?"

Dutton nodded. With one end of the hose in the tank, and the other trailing at random across the parking lot, he put his ear close to the gasoline tank, listening. He grasped the hose and bent it double, releasing it then with a single swift movement, whose efficacy he sought to enhance with a spastic hopping motion.

"I don't believe you can siphon it that way, sir," Albert said.

"Well then, just how *do* you siphon it, Albert?"

"You have to get it started, sir, with pressure of some sort. Then it goes of its own accord."

"Do we have a pump, Albert?"

"Not one that would work on this, sir. Do you really think it's worth it?"

"I guess not," Dutton said.

"I mean, we could just wait a few days until we need gasoline again."

"That's true, Albert." Dutton stood there, lost in thought, frowning at the tank. Finally he sighed. "How *would* you do it, though, I mean if you wanted to? If it became necessary."

"Well, I think what you could do, sir, is take the other end of the hose and put it in your mouth and draw in hard. That gets it going, I believe, so I've heard."

"Hmmmmm," Dutton said. "*You* do it, Albert."

Albert frowned. "Me?"

"Yes, you're the one who knows about it."

"I don't really *know* about it."

"Well, you know more about it than I do. Go ahead."

Dubiously Albert took the free end of the hose, looked at it, brushed the dirt from it, and wiped it hard against his trousers. Then he put it in his mouth and drew air. A second or so later, he gagged and spat out a stream of gasoline. "Good God, Mr. Dutton!" he exclaimed.

"There it is!" Dutton said excitedly. "Lay it down! Give it gravity, Albert! There it is! It's running out good!"

Albert spat and spat again. Dutton chuckled. "Make sure

you don't hold a lighted match to your mouth, Albert. That was nice work, though. *Look* at it!"

They stood there, watching the gasoline flow over the parking lot in a steady stream, and seep into the gravel. After a time, Dutton said, "Check the gauge, Albert."

Albert switched on the ignition and checked the gauge. "It's about three-quarters now, sir."

"Down a quarter?"

"Yes."

"That should do it."

Dutton jerked the hose from the tank, spilling gasoline on his shoe. He tossed the hose aside. "All right, Albert, let's go."

With Albert at the wheel and Dutton in the back seat, they rode into the village, pulling to a stop at the Jolloco pump. The attendant, the same one who had filled the tank that morning, looked at Albert expectantly.

"Would you fill 'er up, please?"

"Went through that one in a hurry, didn't you?" the attendant asked greedily.

Albert got out and slammed the door. "It's only down about a quarter."

"Oh." The attendant began pumping, while Dutton watched from the back seat.

"Four gallons."

"Right." Albert handed over Dutton's credit card. The attendant carried it toward the office, and Dutton got out and followed, stopping to peer at a large banner which flapped in the breeze. PLAY JOLLY DOLLARS, it said. ANY LICENSED DRIVER CAN PLAY.

Beneath this invitation, it said:

Mrs. Angelina Pillsbury won $500.

Mr. E. Brown won $50.

Richard Starbuck won $100.

The names of a number of lesser winners followed.

The attendant handed back the credit card. Albert signed for the gasoline. The attendant then reached into the pocket of his shirt and handed over an envelope.

Albert got back at the wheel and Dutton this time sat beside him in front. "Got it?" he asked. Albert nodded. "Well, let's not open it quite yet," Dutton said.

They had driven perhaps a mile back toward home when Dutton said, "Okay, pull over. Let's have a look." He chuckled with excitement.

Albert stopped the car on the shoulder. "Now then," Dutton said. "In other words, if this is a five-dollar *Dollars*, then we win, is that it?"

"Yes, sir. Would you like to open it?"

"No, you open it, Albert."

"Wouldn't you rather?"

"No, I'd rather you did it."

Carefully Albert slit the edges.

"*What?*" Dutton asked.

"Five thousand," Albert said. "Dollars. Now all we need is the five-thousand *Jolly*."

Dutton's chuckle was high-pitched. "That's something to shoot for," he said.

"It sure is, but, Mr. Dutton, if it's all the same to you,

176

I'd just as soon we didn't do any more siphoning. I can still taste that gasoline. It has a terrible taste."

"Let's not put this one in the glove compartment," Dutton said. "I'll keep it in my wallet. I'll keep both of them."

They drove on. "Of course," Dutton said moodily, "you realize, don't you, Albert, what it is? It's just a sales gimmick, that's all. Just a come-on."

"Yes, I suppose so."

"But on the other hand, they *did* have those people's names listed. It couldn't be rigged. Jolloco is a respectable firm. But the question in *my* mind, Albert, is—well, now we've got a five-thousand-dollar Dollars, I wonder how many five-thousand-dollar Jollys there are in the world. There couldn't be many."

They turned into the entrance and moved sedately up the lane. Rear Guard in all its manicured splendor was spread before their eyes.

"You know, Albert," Dutton said in a faraway voice, "I've never won anything in my entire life. Do you realize that?"

"No, sir, I didn't realize."

"Once I found a quarter in the gutter out in front of the Mar-Tech Club when I was coming out after lunch, but that's the most I've ever found. And I've never *won* anything at all."

Albert nodded. "Well, sir," he said, looking straight ahead, "maybe this will break your streak of bad luck."

21

Unlike Dutton's dinner parties, playing Jolly Dollars involved little or no contact with human beings, nor did it involve the risk of marine disaster or physical injury as had his attempt upon the life of the *Peacepipe Hilton*. It was at first the quiet pursuit of a simple pleasure, and one whose goal was clean-cut and specific.

Mrs. Dutton was highly pleased. She confided to Albert that it gratified her to know that her husband was so absorbed in life. Even though his preoccupation lacked any real substance or importance, she said, it was still very good to know that he had something to look forward to when he got up in the morning.

"This is the way I envisioned his retirement," she said. "Having him happy and relaxed with hobbies and things of a trivial nature."

What should have been apparent to her, Albert thought, as it had long since become apparent to him, was that Jake Dutton could never be relaxed about anything he ever did.

Winning at Jolly Dollars very soon became an obsession.

His quest, although perhaps less nerve-racking than his dinner parties, was hardly less expensive, for Dutton, taking the car out alone and cruising aimlessly about, soon began to waste gasoline at a rate perhaps unequaled in the history of motoring. In a matter of only a few days, he had more than twenty envelopes, including a great many duplications but no match-ups, not even in the $1 and $2 categories. He had a second $5000 Dollars but no matching $5000 Jolly. He also had two $1000 Jollys but no matching $1000 Dollars.

"Son of a *bitch!*" he said heatedly to Albert upon the occasion of slitting open his second $1000 Jolly. "I feel we're hitting all around it, Albert, but we keep missing the bullseye."

Meanwhile at the service station, the list of people proclaimed by the company as winners was growing steadily. A Mr. E. G. Fellows of Starnesburg, Pa., had won himself $5000 and the poster bore not only his name but his smiling, bespectacled, self-effacing likeness.

All this was fuel to the fire that burned within Jake Dutton.

One evening, with his ear to the swinging door, Albert listened to the dinner conversation he was carrying on with Mrs. Dutton.

"I'd just like—just *once* in my life—to *win* something," Dutton exclaimed.

"Well, you certainly deserve to," Mrs. Dutton said.

"When I think of all the contests there are! When I think of all the people in this damned country who are always winning this and that . . . color TV's and whatnot . . . and all the people on welfare and then you see somebody's picture in the damned newspaper who's just won some damned daily double or Irish Sweepstakes or whatnot, and one thing and another . . ."

"I know," Mrs. Dutton said soothingly. "You'd think just the simple law of averages—"

"Limericks! Just take limericks, for example. And then when I think of all the money we've paid out in taxes and never gotten back a plugged nickel except that time I found the quarter in front of the Mar-Tech Club . . . Well, anyway, I'm going to keep on trying on this Jolly Dollars deal until I win something."

"Well, I think you *should*, Jake, if it gives you pleasure."

"It doesn't give me pleasure. *Pleasure?* What are you talking about? It makes me mad as hell, Frances, if you want to know the truth about it. But I'm determined to see it through."

There came the morning in July when Dutton asked Albert to get into the car. Dutton's white hair was slicked down and he wore his hound's-tooth jacket with a dark blue sports shirt. There was a gleam in his eye, as well as a hard, flinty quality in his voice.

"Where are we going, sir?" Albert asked.

"We're going to launch an all-out drive," Dutton said, getting into the rear.

Albert switched on the ignition. "We don't have much gasoline, Mr. Dutton."

"I know we don't, Albert. Stop in the village."

By now, aside from their respective mates, they saw no one else in the world so frequently as they saw the Jolloco attendant in the village. Seeing the Bentley drive up, he came eagerly from the office. "Fill 'er up this morning?"

"Please, Sam," Albert said.

"No," Dutton called from the back seat. "Two, Sam."

"Two?" Sam asked.

"Two gallons," Dutton affirmed.

The pump went *ping, ping* and stopped. Albert started to hand over the credit card, but again Dutton stopped him. "Cash," he said, handing a dollar up to Albert, who passed it to the attendant, who returned a Jolly Dollars envelope with the change. Albert passed the envelope back to Dutton.

As they drove off, Dutton said, "Two-dollar Jolly—son of a bitch!"

Yet it was spoken more with grim determination than with despair.

"Where to, sir?"

"Keep on up to Paxton, Albert."

Dutton seemed not disposed to talk, and when Albert commented upon the great height of the corn or the health of the soybean crop, he got merely a short answer or none at all.

When they reached town, they stopped at the two Jolloco stations that Paxton boasted, settling for a flat dollar's worth of gasoline at each. Grimly, Dutton dropped the offending packets into the large shopping bag in which he now kept his collection.

"Home, sir?"

"No."

"Where?"

"Just drive, Albert."

"Well, north, would you say, sir? Or south?"

"North," Dutton said.

The Bentley purred smoothly along the highway. It was a beautiful day, rather cool for July, as Albert pointed out, and it was not unpleasant to be driving. In the rear-view mirror, he caught glimpses now and again of Dutton's face. It was for the most part stony, and for the most part the eyes looked straight ahead, but occasionally they would dart left and right, now to a Dari-Freez, now to a Stuckey's, taking in with a glance the world which he had tried to leave behind, the world he had forsaken by taking refuge at Rear Guard, and the world which he would not have invaded now had it not been so important to him to do so.

From the look of his eyes, he was intent not so much upon the scenery as he was upon spotting the next Jolloco station, a surmise soon confirmed. "Here's one!" he shouted. "Stop up ahead there, Albert!"

The Bentley rolled up to the pump, a dollar's worth of gasoline was delivered by a sullen attendant, who accepted the dollar and started off with it. "Hey, how about our Jolly Dollars?" Dutton demanded.

The attendant came slowly back, reached into his pocket, and handed over the packet, rather grumpily, it seemed. Albert passed it to the back seat and drove on. He heard the tearing sound, the grunt, and then the rustle as Dutton stuffed it into his shopping bag.

"Keep going, sir?"

"Keep going."

By one o'clock they were nearing the vicinity of Wilmington, Delaware, and faced, in Albert's opinion, a decision. "Do you want me to get on the Jersey Turnpike, sir?"

"Do they have Jolloco?"

"No, sir. I believe Citgo has the concession on the turn-pike."

"Well then, obviously we don't want to get on the Jersey Turnpike, Albert."

"Do you want me to go right on into Wilmington?"

"Skirt it, if you can."

"Mr. Dutton . . ."

"Yes, Albert?"

"Aren't you getting hungry? It's after one o'clock."

"Yes, I could eat, I think. Stop at a Howard Johnson, if you can spot one."

On the lookout now for the familiar yellow-and-blue of Jolloco and the bright orange-and-blue of Howard Johnson, they drove on until Dutton exclaimed, "Well, I'll be damned, Albert. There's a Howard Johnson and a Jolloco right next to each other, side by side. See up ahead?"

"Yes, sir."

"That's luck for you."

"It sure is."

After obtaining another dollar's worth of gasoline and another worthless Jolly Dollars envelope, they pulled into the Howard Johnson parking lot.

At lunch, with his mouth full of cheeseburger, Dutton looked at Albert in a strange way. It was a look, Albert decided, of compassion, a quality which he had never particularly noticed in his employer. "What do you hear from your daughter, Albert?"

"We've had a couple of letters, sir. She's apparently enjoying herself. She's up at Mackinac Island."

"Yes, I know." Dutton paused to chew. "Your daughter, I understand, has always been interested in acting."

"Yes, sir. Ever since she was in junior high school."

Dutton nodded, continuing to chew and continuing to give Albert the same sympathetic look.

"Why?" Albert asked.

"No reason," Dutton said. "I was just interested."

As they were leaving, Albert opened the glass door for Dutton, but Dutton motioned him ahead, giving his shoulder an affectionate clap. "Thank you, sir," Albert said.

"It's okay, Albert."

After lunch, Dutton fell asleep on the back seat, and Albert, doing as he thought Dutton wanted, stopped four times for gasoline while his employer slept on.

Finally, sometime toward four o'clock, he heard Dutton stir and yawn. "Where are we, Albert?"

"I believe we're in Pennsylvania Dutch country, sir. I just saw a Mennonite."

"I must have fallen asleep." Dutton yawned again.

"Here are four more, sir." Albert handed the envelopes over the back seat and heard Dutton muttering as he opened them.

"Any luck, sir?"

"No. NO! The dirty bastards! I'll tell you the truth about it, Albert. It's starting to get my goat."

"I can't say I blame you, sir."

"I'm beginning to feel hatred for Jolloco. Where are they located, Albert? Trenton, isn't it? Their home office?"

"I'm not sure, sir. It probably says on one of the Jolly Dollars envelopes."

"Trenton," Dutton affirmed. "Well, Albert, we might as

184

well turn around and head back the way we came. If we go any farther west we'll be damn near to Pittsburgh. Retrace your steps."

By six-thirty they had done just that.

"Albert, are you getting hungry yet?"

"I could eat, sir."

"See if you can spot a Howard Johnson. Hold on, I think I see one up ahead there. Say, Albert! Do you realize something?"

"Yes, sir. It's the same one where we had lunch."

"It sure is. I didn't see anything wrong with it, did you?"

"No, sir."

This time, however, the place was crowded, and it was past seven before they got a table. They were having dessert and Dutton was speculating bitterly on how many $5000 Jollys there probably were in the world, when a man in the adjoining booth turned and rested his chin on the partition. "You're saving Jolly Dollars too?" he asked.

Albert was facing in the man's direction. Dutton's back was to him. "Yes," Albert said, "but we're not having much luck."

"Any match-ups?"

"None," Albert said. Dutton didn't turn around, pretending to be absorbed in his fudge cake.

"Friend of mine won two bucks," the man said. "Big deal." Dutton muttered.

"I heard you talking," the man said, "and I got to thinking. You got a lot of them? You know—I got to thinking how about if a couple of guys pooled what they had and then if they got a match-up they could split what they won. Who'd ever know? You got yours with you?"

Albert nodded.

"Well, listen. I got a big batch at home and I only live a mile or so. Why don't you follow me over and we'll see what we come up with."

Albert looked at Dutton, whose face gave no indication of his wishes in the matter. "Well . . ." Albert said.

"Look. Are you about finished eating? I'm going to the can a second. Be right back."

Jauntily the man strode down the aisle.

"Do you think we should, Albert?" Dutton asked.

"I don't know, sir. It's entirely up to you."

"I think perhaps not. Let's slip out, shall we? Without any explanation . . ."

Dutton covered the check with a five and a one, and they left hurriedly.

"Shall I stop at this same Jolloco?" Albert asked.

"No, keep going." Dutton sighed. "I suppose it's wrong in a way not to rub shoulders, but the fact is I doubt it would have led to anything, Albert."

"Probably not, sir."

"I have no great desire to meet anybody new anyway. I already know as many people as I care to know."

Albert said nothing.

"I've never really been very fond of others anyway, have you?"

"Others, sir?"

"Other people," Dutton said.

"Other than . . . other than who, sir?"

"Well, other than the people I already know, I suppose, Albert. I feel that's one of the troubles with people in America today, don't you?"

"What's that, sir?"

"They're always trying to get to know a lot of people they don't really need to know."

"That's entirely possible, I suppose. . . . Which way now, sir? Home?"

"How much gas have we, Albert?"

"Just a sliver."

"Hmmm. Shall we give them one last chance? Here's a Jolloco ahead."

While the dollar's worth of gasoline was being pumped in, Dutton leaned tensely forward over the backrest of the front seat. When the envelope was handed back to him, he slit it quickly.

"What luck?" Albert asked.

"A two-dollar Jolly," Dutton said angrily. "That does it. That *does* it, Albert. Never again in this lifetime do I ever buy another penny's worth of Jolloco gasoline. I vow it."

"I can't say I blame you, sir."

"Pull away from the pump, Albert. Pull over there to the side. I have to go to the bathroom." Albert pulled away from the service island and stopped at the edge of the paved area. "This should be okay," Dutton said. "Frankly, I'm not even sure that I want to use a Jolloco restroom, for that matter, but—yes. Yes, I will. Albert, do you have a pen or a pencil? I think there's one in the glove compartment."

Albert handed back a ballpoint pen.

"Thanks." Dutton got out of the car and headed around the side of the building, carrying the shopping bag full of Jolly Dollars.

He was gone quite a long while. When he returned, still

carrying the shopping bag, Albert noticed a curious rattling sound that seemed to come from his pockets.

"Okay, Albert," Dutton said, settling back.

"Home, sir?"

"No. On to Trenton."

"*Trenton?*"

"Trenton."

"May I ask why Trenton, Mr. Dutton?"

"Because that's where the Jolloco home office is. Number 313 Front Street, Trenton."

"But would they be open at night, sir? Their *executive* offices?"

"I hope not," Dutton said.

Albert drove slowly onward, lost in thought.

"Speed it up, Albert. What's the trouble?"

Albert pulled off to the shoulder. It was now past eight and nearly dark. "Mr. Dutton, I feel it's my duty, sir, to ask what you have in mind. I'm not sure it's a good idea to go on to Trenton. It's another hour's drive."

"Are you tired of driving, Albert? I'll drive if you are."

"No, sir, I'm not tired of driving. I'm just wondering what it is you've got in mind."

"You'll see soon enough," Dutton said. "That's the trouble today," he went on bitterly. "Nobody willing to make a commitment."

"I don't quite see the wisdom, sir, of making a commitment to Trenton."

"Albert, I hate to think of you as an employee and myself as an employer, but those are the facts, and if I say we go to Trenton, then we go to Trenton."

Albert maintained a hurt silence.

"Isn't that the way you'd look at it, Albert, if our positions were reversed?"

"If our positions were reversed, sir, I'd say, 'Turn around now, Jake, and let's go home, we've had a long day.'"

"*Jake?*"

"Jake is what I'd call you if our positions were reversed, sir."

"Enough of this nonsense, Albert. Start the car."

"What I have in mind, sir, is the night we took the boat over to the Peacepipe River. If I'd known what you had in mind, I'd have tried to stop you. You could easily have been hurt."

"I have no regrets about that night, Albert. In some ways, it was the high point of my summer. Start the car."

"Mr. Dutton, I feel entitled to know what you've got in mind. I feel it's my moral responsibility to ask."

"All right, Albert, if you drive on I'll tell you while you're driving, but this is costing us precious time."

Albert started the motor and eased back out into the road. "Yes, sir?"

Dutton sighed. "You've noticed the picture of their building, I suppose. The one on the Jolly Dollars envelope?"

"I didn't examine it closely, no, sir."

"It's a new modern building with a lot of glass," Dutton said.

"Hmmmmm," Albert said.

"What do you mean by 'hmmmm,' Albert?"

"You're planning to break some windows. I think that would be a mistake, Mr. Dutton."

"I'm planning to break just *one* window, Albert."

"One?"

189

"Just one."

"And then what?"

"And then I'm planning to empty the contents of this shopping bag through the hole in the window and scatter these damned Jolly Dollars things all over the floor of somebody's office."

"That's all?"

"Not quite all. What I've done is write four-letter words . . ."

"On the Jolly Dollar certificates?"

"Yes. One four-letter word to a certificate, although not always the same four-letter word, naturally."

"That's what you were doing back there in the restroom?"

"That's right, Albert. So. What do you think?"

"I'm not sure, Mr. Dutton."

"Seems harmless enough, doesn't it? No more than they deserve."

"What do you think it will accomplish?"

"I don't know, Albert. I suppose it's only a gesture of protest, a rather feeble gesture perhaps, but still it's mine."

"I've never known you to use four-letter words, Mr. Dutton."

"I don't, as a rule. Anyway, I'm not using them. I'm just *writing* them. You can see the difference."

"Yes, I suppose so."

"Furthermore, I was talking to my nevvew, Nick. He said he was reading about them. He said he read that more people should use them."

"For any particular reason, sir?"

"They act as a purge somehow," Dutton said. "If more

people would use them, it would correct a certain delicate imbalance that prevails in the country today."

"What sort of imbalance would that be?"

"I'm not sure," Dutton said. "I'm just telling you what he told me."

"I don't understand the sudden interest. It seems to me that people have been using them for years. When I was a boy, that's about all I heard."

"Using them, yes, but not writing them," Dutton said.

"We wrote them on telegraph poles."

"Telegraph poles don't get published."

"Hmmmm," Albert said. "In any case, what you've got is a shopping bag full of Jolly Dollar certificates with obscene words written on them?"

"Printed," Dutton said. "With exclamation marks on most of them. I didn't quite finish because I got tired. I did it while I was sitting on the hopper."

"Hmmmm . . ."

"I've spent a great many man-hours on this contest," Dutton said. "They can't be allowed to trifle with a person's life this way."

"It seems to me there should be some other way . . ."

"Well, I can't think of any," Dutton said sharply. "So come on, Albert. You agreed. Speed it up. On to Trenton."

22

It was past nine when they reached Trenton and another half-hour before they were able to find their way to the correct address.

"I guess that must be it," Albert said finally. "See ahead? The white building with all the windows."

"That must be it," Dutton said.

"Yes, that *is* it. See the sign on top?"

Letters of bright blue neon etched the name JOLLOCO across the dark summer sky.

"Don't park too close, Albert. Park about a block away."

"I think you're out of luck, Mr. Dutton. Every window in the building is lit."

"We'll see. Here. Park right here, Albert."

The building was the brightest gem in the diadem of a neighborhood obviously in process of rehabilitation, half slum and half architectural glory.

They got out and stood by the Bentley, peering across at the canopied entrance. "Does that look like a night watchman to you, Albert?"

"He has a uniform on. I guess he must be."

"Why do they keep the lights on all night?" Dutton demanded. "With the electricity they're wasting they could afford to hand out a few winning certificates, the bastards, don't you agree?"

"Yes, sir, they could."

With all the glass, and with the brilliantly lit interior, it was possible to see every stick of furniture in each of the Jolloco cubicles.

"Well . . ." Dutton started walking. "Let's try around back, Albert. I doubt if there'll be any night watchman there."

"Mr. Dutton, let's not do it. I think it's a mistake."

Albert tugged at Dutton's arm, but Dutton jerked away. "Come on, Albert, don't be chicken."

The rear of the building looked very much like the front and was just as brightly lit, differing, however, in that there was no canopied entrance, nor any visible entrance of any kind. Moreover, it backed up to a dark alley lined with darkened, broken-down dwellings.

Dutton reached into his pocket. "Here, Albert."

"What is this, sir?"

"A stone." Chuckling, Dutton patted the pockets of his jacket. They were filled with stones.

"Where did you get all those stones, Mr. Dutton?"

"Back behind the restroom at that last Jolloco station, Albert. Okay. Fire away."

"Why me, sir? Why not you? You're angrier about it than I am."

"I just want you to have first crack, that's all. Just because I'm the employer and you're the employee doesn't mean I always have to go first."

"That's very enlightened of you, Mr. Dutton."

"Fire away, Albert."

Albert tossed his stone with little heart. It bounced off and fell to the alley.

"Here." Dutton reached into his pocket. "Try another one."

Again Albert threw, harder, but this effort too bounced harmlessly away.

"Okay, *I'll* try," Dutton said. He threw with no effect.

"Mr. Dutton, may I make a suggestion? Don't you think these stones are rather small? They're hardly bigger than pebbles."

"Let's keep our voices down, shall we, Albert?" Again Dutton wound up and threw. Nothing happened. "You may be right, though. Come on, maybe we can find something bigger here in the alley. Maybe a brickbat. Ah! Here. Feel."

Albert grasped what seemed to be half a brick with a jagged, pointed end.

"When you think of all the unnecessary miles," Dutton said. "Not to mention what it's cost us in money and energy."

Winding up, Dutton threw. The brickbat struck the glass with a loud report but fell to the ground.

"Damn!" In a rage, Dutton scrambled after the brickbat, reared back and threw it again. And then again and again, each time moving closer until at last he was using the brickbat as a hammer. Finally he became winded and stood there panting.

"Better give up, Mr. Dutton," Albert said. "I'm afraid it's some special kind of unbreakable glass."

Dutton glanced upward. "Maybe it's only these first-floor windows that are unbreakable, Albert. If we could just get up to the second panel . . ."

"Couldn't we just throw at it?"

"No, we couldn't. Don't you see why? We have to have the hole low enough so that we can shove the shopping bag through it and spill the certificates in an insulting way. I don't just want to shove the whole shopping bag through. Here. I've got an idea." Dutton picked up the brickbat. "Let me get on your shoulders and I think I can reach it."

"You mean you're going to *stand* on my *shoulders?*"

"Yes, if you can move up tight against the glass. Bend down, Albert. Wait a minute, dammit, Albert."

"Maybe you should put down the brickbat, sir. It's digging into my neck."

"Sorry, Albert. How's this?"

"That's better."

"Is it getting you in the head?"

"A little. Here. Why not give me the brick and I'll hand it up to you."

"Good idea. Good. Here we go, then." Dutton was up on his shoulders now and clawing at the glass for support. "Move right up against the building. Good. Now we're okay. We're fine now. All right, hand me the brickbat, Albert. Good. Thanks. *Don't!*"

"I was just trying to look up and see what you were doing," Albert explained.

"Well, don't rear your head back like that or I'll lose my balance." Drawing his arm back, Dutton delivered a blow with the brickbat and then a second and third.

"Are you using the jagged end, sir?"

"Of *course* I'm using the jagged end," Dutton said heatedly. Again there was the sound of brick striking glass. "This is the damnedest glass I ever saw in my life," Dutton

195

panted. "Is it conceivable that the second-story panels are also unbreakable?"

"Yes, sir, I think it's conceivable."

"Lemme down, Albert, and we'll decide what to do next."

Albert crouched and Dutton jumped to the ground.

"I suggest that what we do next is leave," Albert said in a guarded voice. "Look, Mr. Dutton."

The night watchman was strolling toward them.

"Okay, let's go, Albert," Dutton said. He picked up his shopping bag and started off.

"Hey!"

Dutton turned.

"Hey!" The night watchman was moving faster now. "Did I hear somebody around here trying to break in?"

"I wouldn't know," Dutton said. "I don't happen to have custody of your ears."

He started off again.

"Hey! Hold it!"

Again Dutton turned. "What is it?"

"Were you trying to break into this building?" the watchman demanded.

Dutton laughed helplessly. "I'll leave it up to this passer-by," he said, turning to Albert. "You, sir, do I look like somebody who would go around trying to break into a building?"

"Certainly not," Albert said.

"Do you see any visible evidence that anyone tried to break into your building?" Dutton demanded. "Just as I thought." He strode onward, followed by Albert.

The night watchman followed but at a slower pace than before.

As they reached the curb at the main entrance, Dutton turned. "I suppose we'd best give up, Albert," he muttered. "Under the circumstances."

"I really think we should, sir," Albert said in a low voice.

Dutton glanced up as the watchman approached. He glowered and then, addressing Albert, said, "I have my car parked just across the way." He pointed to the Bentley. "Can I give you a lift anywhere, my friend?"

"Yes, you could," Albert said. "Thanks very much."

Again Dutton glared at the watchman and then, carrying the shopping bag, made his way across the street. "We failed, Albert," he said, getting in and slamming the door.

Albert started the car and they drove past the main entrance of the building. The watchman stood at the curb and his mouth hung slack.

"What's that fool gawking at us for?" Dutton demanded.

"I'm not sure, sir. I suspect it's because I'm driving and you're in the back seat."

"Hah!"

"Where now, sir? Home?"

"Yes, by all means."

"We'll need some gasoline, Mr. Dutton. We're almost empty."

"All right. Anything but Jolloco."

"Esso?"

"Fine."

Albert pulled into the station. "Fill it, Mr. Dutton?"

Dutton didn't reply, and Albert turned to the back seat. Dutton was slumped wearily against the door, in an attitude of defeat.

"Shall I fill it?" Albert asked.

"We were up against giants," Dutton said. "I suppose that was it. Yes, fill it, by all means. What time is it, Albert?"

"Nearly ten, sir."

"We won't be home until one in the morning. Is that all right with you, Albert?"

"It's okay with me, sir, but I think I'll cut over to the Jersey Turnpike and go down that way, and over the Delaware Memorial Bridge. Mr. Dutton, don't you think it would be a good idea to call home?"

"Yes, you're right, Albert. I'll go do it while the tank is filling."

Dutton got out and entered a telephone booth. Listening to the ping-ping-ping of the pump, Albert watched him. He looked old and very tired, but then, as he began to bark into the phone, he became animated once more.

"That be all?" the attendant asked. "That's six-eighty."

Albert handed him a ten-dollar bill. With the change, the attendant handed him a tiny packet.

"What's this?" Albert asked.

"Tigerino."

"No, thanks," Albert said, handing it back quickly. "We're not much for games."

"You can win money with it."

"No. Thanks just the same. Here. Put it back in your pocket. Don't let my friend see it."

The attendant shrugged and shambled away. Dutton got back in. "Everything is okay, Albert. Mrs. Dutton was getting a little concerned. I told her to go to bed. Jane is typing on the typewriter. What was all that discussion you were having with the attendant?"

"Nothing, sir. He asked me if I knew whose face was on a ten-dollar bill. I said Hamilton."

"Hamilton, of course," Dutton said.

23

It soon became clear that Jake Dutton would regard his Jolly Dollars phase as yet another in a steadily lengthening line of failures, if indeed not fiascos.

There were times now when Albert was forced to ask himself how in God's name Dutton, with his genius for the ill-conceived, his talent for the maladroit, could ever have been the successful head of anything, much less the successful head of one of the largest plastic corporations in America. The answer perhaps lay in the nature of retirement. Even under the best of circumstances, the retirement process was difficult. Dutton had made of it a labyrinth.

Within a very few days following the Jolly Dollars trip, Dutton had become noticeably glum. He had taken to sitting behind the house on a white bench in the sunlight, where often Mrs. Dutton would join him. Albert, from his perch on the mower, would look toward the house and see them there, and to judge by the movements of her head and the way she placed her face very close to Jake's, it was clear that she was engaging him in earnest conversation. After a time, she would stray from the bench over the lawn, loitering by her flower beds, stooping to pluck a weed or perhaps a dead petal.

At cocktail hour, Jake merely toyed with his evening martini, often leaving half of it, staring morosely through the picture window.

"I love the way the reeds bend in the breeze, don't you, Jake, dear?" Mrs. Dutton said.

"Where?"

"Right there along the shoreline," she said, pointing.

"Yeah," Jake said.

"Did you notice, dear, how much nicer the lion's nose looks now?"

"I haven't looked at it," Jake said.

"Well, take a look."

"I will later."

"What did you use, Albert?" Mrs. Dutton asked.

"I used some Vaseline, mum."

Preoccupied with his own misery, Jake continued to sit like an old man in the sunlight, disdaining his pool, his frogman outfit, his boat, expressing no interest whatever in the mowing operation nor in the beautification project which once had so fascinated him.

Even the presence of Nick on weekends brought him no pleasure. Not even Nick was immune from the sourness of his outlook. Hearing from Mrs. Dutton that Nick had called and would be down on Saturday afternoon, Jake only muttered and grumbled. The only reason Nick came, he said, was to wash his car because it was impossible to wash it in Georgetown, and why should he provide Nick with free water?

On the Saturday afternoon in question, Nick arrived and began immediately to wash his car on the parking lot.

As usual, his greeting to Albert was rich with deference. Albert by now found his mere presence embarrassing.

"Good afternoon, Mr. Bagby," Nick said. "How are you, sir?"

Albert winced. He could not help wishing that Nick occasionally would say something coarse or callous.

"I had a nice letter from Beverly this week," Nick was saying. "She says she'll be back sometime between August first and fifteenth. I know you'll be happy to see her."

"Yes," Albert said. "We will."

Nick was stripped to the waist and his body gleamed with moisture, whether from perspiration or because he had accidentally squirted himself Albert could not be sure. Thoughtfully he played the stream of the hose over his right headlight. "I'd just like to say, Mr. Bagby . . . well, it's none of my business, of course, sir, but I think it's very admirable the way you and Mrs. Bagby must have sacrificed to give Beverly a college education. I'm sure you'll never regret it."

Albert frowned. He darted a quick look at Nick's face, which was suffused with right-thinking.

"How is Mrs. Bagby coming with her typing lessons?" Nick asked.

"Huh?"

"Beverly told me her mother was taking typing lessons," Nick said.

Albert looked at the ground. "Yes, she is. She hopes to improve her lot."

Nick nodded. "Of course, for that matter, there's nothing wrong with her present lot."

"That's true," Albert said.

"But you can't help admiring her," Nick said. "Gosh." He cocked his head, listening. "From the sound of it, she's worked up very good speed already."

"Yes," Albert said. "She's done very well. She was told she had a natural aptitude for typing."

"That's just great," Nick said. "How is your father? He must be a wonderful old gentleman. I wish I could meet him."

"Did Beverly tell you about my father?" asked Albert, whose father had been dead for seven years.

"Yes, sir."

"What did she tell you?"

"That he was still in service in England and very highly thought of by the family he works for. How long is it he's been with them? Forty years?"

"Forty-two," Albert said. "A long, long time."

Nick nodded. "That's one of the things you get in Europe that you don't get in this country," he said.

"What are you speaking of?"

"Well, a certain dignity, I suppose you'd call it. There's a dignity and honor attached to being a member of the servant class that's lacking over here."

"I'm going to wring Beverly's neck," Albert said to Jane later that afternoon. He told her of his conversation with Nick.

Jane shrugged. "The lies of the parents, after all . . ."

Dutton, meanwhile, was sinking fast and there came the afternoon when Mrs. Dutton asked Albert for aid. She found him working along the shoreline.

"Oh, Albert," she said in a state of distress. "I'm afraid I need your help."

"Yes, mum?" Albert stood erect and wiped the sweat from his eyelids.

"Oh, I do so love this place. . . ." Her voice became husky. "But, Albert—I'm afraid we may not have it much longer. Mr. Dutton is threatening to throw in the sponge. He's threatening to call a real-estate broker."

"*Mrs. Dutton!* I can't believe it!"

"I'm afraid it's true, Albert, unless you and I together can think of something. . . . Oh, Albert, you see, the trouble with Mr. Dutton is that he worked so very hard all his life that he never really learned how to enjoy himself."

Albert gazed pensively across the river toward the distant cove. "I can't believe it, Mrs. Dutton, I just can't believe it, and it hurts me. You see, the fact is that we like this place so very much, Jane and I, and we like you and Mr. Dutton. We've grown so attached. . . ."

"Oh, Albert," Mrs. Dutton said gratefully. "It's so kind of you to say that, and we feel just the same way about you. I know that if it hadn't been for you and Jane, he would have arrived at this decision long ago."

"But he hasn't actually *arrived* at the decision, has he?"

"No, but he's talking about it, and it petrifies me. We've got to think of something together, Albert. Why don't you join us at cocktail hour this evening, and we'll gang up on him."

"Very good, mum."

"Because you see, Albert—well, some people would say it's because he doesn't have enough to do, but personally I think it's more a matter of his ego. Do you see what I mean?"

"Yes, mum, I think I do."

"He feels he doesn't count for anything in this environment. So maybe we could approach it from that angle. Will you think about it?"

"I certainly will, mum. I'll be thinking while I'm working with these rocks. I get a lot of thinking done when I'm working with my hands."

"Good. Oh, good." Mrs. Dutton sighed. "You know, Albert, I feel I know so very little about you and Jane. I mean, I feel so close to you both, and yet I know next to nothing about your past life or anything. Tell me something about yourself, Albert."

Albert dropped a rock he had been about to set in place. "For a very good reason, mum. I don't think it's proper or fitting, neither for myself nor for Jane."

"To talk about yourself, you mean?"

"That's right, mum. We have our world and you have yours, and there's a wall between. It's simply not fitting."

"Oh, Albert," she said. "How very old-fashioned. And how very charming!"

"Thankee, mum. Well . . . I'll be finishing up me chores, then, and meet you both at cocktail hour."

"Yes," she said, distracted. "Here he comes, Albert. Let's not let on."

Dutton was moving aimlessly over the lawn, disappearing behind one of the willow trees and then emerging.

"Hello, dear," Mrs. Dutton greeted him. "I was just watching what Albert is doing."

Dutton nodded. Then, with a frown, he said, "What *are* you doing, Albert? What is it you're doing with those rocks?"

"Checking erosion, sir."

"Was this something we discussed, Albert? I don't remember asking you to do this."

"I took it upon myself, sir. I noticed the shoreline was being cut away a little in a couple of places, so I thought something should be done about it."

"I see . . ." Dutton still looked dubious. "But where did you get all these rocks?"

"I had them delivered, sir. On a truck. And then I brought them over here in the wheelbarrow."

"Who paid for them?" Dutton asked.

"The rocks? I did, sir. Rocks are the best way to check erosion, you see. And land is just too valuable to let it wash into the river, so to say. So I took it upon myself . . ."

"Oh, Albert!" Mrs. Dutton's eyes were misty. "How very good of you!"

"You mean you paid for these rocks out of your own pocket, Albert?" Dutton asked.

"Yes, sir, I did."

"What made you do such a thing as that?"

"I hate to see valuable land washing away, sir."

During the course of the afternoon, Mrs. Dutton told Albert she had persuaded Jake to have cocktail hour on the boat, and it was there, shortly before six, that he found them, wearing nautical get-up and even striking nautical attitudes reminiscent of their erstwhile friends Clinker and Doris Merritt.

Dutton was standing at the wheel of the boat, turning it listlessly back and forth, while Mrs. Dutton stood beside him, wearing a yachting cap at a jaunty angle over her gray-blue hair.

Seeing Albert, Dutton gave the wheel a final flip and slumped dispiritedly on the light blue cockpit cushions. Removing her cap, Mrs. Dutton reached over to accept the tray which Albert passed to her from the dock.

"Come aboard, Albert," Dutton said without heart. "Where's your drink?"

"I'll come aboard, sir," Albert said, "but I won't have anything to drink, thankee just the same."

He stepped nimbly aboard and sat facing the Duttons.

Dutton was looking at him curiously.

"Is there anything wrong, sir?" Albert asked.

"When did you start saying 'thankee' like that, Albert? You sound like something off a British frigate."

"I wasn't aware of it, sir."

Dutton sipped his martini. "Mrs. Dutton tells me you have something you'd like to say. Go ahead and say it."

"I don't really know exactly what to say, sir. She told me you were considering giving up on Rear Guard, and I must confess it makes me very sad indeed to hear it."

"It's so good of you to feel that way, Albert," Mrs. Dutton said.

"Thankee—thank you, mum."

Dutton said nothing. He was unaccountably silent, peering about the harbor and sipping his martini. Although the sun had not yet set, a waxing moon was visible directly overhead, and the blinking light of the red flasher buoy was beginning to show up.

"When do you plan to leave?" Albert asked.

Dutton frowned. "Hold on, now. This isn't definite yet. I'm just thinking about it."

"I see. Well . . . Mr. Dutton," Albert said thoughtfully. "Do you mind if I say something? You won't consider it disrespectful?"

"Go ahead, Albert. Speak your piece."

"Well, sir, I don't know how to put this exactly . . . but the fact is, sir—well, I'm sure this isn't a *unique* thing. I'm sure it's a problem a lot of retired men have in common, and no disrespect intended."

"*What*, Albert?"

"Well, sir, I just don't think you have enough to do with yourself."

The ensuing silence was broken by Mrs. Dutton's triumphant laugh. "Exactly, Albert! You've put your finger right on it!" She put her yachting cap back on her head.

"I mean, sir," Albert went on. "Not that there's anything basically wrong with sitting in a tree—I have nothing against it—but on the other hand it doesn't really *lead* to anything, so to say."

"My point exactly, Albert," Mrs. Dutton said.

"Now, I remember, sir, one of the gentlemen I once worked for in England. This gentleman had various hobbies —so many hobbies that at the end of the day he was completely done in, sir."

"I *hate* hobbies," Dutton said heatedly. "If there's anything I hate, it's some damned *hobby*."

"Yes, sir," Albert said. "This gentleman felt the same way and I think it's true, sir, more or less of human nature . . . when you stand off from it and contemplate taking *on*

207

a hobby, sir, it seems silly. But then when you get *into* the hobby so to speak, you get immersed and it kind of *grabs* you."

"I think that's a very mature observation, Albert," Mrs. Dutton said. "Very perceptive."

"What am I supposed to do?" Dutton demanded. "Grow African violets?"

"Not unless it should happen to appeal to you, sir. But on the other hand . . ."

"Well, it does not!" Dutton bellowed. "I'd rather be dead and in my grave than spend my days tending to a bunch of goddamned African violets!"

"Jake, please—don't get so excited," Mrs. Dutton said, looking anxiously about the harbor.

"Well, I would and you might as well know it!"

Once more there was a long silence, and Albert, looking down at the water, could see a shaft of moonlight crossing the crimson streak thrown by the flasher buoy.

When he looked up he saw Mrs. Dutton, leaning far back against the gunwale out of range of Jake's peripheral vision, trying to convey something to him, forming words silently with her lips.

Unable to make out what she was saying, Albert raised his eyebrows, shrugged, and then, in a low, soothing voice, said, "I suppose, sir, that what you envisioned when you first came down here—"

"What I envisioned was having some *fun*, for God's sake!" Dutton interrupted. "Hell, I can sit in trees back in New Jersey."

"I'm not sure the tree is the answer," Albert said.

"Of *course* it's not the answer," Dutton shouted. "Who

said it was? But while we're on the subject—if it gives me pleasure to sit up in a tree and look at things, then I'll damn well do it! It's my tree. I paid for it."

In a state of agitation, Dutton got up and took the helm again, twisting the wheel and scowling dead ahead. Mrs. Dutton leaned forward and whispered to Albert, "Don't use the word 'ego.'"

Albert nodded that he understood. "Just as I don't really think the Jolly Dollars contest was the answer, Mr. Dutton."

"I don't want to talk about that," Dutton said.

"You have so much to give, Jake," Mrs. Dutton said. "What happened to your frogman suit? You haven't even touched it. Whatever happened to our plans for going down to the bottom of the river and exploring the oyster beds and everything?"

Dutton remained silent, giving Albert a cautionary glance.

"I think Mrs. Dutton put her finger on it," Albert said. "You're a man with a great deal to give, Mr. Dutton."

"That may be so, Albert. I once thought so. But I've found out something, Albert. I've learned that retirement puts a terrible burden on a man. Do you know what that burden is?" Dutton turned from the wheel. "It's an obligation to be *happy*, and I say the hell with it."

"Oh, Jake . . ." Mrs. Dutton lamented.

"It's true," Dutton said. "I don't mind being unhappy if I'm not paying for it. But if I'm paying to be happy and expecting to be happy because I've made a big investment in it and then I'm still not happy—I'm tired of talking about it. I'm hungry. Let's eat."

"Does that mean, sir, that you've made your decision— to leave Rear Guard?"

"Of course not!"

"Then you may stay?"

"I may and I may not. It's up to me."

"Well . . ." Albert said thoughtfully, "I think the answer, sir, is finding something to do with your time so that at the end of the day you feel as though you've done something that makes you feel better. And maybe to cap it off, an occasional dinner party, or a cocktail party . . . one you could feel was a successful party when you went to bed that night."

"Hah!" Dutton said bitterly. "Nonsense, Albert. Come on, Frances. Let's go eat." Dutton was already on the dock, glaring impatiently at his wife and Albert, who continued to sit in the cockpit. "Come on."

"Mr. Dutton . . . would you give me permission to help, sir?"

"Help what?"

"Help you make your decision. Help plan some of your activities for you, so to say. I might have some ideas."

"Oh, Albert, how wonderful of you," Mrs. Dutton said.

"What kind of ideas?" Dutton asked.

"I'm not positive yet, sir, but if it means saving Rear Guard I'm going to try very hard to come up with something. You see, sir, with the sort of experience I've had—being around a great many retired gentlemen, so to say—I understand some of the problems involved."

"Albert, lemme tell you something," Dutton said angrily. "If you say 'so to say' just one more time, I'm gonna kill you in cold blood."

"Jake!"

"Sorry, sir," Albert said. "It's become a habit. But what about my suggestion, sir?"

Dutton shrugged. "Go ahead."

"Maybe you could just put yourself in Albert's hands," Mrs. Dutton said.

"I'm not putting myself in *anybody's* hands," Dutton snapped. "I never have and never will." Striding along the dock toward the house, he called over his shoulder, "Okay, Albert, go ahead. Do your damnedest."

Albert stepped to the dock and turned to help Mrs. Dutton, who smiled and pressed his hand. "Oh, Albert," she said. "Thank you very much. You're so *very* wise."

"Thankee, mum."

"What do you have in mind?" she asked as they walked along the dock together.

"I'm just not sure, but the two of us, we'll put our heads together—and I have a feeling we'll save Rear Guard yet, mum!"

24

The next morning, while Dutton was in Paxton, Albert and Mrs. Dutton sat on the bench at the bend of the river and put their heads together.

"The reason I didn't want you to use the word 'ego' is

that it would have made him furious," Mrs. Dutton said. "He hates words like that."

Albert nodded. "But just the same, mum, that's exactly what it is."

"He doesn't feel important enough—after having been so very important in his company."

"Mrs. Dutton, mum—is Mr. Dutton good at anything?"

"Albert!" she said reproachfully.

"I mean no disrespect by the question, mum. But what is he particularly good at?"

"He was awfully good at running his company."

"But did he have any sidelines is what I mean to say."

"He was always too busy, Albert."

"Did he ever do any bowling, for example?"

"Bowling? No."

"You see," Albert went on, "if Mr. Dutton were, for example, a retired actor, he might do impersonations at a party. Or if he were a former war correspondent, he could tell of his experiences in little-known corners of the world. Even if he were, say, a retired jockey—"

"Jockey! Oh dear, Albert!"

"Don't despair, mum. I think I may have something."

"Really? What, Albert?"

"Well, as I see it, mum, the problem is a matter of restoring his ego, very true, but it's also very closely tied in with Mr. Merritt. He feels that Mr. Merritt has gotten the better of him and he can't abide it."

"Very true, Albert. The thought of Clinker trying to knife him in the back by trying to steal you—and also the thought of Clinker's, well . . . his popularity, riding around on that big boat and everything . . ."

"Exactly," Albert said. "Well now, as I see it, there are two ways of getting back at Mr. Merritt. One would be a sort of direct revenge, sort of a physical revenge, you might say, and he's already tried—I mean he may have already considered that, but that sort of thing is not practical. Now the other way . . ."

Albert fell silent, thinking.

"Yes, Albert?"

"Well, mum, the other way is a sort of indirect revenge—in other words, covering himself with glory, so to say. Doing something that Mr. Merritt could never ever do and would be envious of. I think if we could bring it off, Mr. Dutton would feel wonderful."

"Yes, Albert, but what on earth would it be?"

Albert chuckled. "It's a wonder to me we hadn't thought of it before, mum. It seems so very obvious. Big game."

"What? Big game—oh." Mrs. Dutton seemed startled. Her eyes began to dart here and there about the surface of the river. "Well . . . you'd have to ask him, Albert. I'm not at all sure how he'd feel about it. You know how very shy he is."

"Mr. Dutton? Shy, mum?"

She seemed confused. "Well, he's shy about certain things."

That afternoon, Albert went up to the balcony and made notes. There were seven heads in all—the lion, the zebra, the wildebeest (or gnu), a cheetah, a water buffalo, another zebra, and an ocelot.

In the local weekly newspaper, Albert often had seen

mention of a group calling itself "Connoisseur's Choice." So far as he could make out, the members met once a month to hear speakers who resided locally but whose experiences were more or less worldwide. Among the topics he remembered reading about were, "How to Catch the Elusive Bone-fish" and "How Many Senses—Is There a Sixth?" and another, "Tench Tilghman—Local Boy Who Made Good."

Bypassing Mrs. Dutton for the moment, Albert took matters into his own hands. Tracking down the club's president, a Mrs. Palatine, he introduced himself and proceeded to sell his client.

"He's a very reticent man," Albert said, "but if by chance he could be persuaded—well, your group would be in for a most interesting evening, Mrs. Palatine."

"And what was his name again, please?"

"Mr. J. K. Dutton. Jake Dutton. He was president of the NuWay Plastic Corporation in New Jersey. They moved down here last fall."

"Yes, but what was this about Africa?"

"He's spent a good deal of time on safari. His house is literally filled with heads—big game animals."

"How very interesting! And you say he's living right here in our midst?"

"On the Swoose River."

"And we didn't even know it!"

"I happen to know that he's shot a lion, a water buffalo, a cheetah, a zebra, an ocelot—let's see what else—oh, a wildebeest, that's like a gnu, you know . . ."

"Oh, yes!"

"*Two* zebras!"

"Heavens! Well—Mr. Bagby, is it? Mr. Bagby, this is most kind of you indeed. How would I go about it? It just happens that our next speaker canceled out on us this *very* morning. Mr. Eggleston. He was to have spoken on 'A Visit to the Home of Anne Hathaway,' but he has a bad case of shingles. So here I'm faced with finding another speaker in time for our next meeting, which is next Wednesday night. One week away. Shall I call him?"

"I'll tell you what. Let me have him call you. I'll be seeing him this evening. I'll have him get back to you, Mrs. Palatine."

"Oh, wonderful. I *do* hope he will do it, because I truly wasn't sure where to turn. 'Through Darkest Africa'—we could bill it something like that, wouldn't you say?"

"I see no reason why not," Albert said.

"And Africa, of course, being of such *particular* interest today . . ."

"Indeed so," Albert said.

As Albert entered the Safari Room at cocktail hour that evening, he could guess from her attitude that Mrs. Dutton had said nothing to Jake about the big-game idea.

"Mr. Dutton," Albert said, sitting on the windowseat, "I've analyzed your problem, sir, and I think I have the answer. I think it all lies in your receiving the recognition you deserve, Mr. Dutton. But the thing is, sir, you're not *giving*."

"Giving what, Albert?"

"Giving of yourself, sir. I mean, there are so very many organizations locally—people who haven't experienced half of what you've experienced. Think of what you could give these people, Mr. Dutton. For example, the group called 'Connoisseur's Choice' . . . You've read about them? Think of what you could do for them, Mr. Dutton."

"*What* could I do for them, Albert?"

"They have speakers, sir."

"They don't want anybody speaking about plastics, I'm sure of that."

"There's so much more to you than plastics, sir."

"For example, Albert?"

"Africa."

"*Africa?*" Dutton looked into his martini glass and then at Albert, incredulously, for some reason.

Mrs. Dutton fingered the buttons of her white cardigan.

"I've taken the liberty," Albert said. "I mean, I happened to bump into the president, a Mrs. Palatine. They desperately need a speaker for next Wednesday night."

Dutton's mouth was working. "Where, exactly, did you bump into her, Albert?" he demanded. "On your lawnmower? You've been mowing the lawn all day."

Albert went doggedly on. "She said she'd be delighted to have you, sir . . . speak to the group about Africa. I told her about all your heads." He waved toward the balcony.

Dutton was up, pacing. He shook his head. "I couldn't do that, Albert."

"Why not, sir?"

"I just couldn't do it, that's all."

"Their speaker for next Wednesday night canceled out. He has the shingles."

Dutton was standing above Albert. "You know, I'm very

fond of you, Albert, and all, but sometimes I think you're one of the damnedest influences a man ever had."

"I don't understand, sir."

"I just couldn't do it, that's all."

"It seems only right, Mr. Dutton, that you should have the recognition you deserve, sir."

Dutton shook his head. "Couldn't do it, Albert."

That evening just before turning in, Albert strolled about the property as he often did. Chancing to look through the picture window of the Safari Room, he saw Dutton up on the balcony, pacing thoughtfully back and forth and pausing now and then to examine the heads of the animals.

Next morning, with Albert supplying the number and spelling the name, Dutton telephoned Mrs. Palatine and accepted.

That afternoon, somebody from the local newspaper called and asked for a photograph. "No!" Albert heard Dutton barking into the phone. "Just head and shoulders. No. No, just a plain business suit. No, we didn't take any pictures on safari, hardly had time. This was a hunting trip, not a photographic expedition. What do you think this is —the National Geographic Society?"

That evening, a photographer came from the paper and took several flash shots of Jake standing on the balcony, next to the head of the lion.

After the photographer left, Dutton said, "Well, Albert, I guess the die is cast, eh?"

"I'm sure you'll never regret it, sir."

From Mrs. Dutton there came a lachrymose sniff.

"I've been thinking," Dutton said, "that with Africa so

much in the news these days, it would seem more pertinent to give more of a generalized talk on Africa."

"I think that's a *very* good idea," Mrs. Dutton said.

"Stay out of this, Frances, if you don't mind," Jake said. Mrs. Dutton left the room.

"Instead of a talk specifically on game hunting," Dutton went on.

Albert nodded. In Dutton's eyes, he noticed a touch of panic, yet his voice was resonant and crackling with determination. He seemed the Jake Dutton of old.

"I may need your help in preparing my speech, Albert."

"I'll be happy to help, sir. In any way that I can."

"I may ask you to stand by me all the way."

"Happy to, sir."

"I don't mind saying that I respect your judgment, Albert."

"Thank you, sir."

"I've been checking to see what the Britannica has to say on the subject . . ."

"Of Africa?"

"Yes. Of course."

"Do you think that's the right approach, Mr. Dutton?"

"I'll decide what the right approach is, Albert."

"Yes, sir."

That night and all the next morning, Dutton was in seclusion. At lunch, he told Albert that he had roughed out a draft of his speech and that he would like to run through it.

218

In mid-afternoon, the two of them took out the boat and anchored in a quiet cove.

"All right, sir," Albert said. "Stand there in the stern and let's have it loud enough so the people in the second balcony can hear it." He gave Dutton a reassuring chuckle.

"Right." Dutton held some typed sheets before his chest. He looked down and then up. "Ready?"

"Ready."

"When you speak of hunting lions in Africa," Dutton bellowed, "there's one thing you should remember. . . ."

The echo of his voice rang around the empty cove.

"Excellent, sir," Albert said. "That was a good big sound. Go on."

"In fact," Dutton shouted, "there are *several* things to remember. One is Africa's size . . . its sheer size. . . ." He consulted his notes. "Africa is a huge continent, with an area of eleven million, two hundred and sixty-two thousand square miles!"

"Yes," Albert said. "That's a nice transition. That information works in very well there."

Dutton nodded, encouraged. "The next thing we must remember," he went on at the top of his lungs, "is that not for nothing is Africa known as the 'Dark Continent.' . . ."

Albert nodded approval. "Remember not to drop your voice, sir."

Gesturing now, Dutton went on. "Its jungles are dense, although, as we shall shortly see, the lion, or King Leo, as he is sometimes known, keeps for the most part to the savannah country. Who here has ever been to Savannah, Georgia? Raise hands. You'll know then what I mean by savannah country."

"Damned good!" Albert said.

Dutton nodded with satisfaction. "Albert, there's a bottle of bourbon in the cabin there. Bring it out."

"You know what bourbon does to you, sir."

"I can't help it, Albert. I'm nervous. I feel like some bourbon."

Albert produced the bottle, and Dutton took a generous gulp. "Here, Albert, have some."

"Thank you, sir." Albert tilted the bottle and wiped his mouth.

"Ready?"

"Yes, sir, ready. Go ahead about Savannah, Georgia."

Dutton frowned. "That was just—"

"Yes, of course. I mean about the savannah country."

"Okay. Savannah was originally a meadowland or large—"

"Do it in your speaking voice, Mr. Dutton."

"Right." Again Dutton's voice became a bellow. "Savannah was originally a meadowland or large grassy treeless tract, but now also including level areas with tall grasses and isolated clumpy trees, as in Nigeria, where the more appropriate name would be *park* savannah, you see?"

Albert nodded. Dutton went on:

"It was, moreover, in savannah where man's earliest ancestors stood erect on their hind legs, giving them a considerable advantage over their four-footed adversaries, because they could see over the tall grass and detect the presence of danger."

Dutton paused. "Do you really think we should leave that in?"

"It seems pertinent to me, sir. You know, actually, Mr.

Dutton, you've done a great deal in a very short time. I'm beginning to be enthusiastic about this."

Dutton grinned. "I'll have another nip of that bourbon, Albert. It doesn't sound bad at that."

"Your voice is absolutely great, sir. You have a very good voice. It really awakens echoes, so to say. Sorry."

"That's all right, Albert."

"So to speak," Albert said.

"I always did have a big voice," Dutton said. "When I used to address our people back at the plant . . . well, I always had very good reactions, a lot of compliments and so forth. Well, now where was I?"

"About man standing up in the grass."

"Oh. Right." Again Dutton consulted his notes and then looked up. "What's this bastard doing, Albert?"

A small outboard motorboat was circling. Its sole occupant looked at them curiously, then zoomed away.

"Now then," Dutton shouted, glancing at his notes. "Who here would believe that Africa is largely a plateau? Raise hands. Well, you're in for a surprise. It is indeed largely a plateau, this contrasting very strikingly with Eurasia, in which fold-mountains of successive series in diverse stages of denudation occupy a large proportion of the surface!"

"I wouldn't read that part so fast, sir. You're slurring it. Slurring your words. Make each word distinct."

"I did rush it, I'll admit."

"It's okay to do it out here in the boat, but when you get up in front of the audience I'd hit each word hard."

Dutton nodded. Glancing at his notes, he raised his eyes and swept his imaginary audience. "What, you may ask, does all this have to do with hunting a lion?"

"Sir . . . wait a minute." Albert shook his head. "I think we should leave that out. It plants a question in their minds that might otherwise not be there."

Dutton nodded. "I think you may be right, Albert." He took a pencil from his pocket and crossed out some lines. "Okay. Good."

"Go right ahead, Mr. Dutton."

"That's all."

"That's *all?*"

"I mean, that's as far as I've gotten. I'll work on some more tonight. But as a starter, how do you like it?"

"I think it's great, Mr. Dutton. I think it has just the right tone."

"I was hoping you'd like it," Dutton said.

"I really do. Very much, sir."

"I think you've had enough of that bourbon, Albert. Put it back in the cabin."

"Yes, sir." Albert put the bottle back in a drawer and emerged. "Well, who's going to hoist the anchor?"

"You are, Albert. Who in the hell do you *think* is going to hoist the anchor?"

"Yes sir," Albert said sullenly.

"Good start, eh, Albert?"

"Very good start, sir. I have confidence you'll knock 'em dead."

That evening at bedtime, Albert asked Jane if she happened to have any books on lion-hunting.

"No," she said.

"None?"

"None that I can think of, except—well, that's fiction, though. 'The Short Happy Life of Francis Macomber.' Ernest Hemingway."

"Is it long?"

"It's a long short-story."

"Do you have it?"

"Why?"

"For Dutton. He's going to give a talk on big-game hunting next Wednesday."

"How nice. Can we go hear him?"

"I'm planning to. Where is this thing?"

"It's in a collection of short stories somewhere. I'll find it for you tomorrow morning."

"Okay. What's it about?"

"Oh . . . about a man named Macomber who's a coward and then gets brave. He's scared to death and runs away and the white hunter has to shoot the lion for him and then there's a lot of hanky-panky between the white hunter and Macomber's wife."

"Is that all?"

"No. Overnight, Macomber gets guts and the next day he stands up to the lion, or maybe this time it's a water buffalo or a rhino, I don't remember. So his wife shoots him in the head."

"*What?*"

"She pretends to be helping him, but actually she shoots him because she's seen the change in him and she doesn't *want* him to be brave. She likes him being a coward because he has a lot of money and that's the only way she could abide the marriage."

"Oh. Well, find it for me in the morning."

The next morning, book in hand, Albert went over to the Safari Room and read the story. When he was finished, he tossed the book carelessly on the windowseat.

25

All during the rest of the week, Dutton and Albert followed the same routine, working at night to collect their material, revising and polishing it, smoothing out transitions here and there, and occasionally substituting "punch words," as Dutton termed them, for the phrases offered by the encyclopedia and two other reference books that Dutton had gotten from the local library.

Afternoons found them on the river rehearsing, speaker and audience. It was a time of pleasure for them both, and Albert, in a mood of self-congratulation, made a point of remarking to Mrs. Dutton on the change in her husband, for Dutton once again was riding a crest, approaching the big night with supreme confidence.

By common agreement, both Mrs. Dutton and Jane were denied a preview until all was perfection.

On the night before the lecture, there was a dress rehearsal in the Safari Room. Dutton stood on the balcony next to the lion's head and gave his entire speech, although, Albert noted, he was not nearly so effective as he had been in the boat, perhaps because Jane and Mrs. Dutton were not so responsive an audience as he, Albert.

They listened intently enough, yet Albert could not help noticing the strange expression that crossed Jane's face when Dutton came to the section of his speech wherein he described a lion's voice as a "loud and characteristic roar," going on from there to a brief description of the "lionfish, so named for the stripes which give a manelike effect."

When Dutton finished, Albert clapped vigorously, and Mrs. Dutton and Jane joined in. "Bravo," said Jane matter-of-factly.

"Well . . ." Dutton came down the spiral staircase. "How did it go, ladies?"

"Fascinating," Jane said.

"Frances?"

"I think it was very nice, Jake."

"Convincing?"

"Well, *I* was certainly convinced." Jane said.

Yet, as the evening progressed, Albert noticed Mrs. Dutton's long, long silences, and the emanations of doubt she was giving off seemed to have the effect of attrition on poor Jake.

To Albert, it seemed clear that to be at his best Jake would have to be drunk for the occasion and that it would be well if, somehow, the audience were drunk as well.

"Mr. Dutton . . ." He buttonholed Jake just before bedtime. "I hadn't heard that stuff about the lionfish before. I'd leave that out, if I were you."

Dutton looked hurt.

"I mean," Albert went on. "It's fascinating of itself, but I'm not sure it's germane."

Dutton scowled and passed on.

In bed that night, Jane said, "That was simply terrible, Albert. Are you really going to let him give it?"

"Don't be ridiculous, Jane. Have you ever known anybody who could stop Dutton from doing what he wants to do?"

"Something has occurred to me, Albert."

"What?"

"Do you think he's really and truly been big-game hunting?"

"I certainly have no reason to doubt it. Those heads didn't walk into the house and jump up on the wall, did they?"

The next morning, Jake stayed in his bedroom and when, after lunch, Albert suggested a final rehearsal, Jake demurred.

"I have some new material I'm working into it, Albert," he explained curtly. "I think it's going to strengthen it a great deal. You'll see."

"Could I hear it?"

"No. There won't be time."

The lecture was to begin at 8:30. After an early supper, the four departed at a quarter of eight, Albert at the wheel of the Bentley, Dutton beside him, and the ladies in the rear.

Jake had declined his usual martini before supper, but now, Albert noted, nipped at intervals from a bottle which he had ill-concealed in a brown paper bag.

"Jake," Mrs. Dutton called from the back seat. "There's one thing I do hope—"

"Don't bother me, Frances!" Dutton said. "I'm concentrating." His voice dropped to a mutter. A sheaf of onion-skin pages lay on his lap. Taking his eyes from the road momentarily, Albert glanced over and saw the words, "memsahib go push-push . . ." They had been crossed out with a pencil.

Dutton kept muttering to himself, rehearsing, scowling, and reaching now and again to the floor for his bottle.

"Jake . . ." Mrs. Dutton chided. "You know what that stuff does to you, dear."

"Tonight's tonight. Tomorrow's tomorrow. Keep quiet."

They rode on in an uneasy silence, broken only by Dutton's muttering. As they reached the lecture hall, Dutton folded his papers, reached for the door handle, thought better of it, reached for the bottle instead, took a nip and then wrapped the bottle carefully in the paper bag. They all got out.

"Albert," Dutton said in a low voice as they walked from the car. "You might as well know. I've taken an entirely new tack. I'm not using *any* of the stuff we rehearsed. It was far too dry."

Albert nodded. "Just so you think you're doing the right thing, Mr. Dutton."

"Just trust me."

Albert hung back for the ladies, opening the door. Dutton immediately was seized upon by Mrs. Palatine, a wraith in chartreuse, who steered him toward an eager semicircle of elderly club members. Immediately he was the center of attention.

"Frances . . ."

Dutton drew Mrs. Dutton into the group, totally ignoring both Albert and Jane, who thereupon had no choice but to sideslip away.

Albert was incensed. "The old son of a bitch!"

"Why?" Jane asked.

"He still thinks of us as servants. I hope he falls on his face!"

"Isn't that Mr. Merritt?"

Albert turned, and there indeed was Clinker, seated alone in the last row, looking ponderous and sweaty in a white jacket.

"It looks like a full house," Jane said.

"I hope they're not disappointed," Albert said grimly.

So saying, he steered his wife to a seat in the second row, noticing soon that Dutton had excused himself from the admiring group and disappeared, doubtless to find seclusion where he could fortify himself from the bottle.

He reappeared just minutes before Mrs. Palatine stood at the rostrum to say:

"We are truly privileged tonight to have with us a man who comes to us as president and founder of one of the largest plastic companies in the entire United States. Yet . . ."

Mrs. Palatine turned to Dutton and smiled. "It is not as a plastics expert that Mr. J. K. Dutton comes to us tonight . . . but as a lion-hunter . . . a man well versed in the ways of Africa, which, as we *all* know, is of especial importance today."

Dutton sat by, grinning broadly, no longer nervous. His foolish grin indicated, Albert felt sure, that he had been nipping heavily from his bottle and now faced the occasion with aplomb, with indeed as much certitude and brashness as he had displayed in the boat.

"And now, Mr. J. K. Dutton!"

Dutton walked carefully to the lectern. His eyes had a defiant glint. "Mrs. Palestine," he began, "ladies and gentlemen of the Connoisseur's Club—connoisseurs all, I trust—when Mrs. Palestine first asked me to address you tonight, I wondered about the approach I should take. Do these people, I asked myself, want to hear facts about Africa that they could read in any encyclopedia? Are they interested in knowing that the area of Africa is eleven million, two hundred and sixty-two square miles? Or that Africa is, largely speaking, a plateau? I decided the answer was no. What these good people would like to hear, I decided, is what it *feels* like to hunt a lion. The sights, the sounds, the smell, the texture of fear and the tissue of bravery . . ."

"Wow!" Jane whispered.

"*Because,* ladies and gentlemen, a lion-hunt can be a fearsome thing, even to the brave."

Dutton nodded emphatically and adjusted his onionskin pages.

"For more years than I care to remember, I had wanted a crack at Old Simba, as King Leo is known in Africa. My chance came in 1956, and there were three of us, my wife, myself and our guide, the so-called white hunter, a stocky, blond man named Bates, very red-faced from the sun."

Albert glanced at Mrs. Dutton, who sat in the row ahead, three chairs to the right. She seemed tense.

"My wife, Frances, and myself, what we did was fly to Nairobi," Dutton went on, "where we met Bates and headed then straight into lion country—Tanganyika, which now, of course, is known as Tanzania, but in 1956 was still Tanganyika."

Albert noted appreciative nods from the obviously well-informed audience.

"With us, of course," Dutton was saying, "were the usual group of gun-bearers and beaters, and here, to diverge for a moment, is an interesting thing about the dress of a gun-bearer. You've all seen them in the movies, I'm sure, with those tall red caps that make them look like they should be named Abdullah—but in reality your typical gun-bearer won't dress like that. Your typical gun-bearer will wear a *knitted* cap, along with a khaki tunic and shorts and, it's interesting to note, *rubber* sandals. . . ."

Dutton paused. The audience did not seem overly impressed with the information they had just been given, but on the other hand they were still very much with him.

"Now then . . ." Dutton went on. "Unless you've actually heard the roar of a lion, it's hard to appreciate the feelings that it can stir up. Just for the sake of curiosity, I had a look at the encyclopedia, where I read that the voice of a lion is a 'loud and characteristic roar.' Well! Accurate enough so far as it goes, but it doesn't begin to tell it all. Not by half."

Albert, glancing now and then at Mrs. Dutton, saw that she had taken out a pack of Life-Savers and was fumbling with the foil wrapper.

"The night I heard my first lion, ladies and gentlemen, I

230

was in the tent, half-asleep on my cot. When I say I heard my first lion, I mean, of course, in the jungle, not in a zoo, where it's an entirely different matter. When I heard that lion roar, I woke up fast. It was a very deep sound, and at the end there were a series of coughing grunts that made him seem almost as if he were right there in the tent beside me, or at least just outside the flap. Ladies and gentlemen, I don't mind saying that for the first time in my entire life, I knew the meaning of fear. There would be no point in my denying it to you now, at this point, so many years after the fact.

"What I did not know at that moment was that there is an old African proverb, or saying, to the effect that even a brave man is always frightened three times by a lion: when he first sees his tracks, when he first hears him roar, and when he first confronts him face to face. But that night, lying there on my cot and listening to the lion roar, I knew nothing of the proverb—and I was afraid."

Dutton, with a casual glance at his notes, went on in a voice vibrant now with confidence that he had his audience firmly by the throat. "Tomorrow we go lion-hunting, I told myself, and tried my best to sleep, but the fact is that I lay awake until dawn, an important fact to remember. I didn't sleep. I just lay awake, listening to the lion and hating the sound of it. In the morning, at breakfast, I was nervous, and I believe it showed. Several times I noticed Bates, our white hunter, looking at me quizzically. He gave me a briefing before we left camp, telling me at what range to shoot and suggesting that I aim for the lion's shoulders in case we got a shot at it.

"It was still very early when we left camp—Bates and I

231

and my wife, Frances, traveling perhaps half a mile by motor car until we spotted the lion near the bank of a stream. 'There he is!' my wife said excitedly. 'Yes, get out and take him!' Bates suggested."

Albert saw Mrs. Dutton, eyes straight ahead, pop a Life-Saver into her mouth.

"Getting out of the car, I walked a few steps toward the lion, feeling rather wobbly. Then I fired. The lion was wounded, but had enough strength left to skulk off into hiding. 'I believe you have gut-shot him,' said Bates scornfully, 'and now he has disappeared into the high acacia grass.' 'What do we do now?' I asked. 'What do we do now?' echoed Bates. 'We finish him off, of course.'"

"Albert!" Jane whispered.

"What?"

"What's he doing?"

"God knows."

Dutton continued before an audience now rapt. "I was frankly skeptical. Suddenly the lion appeared from nowhere and gave its rush. 'Shoot!' exclaimed Bates, but something inside me froze. At the sight of that lion, something happened to me so that nothing else would do but that I turn tail and run back to our Land-Rover and join my wife, Frances. I heard a loud report. Turning, I saw the lion motionless at Bates's feet. 'There's your lion,' Bates said with thinly veiled scorn."

"Albert, for God's sake!" Jane whispered tensely. "Did you do this?"

"Do what?"

"Put him up to this?"

"Put him up to what?"

Dutton, after a dramatic pause, had continued. "All during the ride back to camp," he said, lowering his voice, "there was silence in the Land-Rover. My wife's attitude toward me changed radically. It was as if she thought me a coward, and at that moment I thought so myself. It was not a pleasant feeling.

"Now let me say that my marriage, if I may say so, is a very good marriage and has always been a good marriage. Never in my life have I ever had any reason to question Frances's loyalty—and yet that evening in camp I noticed that she was somehow beginning to play up to Bates, the white hunter."

Albert heard a loud click, indicating, he felt, that Mrs. Dutton had just bitten a Life-Saver in half.

"Surely it must be my imagination, I thought to myself at supper. My imagination must be playing tricks on me. That was it, I concluded. That evening, Bates seemed to sense some of the things that were going on in my mind about the lion, for just at bedtime he told me the proverb about the brave man fearing the lion three times before his fear can be conquered. This made me feel a great deal better, and, as I lay there on my cot, reviewing the day's events, I also consoled myself with the thought that on the previous night I had had a very poor night's sleep. By the time I drifted off, I had arrived at the conclusion that my running from the lion was due not so much to cowardice as to the fact that I had slept poorly.

"It's necessary at this point to digress for a moment to point out an interesting thing about Bates, our white hunter. On all his safaris he carried a double-size cot to accommodate any windfalls that might happen his way.

233

This much I knew because I had seen his cot. Sometime in the middle of the night, I woke up. Until that moment, I had slept very soundly and well. When I woke up, however, I noticed that Frances's cot was empty. . . ."

Mrs. Dutton was staring straight ahead, frozen, lips parted.

"In the light of our marital history," Dutton went on, "it seemed inconceivable to me that she had decided to break faith over the matter of the lion—and subsequent events proved me right. I lay awake, listening intently, and in fifteen minutes or so, she returned to the tent, explaining that she had been unable to sleep and had merely stepped outside for a breath of fresh air. I was satisfied with this explanation and went back to sleep, sleeping quite soundly until morning, and waking much refreshed."

For some time now, Albert's attention had been distracted by a deeply tanned man in a light gabardine suit, sitting on the aisle in the first row. He had been frowning from time to time and now, as Dutton told of waking much refreshed, the man burst into laughter, which was answered with glares from other members of the audience.

Dutton frowned slightly, but went on, undaunted. "That morning, I suggested that we go after another lion, but Bates at first objected. He said there was no reason on earth why I shouldn't simply take home the head of the lion he had shot for me, but this struck me as very wrong. 'No,' I said, 'I won't do that, Bates.' Nothing would do but that I go after another lion. Bates shrugged and off we went in the Land-Rover. I must say that I felt marvelous, and both Bates and Frances must have noticed the change in me, because they kept giving me glances from time to time.

I was no longer afraid. I had slept beautifully and I kept thinking about the proverb. As we rode along in the Land-Rover, I found myself grinning from time to time with confidence."

"Albert! You should be ashamed of yourself!" Jane whispered and glared.

"For what? I didn't do a damned thing, I swear it."

"You're lying," she whispered fiercely.

"What's wrong? I think it's good."

It was at this point that the tanned man at the end of the row began to choke violently, conceivably with laughter. Unable to stop, he got up from his seat and hurried down the aisle and away.

Dutton glared after him, and then resumed. "Again we found our lion, and although this time I tried hard to take him in the shoulders, as Bates had told me, I saw that once again I had gut-shot him and once again the lion skulked off into hiding." Dutton paused dramatically. "Ladies and gentlemen," he said, "I realized that I had now reached perhaps the most critical point in my entire life. How would I react?

"When the lion charged, I learned the answer. I stood my ground and pumped lead. On came the lion in his death charge. I raised my rifle and took careful aim. At that moment, I heard the zinging sound of a bullet passing close to my ear and then the dull thud indicating that it had lodged deep in a nearby tree. Once more I fired. The lion dropped dead at my feet.

"Turning, I saw Frances, my wife, standing next to the car, a rifle in her hand. Thinking the lion had been about to get me, she had tried to help out by firing, but she had missed and struck a tree. 'Hey, honey,' I shouted at her. 'You almost got *me*, that time!' She then explained that she had been trying to save me when the lion made its charge.

"You can well understand that this time the trip back to camp in the Land-Rover was an entirely different sort of trip. I felt good inside, and Frances and Bates looked at me with respect, and I mention all this not to blow my own horn, ladies and gentlemen, and I hope you will accept it in the spirit in which it is told. I simply mention it to underscore the fact that a lion is indeed a fearsome object and no man who fears Old Simba should ever be ashamed. The rest of that day we spent lounging about camp while the native boys skinned my lion, which was at last truly mine. It is the head of that lion which today adorns my home, and in closing I should like to say that anyone who cares to drop by and take a look is most welcome to do so and I should like furthermore to say to the club—thanks for being such a wonderful audience."

Dutton smiled, nodded, gathered up his notes and went back to his seat. The applause was most generous.

Part *Four*

26

The night of the lecture on lion-hunting was the high point of Jake Dutton's summer, or conceivably the low point, depending upon how one viewed it.

Having created his own spell, Dutton for a time remained under that spell, and for a few days at least he even seemed to be under the impression that he had scored a triumph which would at last permit him to know the true sweetness of retirement.

That he should have felt so was hardly surprising, Dutton being Dutton, for the twice-weekly newspaper carried a full account of his lecture, even including a brief description of his physical appearance—"white-thatched and wiry."

Moreover, the very day following the lecture a middle-aged couple arrived in a Cadillac, responding to his generous blanket invitation to members of the Connoisseurs to drop by and see his heads.

Albert was in the kitchen when he was summoned to bring light refreshment to the Safari Room. As he carried the tray down the hall, he overheard Dutton and his visitors up on the balcony. The lady was congratulating Dutton for his candor in acknowledging his own fear. "The whole way you told about feeling afraid was so wonderfully humble and full of self-awareness," she said. "Not many men would have admitted feeling that way. It was so—human."

Setting the tray on the coffee table, Albert turned back down the hall. "Yes, well, fear is a very complex subject," Dutton bellowed graciously.

Albert paused, listening.

"It's not really so black and white as people seem to believe," Dutton went on. "It's more of a gray."

"Oh, I'm so glad to hear you say that," the lady replied.

"What's this one?" the husband asked in a voice betraying little interest.

"This?" Dutton replied. "This is your wildebeest . . . very much like your gnu."

"I wonder if I could take your picture," the husband said, once more in a listless voice.

"I just gave him that Polaroid for his birthday," the wife said. "He didn't want it but he got it, and I'm determined he's going to get some use out of it."

"Over by the head of the lion, how about?" the husband said.

"Don't see why not," Dutton replied with a chuckle.

There was a moment of silence, followed by conversation having to do with the reason Dutton saw fit to display two zebra heads instead of one, followed then by another pregnant silence which meant, Albert judged, that the picture was about to be disgorged by the camera.

"It's all *blurred*," the wife said. "You're terrible, Manley. Why didn't you read the instructions?"

240

"I didn't ask for the damn thing in the first place," the husband retorted.

Dutton suggested he take the picture again, and then offered to show them about the grounds, but in each case the husband gave a curt demurral, pleading a dental appointment.

As they left, Albert hurried forward to hold the front door open for them, following them outside and watching as Dutton stood on the parking lot and waved a jaunty farewell to the Cadillac.

When they had gone, Dutton turned back toward the house. "Well, Albert," he said, grinning, "I guess we're really in for it now. I'm afraid it's going to be a damned nuisance."

It was clear that he thought the floodgates were about to open, and that hardly a day would pass without someone dropping by to have a look at his collection of heads.

Albert, however, could not escape the conclusion that the couple had dropped by only because of the wife's determination that her husband should damn well get some use out of the camera.

As day followed day and it became apparent there would be no more visitors, the spell holding Dutton seemed to grow flimsy, and the change was pronounced, not only in Dutton himself, but in Mrs. Dutton.

Sitting on the bench behind the house in the August sunlight, or sitting in the Safari Room at cocktail hour, they seemed to be a couple in a state of anxiety, two aging people knowing the ax must fall and simply waiting to feel the blade.

It was with an attitude of sadness that Mrs. Dutton watered and tended her flowers now, as if she knew they might not be hers to water much longer.

And Dutton's collar, particularly when he wore a necktie for supper, looked far too large for his neck, a sight which somehow caused Albert to feel great pity.

Bringing in their drinks, Albert would find them almost invariably sitting in a sort of conspiratorial silence, or else discussing how much shorter the days had become. They struck him as a couple seriously considering flight, and there was an afternoon when he thought they had indeed fled, so long were they gone off in the Bentley, but finally they returned, just before supper, with no explanation for their protracted absence.

Beverly sent a card announcing she would be back on August 14. Jane meanwhile, to Albert's great surprise, finally finished her book and mailed it off to a literary agent. Thereupon, she had so much time on her hands that Albert found her a nuisance, particularly since she seemed bent upon blaming him for the hoax which Dutton had visited upon the Connoisseurs.

"I'm sure you deliberately left that book where he would find it," she said.

"That's not true," Albert said heatedly. "Why would I do such a thing?"

"That's what I keep asking myself," Jane said. "Why indeed?"

242

"I left it on the windowseat in the Safari Room. How was I to know?"

She shook her head. "I'm sure he's going to get caught, and if he does it'll be your fault."

"How will he get caught?"

"He'll be exposed, I'm sure of it."

"How? Not in the newspapers. They can't take a chance on libel."

"That horrible Mr. Merritt, don't forget. I don't trust him."

"Clinker Merritt doesn't strike me as a heavy reader."

"You did a very cruel thing, Albert."

"I wish you'd never finished your damned book," Albert said.

He had not realized how well off he had been, for when she was not lying on the bed or lying by the pool, she was off in the station wagon, spending money unnecessarily, spending money out of sheer ennui, and he could see now that there were great advantages in having her engrossed in her career.

Her pity for the Duttons took care of some of her energy. So great was her pity and so copious her leisure that she began to spend unwarranted time in the kitchen of the big house, digging into recipe books and coming up with mousses and casseroles which she hoped might please them.

After supper, Mr. and Mrs. Dutton would wander out to the kitchen. "My, my, Jane," Dutton would exclaim, patting his stomach. "You're going to make us so fat we won't be able to walk."

Perhaps because of the humility in his voice, perhaps because of the collar that was too large for his neck, or perhaps because of his newest project (making a scrapbook on the genealogy of Mrs. Dutton's family), Jane found it too much to bear and would turn toward the stove, brushing away a tear.

Having been Dutton's subaltern in many a bizarre episode, Albert felt he knew the man better than Jane did, and to know him was to know the brass of which he was made. Hence, Albert found it impossible to believe that Dutton could ever remain humble for long. No matter what the obstacle, no matter what the pitfall, he felt that Dutton's insensitivity would see him through.

Yet, for the moment, Jake continued to show all the attitudes of a man who knew he had done wrong and was awaiting punishment. And while he waited, he busied himself with paste pot and scissors in quiet pursuit of a contemplative pleasure, covering the first page of his scrapbook with the meticulously lettered inscription: A HISTORY OF THE FAMILY OF FRANCES DUTTON, BORN FRANCES CLAGGETT, 1635 TO 1968. PREPARED BY J. K. DUTTON.

When Mrs. Dutton protested mildly that his inscription not only implied her death but implied as well that she had lived 333 years, he told her that she was missing the point—that the dates referred to the longevity of her family, not to herself as an individual, and to stop being dumb about it.

On August 14, Beverly returned. Albert rented a rowboat for her from one of the boatyards and Beverly, loading it with books, magazines, suntan lotion, and transistor radio, would row over each morning to the quiet cove across the river, tie up the boat to the branch of a tree, and stay there until late afternoon. It was a routine that lasted, however, only a very few days because Nick arrived and promptly took over Beverly's days and nights. Nick, Beverly explained, was on his vacation.

"He's serious about you, isn't he?" Albert asked.

"I don't know," Beverly said.

"Are you serious about him?"

"He's nice. He's very kind."

Beverly and Nick spent their days lounging about the swimming pool, or taking long trips in Nick's sports car. A few times, Nick dutifully borrowed the Thunderbird and took Mrs. Dutton and Jane along as well.

Dutton seemed hardly aware of their absence—nor, for that matter, had he seemed to take any particular notice of Beverly's arrival; not even Nick's. He just kept plugging along at his genealogical project with little apparent interest in his environment, except to make certain that either Mrs. Dutton or Albert, one or the other, was on hand at all times to give him solace and comfort in case he should need it, or to provide an audience in case he had something to say.

Privately Albert was inclined to agree with Jane that Clinker would not let the hoax pass unnoticed and, watching Dutton at his paste pot, he could not help but be impressed by his stoic bravery. He was neither fleeing nor was he asking quarter. He was merely scissoring and pasting, and occasionally staring at the wall.

Clinker struck on the day that Nick took Beverly, Mrs. Dutton, and Jane on a seventy-five-mile expedition to a seafood pageant, highlighted by a so-called Crab Derby, in which hardshell crabs started at the center of a very large circle and raced to its perimeter.

In mid-afternoon, Albert was riding the mower and checking erosion when, chancing to look downstream, he saw the familiar hulk of the *Peacepipe Hilton* lumbering up the river in his direction.

It obviously had been spotted at about the same time by Dutton, who was so excited by the sight of it that he came running from the house, carrying his paste pot.

"Hark, Albert!" Dutton was shouting and gesticulating, trying to get Albert's attention. Albert, who had been having difficulty with the motor, kept right on mowing. He knew, however, that in moments of potential excitement, Dutton could not bear to be alone, and even though he pretended not to hear, he knew that he was being summoned to report to the riverbank to share what Dutton was experiencing.

"Look, Albert," Dutton shouted, pointing downstream as Albert arrived on the mower. "Isn't that Clinker's boat I see? Turn off that damned engine, Albert, I can't hear anything."

"Yes, sir, I believe it is," Albert said, killing the motor.

"Where do you suppose the silly son of a bitch is going with it?"

Albert peered against the sparkling blue of the river. "I guess he's going to turn in at one of the boatyards. That's what it looks like to me."

Together they watched, waiting for the *Peacepipe Hilton* to leave the channel and turn off, but it kept coming, the sun glinting on its blue and white paint, and occasionally glinting on something that most likely was a beer can, Albert thought, for now it was close enough for him to make out the figure at the helm, on the very topmost of the many flying bridges. The shock of thick white hair and the occasional glint of sun on metal could only mean that it was Clinker at the controls.

"Damn fool," Jake said. He turned to go back to the house, but then paused, looking again downstream. Clinker was moving steadily ahead, creating, even at medium speed, a wake and wash that were awesome. To look downstream beyond him, at the course he had covered, was to see small boats on both shores careening crazily at their moorings.

As the monster ship moved steadily closer, it was possible to make out other figures aboard, and soon Albert saw that there were three men, all stripped to the waist in the warm sunlight, lounging about the cockpit.

Less than a hundred yards away now, Clinker cut his speed slightly but still did not change course.

Dutton had seen enough. He moved hastily toward the house, still looking over his shoulder. "Keep on mowing, Albert," he said. "Just act like you don't see him."

Albert looked dubious. The *Peacepipe Hilton* was so huge that it was hard to pretend not to see it. He was bending over the mower, reaching for the starter strap, when he heard himself hailed.

"Hey, Al!" He looked up. Clinker was standing at the helm and waving. "Clink Merritt. How you doing?"

Albert waved a hand in greeting and bent to the mower again. He wound the strap tightly and jerked, but nothing happened. Bending once more, he glanced up. The boat now was nearly abreast of Dutton's bulging point of land.

With some irritation, he noticed that its wake was sending good solid waves lashing against the shoreline, the sort of wash that could undercut the bank and create more erosion.

"Hey, Al!" Clinker yelled again. "Come on aboard!"

Albert could make out the other three men clearly now. All held glasses in their hands, all were sprawled about in lounge chairs, and all seemed hilariously high-spirited.

"Hey, Al! Don't tell me you're still working for *Jake!*"

Albert addressed himself to the starter again, jerking three times without effect.

When he looked up again, he saw that the big boat had nosed just barely out of the channel and was now motionless in the water.

"Leggo the hook!" Clinker yelled.

A second later, there was an enormous splash. The *Peacepipe Hilton* had dropped anchor within fifty feet of Dutton's land.

Frowning, Albert looked at the boat and then at the water, noticing that the tide was unusually high.

Clinker by now had come down from the flying bridge and was seated with his cronies on the main deck. Although Albert could hear a continuous low hum of conversation and chuckling, he could not make out what they were saying unless they yelled. Intermittently there was the rise and fall of boisterous laughter.

"Hey, Al!" Clinker was standing at the rail now, high above the water, a can of beer in one hand, a highball in the other. "Come on aboard. Have a drink with us."

Albert pointed to the mower and spread his hands in a helpless gesture.

248

Clinker turned away and then immediately moved to the rail again. "Hey, Al!" he yelled. "Where's Bwana?"

At this there was a loud burst of laughter, led by Clinker himself.

"Where Memsahib?" Clinker shouted, and again the ship's company broke up.

Clinker was pointing a finger toward the house. "Tell Bwana buy self-starter, Al," he bellowed. "Tell that cheap old son of a bitch you tired of going push-push!"

Once more Clinker knew the glory of fracturing his audience, abetted no doubt by their states of intoxication. They had the look, for all the world, of four men who had been drinking in the hot sun since very early in the day. His cronies were roughly his age or younger, all tanned and fit-looking.

At this point, still unable to start the mower, Albert headed back to the house to find Dutton.

He found him in the Safari Room, looking badly shaken. He was seated at a card table near the picture window, with his scrapbook, scissors and paste pot arrayed before him, trying with little success to concentrate on the faded, yellowed photograph of a lady with a Gibson Girl hairdo, topped with a huge white bow of ribbon. Although he was still applying paste to the photograph, he had already printed a legend beneath the space where it was to be pasted: *Anna L. Claggett, Mother of Frances Claggett Dutton, Wife of J. K. Dutton.*

Through an open window, Albert could clearly hear the metronomic rise and fall of boisterous laughter from the ship anchored so flagrantly off the Dutton headlands, and it was evident that Dutton had heard all.

249

"Ahoy, ashore!" Clinker yelled now. "Ahoy, I say! Where in the hell is Bwana Dutton?"

Dutton's lips moved. His face was pale with fury.

Clinker bellowed in a voice choking with laughter, "Anybody inside there who can teach me how to shoot a lion?"

"*Gun-bearer!*" shouted one of the cronies.

"*Lion-skinner!*" shouted another.

"*Sons of bitches!*" muttered Dutton. "Albert . . ." His hand trembled as he held the paste brush to the reverse side of Anna Claggett's likeness. "Go order them off the property, Albert."

Albert looked through the window. "How can we do that, Mr. Dutton? They're not *on* the property."

"They're on my water," Dutton said.

"You know better than that, sir."

Dutton looked helplessly through the window, and Albert followed his gaze in time to see an empty beer can, describing an arc in the sunlight, landing in the yard.

Dutton was up like a shot, dropping the photograph paste-side-down on the card table and rushing from the house, followed by Albert.

"You sons of bitches!" Dutton screamed. "Quit throwing beer cans in my yard!"

Picking up the beer can, he hurled it, aiming for the hull, but the can fell short, making an entirely unsatisfactory and even rather dainty splash in the water.

From the *Peacepipe Hilton* there came derisive guffaws.

"Use a rifle next time, Bwana, you'll get more distance."

Dutton advanced to the very edge of the bank, a diminutive figure in his small white sneakers and blue nautical blazer. "Get the hell off of my water, you dirty scut-bastards!" he screamed.

He was answered only with laughter.

"I'm giving you fair warning, Merritt!" Dutton yelled. "If you don't take that lavender outhouse away from here, I'm calling the Coast Guard."

Albert grinned with approval. Dutton, turning abruptly, strode back toward the house, followed by waves of laughter and derogatory remarks. "C'mon, Albert," he said curtly.

Reaching the base of the tree, Dutton paused and looked up, as if seriously considering taking solace in its branches. Instead he put his hand on Albert's shoulder. "Albert," he said, "we've been through a lot together. What do you suggest?"

"I'm really not sure, sir," Albert said. "It wouldn't do any good to call the Coast Guard. They're on a public waterway."

"I realize that, Albert. I'm no fool. I was just bluffing, that's all."

Albert grinned. "I think the best thing, sir, is to ignore them."

"Perhaps." Dutton's eyes now gleamed with something of their old-time demented quality. *"But I can't stand it!* I can't just sit here and let him *get away with it,* Albert, don't you realize?"

"Yes, sir, I understand how you must feel."

"What are you grinning about, Albert?"

"I'm not sure, sir. I'm just glad, I guess, to see your spirit returning, so to say."

"I just had a thought, Albert," Dutton said grimly. "Do

you happen to know where you might lay your hands on this week's tide table?"

"The one the newspaper carries? Yes, sir, I have a copy of this week's newspaper in my room."

"Would you mind getting it, Albert?"

Albert found the newspaper under his bed. Running down the stairway, he hurried back to the house and found Dutton in the Safari Room, perched on the windowseat, glaring at the *Peacepipe Hilton*.

"I did happen to notice, Albert," Dutton said, turning the pages, seeking the tide table, "that when they dropped anchor the tide was higher than usual. At least a foot higher than the usual high tide."

"I noticed the same thing, sir. I was checking for erosion and I happened to notice how high the tide was, and I thought to myself that it was only because of the abnormally high tide that they could even leave the channel and drop anchor. That and the fact that they're very drunk."

"What time is it now, Albert?"

"It's about four-thirty, sir."

"Hmmmm," Dutton said, studying the tide table. "Flood tide was at three-fifty. How long would you say they've been there? About half an hour?"

"Just about, sir."

"That must mean, then, that it was at almost the exact peak of the tide that they dropped anchor. Does that make sense to you, Albert?"

"Yes, sir."

Dutton nodded. "Good."

"I do hate to see you taken advantage of, sir, and that's a fact."

"Thank you, Albert. Son of a bitch!"

"What's wrong, sir?"

"They just threw another beer can on my lawn!"

"I'd let it stay there, sir, at least for the time being."

"I'll busy myself with my scrapbook awhile longer. This was Mrs. Dutton's mother. Handsome lady, wasn't she?"

"Indeed so, sir. Very pretty eyes."

"You go on with your mowing, Albert."

"I can't get the engine started for some reason, sir."

"Well, tinker with it, Albert. Or just let it sit there. I don't really give a damn."

As Albert headed from the room, Dutton was humming an old-time tune. He stopped humming abruptly and cursed.

Albert paused. "What's wrong, sir?"

"Nothing, Albert," Dutton said with irritation, but Albert could see that he had pasted Mrs. Dutton's mother to the card table.

"What time is it now, Albert?"

"It's twenty minutes of five, sir."

27

Leaving Dutton with his scrapbook, Albert went out and tried to start the engine again, while empty beer cans continued to pelt the lawn.

Again and again he tried to start it, without success, and finally headed for the garage to get some more gasoline, with the intent of priming the carburetor. On the way to the garage he came upon Dutton, returning from the direction of the swimming pool and pausing for a moment to hold his breathing-tube up to the sun.

Remarking that the days were fortunately getting shorter, Dutton continued on to the house, while Albert carried the gasoline can back to the mower, poured some into the carburetor and tried, still without success, to get it going.

From time to time, he took note of the water level. By six o'clock, it had fallen at least a foot and a half, he judged, and by now the drinking cronies were louder and even drunker. The beer cans were coming in a steady hail.

At six-thirty, Dutton called him in and asked him to warm up some soup for their evening meal, suggesting that they eat it together in the Safari Room, where they could command a view of what went on outside.

"What kind of soup, sir?" Albert asked.

"Cream of tomato would be nice, Albert."

Albert prepared the soup and they ate it at Dutton's card table, from which by now he had cleared away his scrapbook and other paraphernalia, stripping for action.

"Do you notice something about that boat, Albert?" Dutton held a spoonful of soup suspended before his lower lip. "It's not rocking."

Albert peered through the window. The sun was low in the sky, and a huge bulking shadow fell over the water from the *Peacepipe Hilton*.

"What I mean, Albert, is that when a boat is afloat it has

254

a little *motion* to it. That boat is just sitting there in a rigid sort of way. I believe they're already aground."

Albert nodded. "I believe you're right, sir. I'm not sure they realize it yet."

"Clinker, of course, has always fancied himself something of a seaman. He belongs to something called a power squadron."

They had finished their soup and were nibbling on brown-edge wafers when they heard the roar of an engine, a rasping sound, and then several voices shouting all together.

"Hard aground, Clink!" one voice shouted, louder than all the rest. "Cut the engine, cut the engine, for God's sake! Propeller's hitting! You'll ruin the screw!"

The sound of the engine died and the four aboard the *Peacepipe Hilton* could now be observed in the twilight, hanging over the rail, peering down into what could only be very shallow water by now.

"The way I figure it, Albert," Dutton said, "there won't be another flood tide until around four-thirty in the morning, am I right?"

"Yes, sir, that's about right."

"This tide now will keep going out until about ten-thirty tonight, I'd say, and then it starts coming in again, but it won't reach its crest until four-thirty a.m."

"Right," Albert said. "They don't seem very worried, though, do they?"

It was apparent that Clinker and his cronies were far too drunk to care. Occasionally, one would stand on the main deck with legs spread apart and move his torso from side to side, in the evident hope that the *Peacepipe Hilton*, with all its untold tonnage, might somehow be rocked free. Failing, he would resume his seat in one of the lounge chairs and reach philosophically for the bottle, or perhaps another can of beer.

As the tide continued to run out, the *Peacepipe Hilton* looked ever more absurd with its vast hull emerging steadily from the water and its ungainly lines revealed until, just before dark, it looked not unlike a small hotel perched lopsided on a sloping foundation.

It was perhaps nine-thirty when Clinker's voice rose angrily on the summer air. "All right, shut up!" he bellowed at one of his shipmates. "How in the hell do you propose I get it off—pick it up in my arms and carry it out to deep water?"

The stricken ship was now showing its running lights, even though it was running nowhere whatever. The cabin lights were also ablaze.

"Ahoy, ashore!" Once more, Clinker's voice.

With a faint smile, Dutton strode over the lawn. "Ahoy!" he called.

"Ahoy!" Clinker replied. "Is that you, Jake?"

"Is that you, Clink?"

"Ahoy! Hey, Jake, is it okay if we come ashore and use your phone?"

"Are you aground?" Jake inquired.

The answer came from one of Clinker's cronies, in a low voice which carried, however, quite distinctly across the water: "What the hell's it look like, Bwana?"

"Shut up!" Clinker said fiercely. "Yeah, Jake, hard aground."

"Ahoy," Dutton said. "That's a damn shame. How did it happen, do you suppose?"

"Okay if we come ashore and use your phone, Jake?" Clinker asked once more.

"Stay where you are," Dutton replied. "Just tell me who to call. I'll call for you."

"Will you call somebody to haul us off? I'd sure appreciate it, Jake."

"No trouble," Dutton replied. "Glad to do it."

As he strode back over the lawn toward the house, Albert could hear him chuckling in a breathless, exhilarated way. "What are you planning to do now, Mr. Dutton?" Albert asked.

"You just stand over on the shore there, Albert, and if they say anything—"

"What are you planning to do, Mr. Dutton?"

"Just tell 'em I'm from the towing service, Albert," Dutton said and strode happily into the house.

In a half-hour or so, standing obediently and watchfully near the shoreline, Albert heard a commotion in the water. In the lights from the ship, he saw then the faint gleam of the breathing-tube moving slowly along through the darkness, slowly and jerkily and not close down to the surface as might have been expected, but sticking up a good three or four feet above the water.

The breathing-tube passed from view for at least thirty seconds and then, with a loud wallowing sound, Dutton, having either run aground or experienced trouble in breathing, suddenly did a rolling twist so that he became fully visible, the lights from the ship gleaming on the wet sheen of his frogman's suit.

There was an immediate reaction from those aboard the ship, who until then had apparently noticed nothing out of the ordinary.

"Hey, Clinker!" one of the shipmates yelled. "Here's the monster from the black lagoon! All hands on deck!"

"Who in the hell are *you?*" Clinker demanded, leaning over the rail.

"It's okay, Mr. Merritt," Albert shouted reassuringly. "It's the man from the towing service. He's sizing up the trouble."

Dutton now was standing in water that reached barely halfway up his shinbones.

"How's it look?" Clinker addressed him.

Dutton shook his head.

"He can't talk with his helmet on," Albert explained.

"What in the hell is he doing with that brace-and-bit?" Clinker demanded.

"That's not a brace-and-bit, Mr. Merritt," Albert explained. "That's an electronic testing device. The people at the towing service said it was necessary to test whether it's hard bottom or soft bottom."

"God Almighty!" Clinker shouted. "What the hell kind of a towing service did you *call?*"

"I'm just telling you what they told me," Albert said.

"Where's Dutton?" Clinker asked sharply.

"Up in the house," Albert replied.

Shaking his head dubiously, Clinker leaned over the rail, looking down at the water.

Dutton meanwhile had submerged again, although not very successfully. He seemed for the most part merely to be wriggling about in the mud.

Finally he disappeared altogether, and a few minutes later Albert heard him call from the shore, perhaps a hundred yards off in the darkness. Albert was about to leave his post when he paused, his attention arrested by the sight of Clinker Merritt hanging over the side of his ship and retching mightily.

Hearing a low whistle, Albert trotted through the darkness to meet his employer. "Couldn't get any kind of leverage," Dutton said, panting heavily. "Water's too shallow, Albert. Have to do something else. Wait here a minute."

Dutton disappeared into the house. A few minutes later, he returned with a flashlight and what seemed to be a large sheet of cardboard. Together they headed down to the dock and climbed aboard Dutton's boat.

"Now first off, Albert—have you ever had occasion to pump out the bilges in this boat?"

"You never told me to," Albert said.

"No need to apologize, Albert. Well now, I know for a fact that this thing here is the bilge pump, and here's the hose. What we do is hang the hose over the side like this and pump. Go ahead, Albert. Pump."

Albert pumped and heard a stream of water shoot into the river.

"Wow!" Dutton exclaimed. "That bilge water sure stinks, doesn't it?"

"Yes, sir, it certainly does."

"That's enough pumping, Albert, for the time being. Hark!"

They fell silent, listening. From downstream there came what sounded like a very nasty argument aboard the *Peacepipe Hilton.*

259

Chuckling, Dutton picked up the large sheet of cardboard.

"What's that, sir?" Albert asked.

"I just lettered it sloppily," Dutton said. "It's not my best lettering, but it's good enough, wouldn't you say?"

Dutton played the flashlight over the cardboard and Albert read:

ACE TOWING SERVICE

"Good enough?"

"Yes, sir, I should think so," Albert said.

Dutton placed the sign just below the gunwale against the hull. "A couple of thumbtacks should hold it," he said. "There." He hammered at first one thumbtack and then the other with the end of the flashlight. "Now. What we want to do, of course, is get as close as possible but not so close that *we* run aground ourselves."

"Are you actually planning to tow them off, Mr. Dutton? Or squirt them with bilge water?"

"Never mind, Albert. Don't concern yourself. You just follow instructions and don't give me any of your doctrinaire liberalism."

"Mr. Dutton, I'm not sure about all this. We've proved we're really not expert at handling boats."

"Nonsense, Albert." Dutton touched the ignition and the motor roared. "Cast off the ropes, Albert! Hurry up!"

Albert did as commanded and came scrambling back to the cockpit. Slowly they inched their way backward out of the slip.

"All right, Albert, get that long rope out of the cabin there, on the seat next to the icebox. Good. Just drop it on the cockpit cushion there. Yes, we're going along very nicely, Albert. See?"

They were indeed, Albert conceded, moving with more style and grace than was their custom. Beyond the bend, he could see the *Peacepipe Hilton*, lights blazing. As they drew closer, he could see that the water was lapping a little higher against the giant hull than it had been when Dutton was flopping about in his frogman's suit, so it seemed reasonable to conclude that the tide had turned and was now coming in, although still a long way from high.

Muttering to himself, Dutton jabbed at the gearshift, and the boat, now evidently in neutral, began to lose speed. "Now, Albert," he said. "I don't want them to hear my voice, naturally. What I want you to do when we get in hailing distance is just ask Clinker if he's ready to be hauled off."

"Do you really think the tide's high enough, sir? Shouldn't we wait until the tide gets a little higher?"

"*Albert!*" Dutton said with exasperation. "I don't like to be curt with you, Albert, but just do as I tell you. After all, it's *his* boat. It's up to him."

From the *Peacepipe* now there came a cry of drunken glee, and then a chorus of huzzahs heralding the appearance of the Ace Towing Service.

"Ahoy!" Albert ventured as Dutton covered his face again with the frogman mask. "Ahoy—Mr. Merritt!"

Merritt's three shipmates were lined up expectantly at the rail, but he was not in evidence.

"Where's Mr. Merritt?" Albert called.

"Down below," was the reply. "Puked and passed out. Come on, Ace, let's get with it. Throw us a line."

"You'd better back water, Mr. Dutton," Albert warned.

"We're gliding, Albert."

"I know, but we're gliding a little too fast. We had too much momentum." Albert reached for the gearshift, but Dutton shoved his hand away.

"Mr. Dutton—"

"All right, Albert, I'll handle it!" Dutton growled from within his headpiece. "Whose boat is this, yours or mine?" Dutton shifted to reverse. "Don't sulk, Albert, at a time of crisis. Look alive. Ask them if they're ready to be hauled off."

Dutton's boat by now was at the very edge of the channel and no more than thirty feet from the stern of the *Peacepipe Hilton*.

"Ahoy," Albert said in a listless, unnautical way. "Are you ready to be hauled off?"

"Hell, yes!" one of the cronies shouted. "Let's get on with it, Ace."

"Tide's still low," another said. "Maybe we'd better ask Clink."

"The hell with Clink, he's out cold. Come on, Ace, toss us a line."

"Take the rope there, Albert," Dutton said.

"You're going to have to back up to it, Mr. Dutton. Stern to stern. Do you think you can manage?"

"Tie your end on the cleat back there in the back, Albert," Dutton said. "Ask if they're all set."

"Okay?" Albert called.

"Okay," came the reply. "Give 'er hell."

Albert would never know for certain whether the fate that befell the *Peacepipe Hilton* was something that Dutton had deliberately premeditated, or whether it was, in the end, merely accidental.

That Dutton wished the ship ill was beyond doubt. Yet his seamanship was so poor, had been tested and found wanting so many times, that what happened to the ill-fated vessel might have been, as Dutton was to claim, merely an unfortunate accident.

It all happened, moreover, with such swiftness, and with so many spastic, jolting maneuvers, and was accompanied by so many rasping, nerve-racking noises, that Albert would have been hard put in any event to perceive it in clear sequence.

He had a jumbled memory of Dutton heading slowly and sensibly out into the channel until the line became taut; of a sound that indicated the bottom of the stranded ship was sucking grudgingly free of mud, and a rasping sound indicating that its bottom was passing over something considerably more abrasive than mud; and then of a disheveled and distraught Clinker Merritt, rushing into view on the afterdeck, screaming at the Ace Towing Service to cease towing, and then berating his drunken cronies for having permitted the towing operation to begin—and all accompanied by the violent outbursts of Dutton's engine as he revved it higher and higher until it became a thin, frightening whine.

Abruptly the tension slackened, and the *Peacepipe* was free, a fact attested by the loud cheers that came from the afterdeck. There were even shouts of commendation for the Ace Towing Service, although not from Clinker Merritt.

Albert heard the *Peacepipe*'s motor roar into action. The other end of the tow-line came whistling over his head. He grabbed it, coiled it up, and dropped it into the cockpit.

The two craft were, at this point, still stern to stern. "Now then, Albert . . ." Dutton was jerking at the gearshift, his engine still revved up high. And then came the moment of doubt.

For suddenly Dutton was moving backward at an alarming rate of speed, and although warnings were cried both by Albert and those aboard the target vessel, there was a horrible crash as Dutton struck the stern of the *Peacepipe* a blow which although it elicited from Dutton a "Whoops!" may in the end have been totally gratifying to him.

Certain it was that he had no trouble whatever in now shifting to forward and moving out into the channel, nor did he have any trouble in throttling down the engine to a murmur.

"Good God, Mr. Dutton," Albert said with awe. "Did you do that on purpose?"

"Of course not, Albert. The gear got stuck. They're not hurt, anyway. Here they come."

"May I make a suggestion, sir? I'd suggest we keep out of their way. They sound mad as hell."

"What about?" Dutton demanded. "We pulled them off, didn't we?"

The *Peacepipe Hilton* by now had gotten itself turned around and squared away and was heading slowly out toward midchannel, although it seemed in no hurry. Above the steady drone of its motor, Albert could hear cries of lawsuits and slurs against the Ace Towing Service, and then Clinker's voice, rising above all: "Ace Towing Service, hell! Dutton, you murderous bastard, I'm going to kill you!"

The *Peacepipe Hilton* was headed directly now for the rescue vessel, and Dutton, displaying remarkable control, kept his own engine throttled down and began a wary circling maneuver.

"What shall we do, Albert?" he asked. "Make a run for it?"

"I don't know, sir," Albert said miserably. "I'm sure he can outrun us."

"Do you suppose we should abandon ship, Albert?"

"I don't know, sir. It's up to you. I know he's gonna ram us, though."

Feeling it was no longer fruitful to maintain his disguise, Dutton stripped his frogman mask away and, holding the helm with one hand, used the other to scratch vigorously at his head, so long imprisoned by its rubber headpiece.

"I'm going to make a run for it, Albert," Dutton said. "There's no other way."

"All right, sir— Wait! Something's happened!"

Although the *Peacepipe*'s intent had seemed quite clear and its course totally menacing, it was now losing ground, faltering.

Abruptly from one of the ship's company there came a cry of distress: "Hey, Clink! We're sinking! She's got a hole in her!"

All four rushed to the stern and peered over.

The *Peacepipe* indeed had lost what speed it had and was already undeniably lower in the water.

"*Sinking?*" Dutton exclaimed. "How *could* they be, Albert? Unless we hit 'em a better clip than I thought."

"We hit 'em a good clip, sir, no doubt of that," Albert said.

The sounds emanating from the stricken vessel now were totally chaotic. Mingled with Clinker's piercing shrieks of hatred were his cronies' shouts of drunken alarm. First one, and soon all three were singing, "Nearer, My God, to Thee."

Clinker's voice rose above the singing: "Abandon ship! Man the life raft!"

A huge orange life raft was tossed overboard. All four men jumped into the water and climbed into it.

"I guess we'd better go help," Dutton said.

"I wouldn't do it if I were you, Mr. Dutton. They'll be okay. It's only about a hundred yards to shore anyway."

"Nonsense, Albert. They may need help."

"If you ram the life raft, sir, you may kill somebody."

"I have no intention of ramming the life raft, Albert."

"Keep your speed very low, sir. Take it out of gear. Out of *gear*. Put it in neutral. Oh, my God!"

"We're okay, Albert. Don't get excited."

They were gliding toward the life raft. Paddles were brandished as they approached. "Keep clear, Dutton!" Clinker screamed. "Keep *clear!*" In Clinker's voice there was sheer terror.

"Ahoy!" Dutton called. "We'll stand by to pick up survivors."

"Stay away! Stay away! Dutton, you son of a bitch, stand clear, I say!"

"Don't call me a son of a bitch, you scut! I'm here to give you any help I can."

"Get out of our way, Dutton! Let us paddle clear. Can't you see it's sinking, you dumb bastard! We'll be sucked down into the vortex."

Aboard the life raft, paddles were being plied in a frenzy, although there was some evidence that the two paddlers were paddling at cross-purposes, for the life raft kept describing a circle.

266

"Man the pump, Albert!" Dutton said, grabbing the end of the bilge hose.

"But, sir—" Albert protested. "Don't you think that would be a little too much?"

"I suppose maybe you're right, Albert."

"I think it would be excessive, Mr. Dutton. I really do."

"She's going!" Those aboard the life raft were shouting in alarm, looking up with awe at the huge bulk of the mother ship, which was indeed making a curious sucking, gurgling sound.

"Oh, God!" Clinker moaned. "Dutton, you dirty dumb bastard!" Grabbing one of the paddles, Clinker hurled it at Dutton's boat. It struck the bow a glancing blow.

"Pump, Albert!" Dutton screamed.

"Mr. Dutton . . ."

"Pump! Pump!"

"Paddle clear!" Clinker shouted. "She's going fast!"

At that moment, Clinker received a spurt of bilge water directly in the face.

"Pump, Albert, pump!" Gleefully, Dutton trained the hose full on the life raft, disregarding the piteous cries of those aboard. "Pump! Pump! Pump!"

Carried by its momentum beyond the life raft now, the rescue vessel circled about. "Heading for home now, Albert," Dutton said happily.

Looking backward as they headed steadily upstream for the dock, Albert saw the bulk of the *Peacepipe Hilton* settle lower and lower and then, with an abrupt jolt, come to rest.

So deep was its draft that even though it had sunk in

the very middle of the channel, a good three-quarters of it remained visible, towering over all, indomitable.

"Well, Albert," Dutton said with a chuckle. "We finally sank the *Peacepipe Hilton!*"

"Yes, sir," Albert said.

28

The weekly newspaper was published each Tuesday and Friday. Feeling a very strong premonition, Albert hurried to the local drugstore early Tuesday morning, bought a copy, and quickly scanned it. He found nothing.

Tuesday, as it happened, was the day following the sinking of the *Peacepipe Hilton*. Not until Friday was it succored—by a highly legitimate towing and salvage company. It rested in the mud for three full days, an inert pastel promontory, an ungainly hippo, stricken in midchannel, a menace to navigation, and for three days a ready reminder, if reminder were needed, of the events that took place on the night of its demise.

For Dutton, it was a reminder of triumph, of glory. During the three days the ship remained unsalvaged, Albert observed his employer advancing several times daily to the utmost point of his land and gazing toward the stranded vessel with a smile of satisfaction. After fifteen minutes or so, he would turn away, chuckling and shaking his head.

So far as Albert knew, Dutton did not recount the details of his triumph to Mrs. Dutton. Albert, however, told Jane and Beverly everything following their return from the Crab Derby the next day. Jane expressed concern that Dutton was now in for real trouble, while Beverly contented herself with the observation that any society of which Jake and Clinker and in fact her own father were members deserved to perish in whatever holocaust history might offer.

Dutton, however, was much too pleased with himself to worry and, as usual, when he became pleased with himself he was intolerable. Albert had always found him at his best when he was at his most miserable, enmired in sorrow and defeat. A triumph of any sort, however petty, sent him into a manic, euphoric state in which he quickly became a supercilious braggart and which, among other things, brought back all his atavistic feeling for the division between what he still regarded as the classes.

At such times, as Albert well knew, even he himself was not immune to Dutton's smugness.

On Thursday afternoon he chanced to pass Dutton on the parking lot. Dutton, not speaking, looked at him in a peculiar way, giving him a sidelong glance that seemed to reflect a certain conflict. What he evinced was not anger, not quite anger, and yet it seemed somehow related to anger. It also showed anxiety, and was in some respects even a plea, however unspoken and however, at that point, ambiguous.

So aware by now of all the nuances of his employer's behavior, Albert was puzzled by this one.

Twice more that day he chanced to pass Dutton and twice

more Dutton failed to speak, although the glances he now gave Albert were glances of clear-cut accusation.

At cocktail hour, he was rather silent, rather thoughtful, whereas the previous evening he had taken great pleasure in perching himself upon the wide windowseat and gazing happily downstream through the picture window at the immobile *Peacepipe Hilton.*

After supper, Albert was told by Mrs. Dutton that Jake would very much appreciate it if he would come and have a few words with him. He was in his tree.

"You wanted me?" Albert asked, standing close to the trunk and looking up. In the darkness, Dutton was barely visible, only a shadowy outline against the evening sky.

"Good evening, Albert," he said. "Care to nip up?"

Dubiously, Albert climbed to the first branch and there stopped.

"Have a seat, Albert. Make yourself comfortable. Actually, I hardly know how to begin, Albert. Whatever I say, I want you to accept it in the spirit in which I offer it. How could I ever feel anything but affection for you, Albert, after all we've been through together?"

"I don't know, sir," Albert said.

"That was certainly a wonderful experience the other night, wasn't it, Albert?"

"You haven't heard from Mr. Merritt?"

"No," Dutton said. "Why?"

"I was just wondering. I can't help feeling that you *may.*"

"The hell with Mr. Merritt, Albert. Mr. Merritt is not what I wanted to talk to you about."

"All right, sir, what is it?"

"Well now, as fond as we are of each other, Albert—and I

think I can safely say that it's mutual, I mean that you're fond of me too. I'm sure you must feel it."

"Feel what?" Albert asked.

"Our fondness for each other. But I can never be quite sure whether you feel the—the other thing."

"What other thing?"

"Well, I suppose you'd call it an invisible barrier, Albert. It's there, of course, even though at times it may seem that it's *not* there. Actually, Albert, I don't really like the idea of classes any more. I've been doing a good deal of thinking about it lately, and I really think class distinctions are a thing of the past. They have no place in America. So let's not even speak of classes, shall we?"

"I *wasn't*," Albert said.

"Of course not, and neither was I," Dutton said, gaining assurance. "Let's simply use such words as background and environment—of shared experience and whatnot." Dutton paused. For a long while he was silent. Presently he sighed, and at the same moment a faint breeze sighed in the tree. "Actually," he said, "except for the fact that the days are getting shorter, there's no sign that autumn is so near."

"And winter," Albert said grimly.

"What, Albert?"

"I say, or that *winter* is so near."

"That's true . . . but why do you say it in that tone of voice, Albert?"

Albert did not reply.

Again Dutton was silent. Finally he gave a rueful chuckle. "I just can't do it, Albert. I can't go on. I'm afraid that no matter how tactfully I say it, your feelings will be hurt."

"What are you trying to say, Mr. Dutton? Say it."

Again there was a prodigious and regretful sigh. "Albert, let me say first off that I think your daughter, Becky, is just as cute as she can be, and Mrs. Dutton agrees. We both think the world of her. And I want her to be happy, just as I'm sure *you* want her to be happy. I think she's just as cute as a button. And we don't want her to be hurt, do we, Albert? Do we? Want her hurt? You haven't answered my question, Albert."

"What question?"

"Do you want her hurt?"

"Do I want her *hurt*? My God, Mr. Dutton! Of *course* I don't want her hurt. Some questions don't really *need* answering."

"I can tell you're becoming offended already, Albert."

"Not necessarily. But this is as good a time as any to tell you that you can ask some of the most damn-fool superfluous questions I've ever heard, and I've answered every damned one of them all summer long."

Dutton seemed offended. "I'll let that pass, Albert," he said morosely. "I won't take up the challenge, because I'm fond of you and because I suspect—I can *judge*—that you already know what I'm about to say and I can understand your hurt."

"What are you trying to say?" Albert asked, snapping a branch. "What are you talking about?"

"About my nevvew Nick wanting to marry your daughter, Albert."

"What!"

"Yes. And in spite of his fondness for liberal causes and all, I just don't think your daughter and Nick would ever be happy together."

"Oh, my God!" Albert said.

"I can appreciate the way you feel about it, Albert, and I can appreciate the way Becky's going to feel—her disappointment. And I'd like very much to do something that will soften the blow, not only for Becky but for you and Jane."

"Mr. *Dutton!*" Albert pounded his fist on the limb. "I can assure you my daughter has absolutely no intention—"

"What I'd thought of doing, Albert, was treating her to a nice trip to Europe. Maybe she could go to one of those high-class cooking schools in Paris, where she could take fancy cooking lessons, which would always stand her in good stead no matter what her future should turn out to be. All at my expense, of course."

Choking with rage, disgust, and something very close to hysteria, Albert slid down the tree and stalked off.

Beverly was still out when he went to bed that night. The next morning when he awoke she was still asleep.

"Bev . . . wake up. I want to ask you something."

Beverly groaned.

"Open your eyes and look at me. This is very important."

"What, Daddy?"

"Turn over and open your eyes. Look at me."

Groaning, Beverly turned over and opened her eyes, immediately closing them. "I can hear."

"Has Nick asked you to marry him?"

"Yes."

"Are you planning to?"

"Of course not."

"Open your eyes."

"I can't. He wants me to marry him, but I'm not going to. Except I don't know how to get rid of him without hurting his feelings. He won't take no for an answer. Is that enough? Can I go back to sleep now?"

"Yes, you can go back to sleep now."

That day, Friday, the local newspaper came out again.

Clinker's revenge took a form that Albert found not only ingenious but altogether rather delightful.

Dutton, unbeknownst to Albert (it was, after all, a fee hardly worth mentioning), had been paid fifteen dollars for the lecture he delivered before the Connoisseur's Choice Club. Accepting the money may have been one of the larger mistakes of his life.

Through one of the more prominent lawyers in the area, Clinker had filed a lawsuit at the county courthouse in Paxton, naming Jake Dutton as defendant.

The lawsuit relied upon an ancient statute originally put on the books to protect guileless rural audiences from being defrauded by the operators of medicine shows once popular in the area—shows offering bottled medicine and dancers specializing in the so-called hoochy-kooch, or, as it was sometimes spelled, hootchy-kootch.

In the lawsuit, Dutton was accused of accepting money fraudulently and was being sued by Clinker for recovery of Clinker's two-dollar admission fee, plus certain damages alleged to have been suffered by Clinker by virtue of having been enticed to a performance "shot through with fraud, deceit, and outright falsehood."

Contained as they were in the lawsuit, the accusations

were hence privileged material and they offered Dutton no grounds for a countersuit of libel.

The story was on the front page, under a headline reading:

SUIT ACCUSES
SPEAKER OF FRAUD

The story quoted the lawyer's brief as alleging that Dutton's speech was "specious in every respect."

"Plaintiff alleges," the story said, quoting the brief, "that he has known J. K. Dutton his entire life and is prepared to swear that the said J. K. Dutton has never shot a lion and has never set foot in Africa . . . and that the said J. K. Dutton did willfully and maliciously describe to members of said club an adventure totally without basis in fact, accepting money for said speech under patently false pretenses, having, furthermore, taken and rendered in his own words and embraced as his own, the events chronicled in a work of fiction by the late Ernest Hemingway."

29

Even then, it seemed for a short time that Dutton might fight on. Knowing the man as he did, Albert would hardly have been surprised, for Dutton's vision of things was, of course, peculiarly his own.

Stranded as he was in the community mainstream, his flanks exposed to the pitiless scrutiny and contempt of all, he was still capable, Albert knew, of taking up the challenge, hiring a lawyer, and careening like a wounded gnu into the arena to give the lie to Clinker's charges.

He won an unexpected ally in Jane—Jane, who from the very first had felt for him more pity than scorn, and whose pity had, as time passed, verged upon outright affection. Having read the article in the paper on Friday, she had seemed all through the day very close to tears. She had even seen fit to attack Albert—with no provocation whatever, in the latter's opinion. "You seem positively *glad* about it," she said.

"I'm not glad at all," Albert replied. "Why should I be glad? But God knows he brought it on himself."

"Poor old fellow," she said.

"If he'd been content with simply ramming the boat, that might have been interpreted as an accident," Albert said.

"Why he had to insist upon squirting them with bilge water when they were already in the life raft and the ship was sinking—that was just plain malice, Jane, you've got to admit."

"Why didn't you *stop* him, Albert?"

"He's not the type one stops," Albert said.

"You could have stopped him if you'd really wanted to."

"Hah!" Albert said.

Jane glared at him.

On Sunday evening, as Albert placed dessert before the Duttons, Jane came bursting into the dining room, wearing the same Colonial Williamsburg costume she had been wearing all through the summer.

"Mr. Dutton!" she exclaimed. "I just can't let another minute go by without telling you that I think that story in the paper was outrageous! You should sue that man!"

Dutton glanced up from his lemon sponge. Up to now, he had not mentioned the article and, save for a certain slump in posture and a dejected shambling stride, had given no sign that he had even read it, although surely he had.

"Thank you, Jane," he said with great dignity. "I'm still mulling over what course of action to take. I'm consulting my lawyer, Squire Mulligan, in the morning. . . . Albert, I wonder if we might have a little pousse-café."

"I beg your pardon, Mr. Dutton," Albert said. "What is it you want?"

"A little pousse-café, if you please, Albert."

Albert glanced from one to the other. Dutton was looking

at him expectantly. Mrs. Dutton was gazing with melancholy at the tines of her fork.

"Pousse-café. Pousse-*café*." Dutton frowned.

Albert withdrew to the kitchen, deciding to do nothing.

"Yes, Jane," he heard Dutton say. "One hardly knows how to react to such poppycock. My first reaction was simply to ignore it . . . to let it find the oblivion it deserves."

"Oh, but he shouldn't be allowed to get away with it," Jane protested.

"That's in line with my present thinking," Dutton said. "After all," he went on with a distinct note of bluster, "I could have him behind bars for such a malicious trumped-up charge."

"I'd be willing to testify, Mr. Dutton, if you'd like me to," Jane said.

Albert, watching and listening through the slit, grimaced.

"Oh, Jane . . ." Mrs. Dutton said with gratitude, although not happily.

"I realize, ma'am," Jane said, "that it would be embarrassing for *you* to testify. Naturally it would. But I could. I'd be glad to."

Dutton cleared his throat. Albert saw him smile faintly and cast his eyes down upon his half-eaten lemon sponge.

"I will testify," Jane went on, "that I accompanied you two on a trip to Africa, whenever it was, whenever you say. And that it all happened exactly as you said it did, regardless of Ernest Hemingway."

"That's awfully kind of you, Jane, dear," Mrs. Dutton said. "But . . . I'm not sure it would be wise."

"I can say," Jane continued with heat, "that we all went on safari together, and that you didn't kill the lion the first

278

day, but then you did on the second day. And I could tell how Mrs. Dutton tried to save your life, by shooting when the lion charged you. After all, Mr. Dutton, things *can* happen. So far as anybody knows, it's *true*."

Dutton seemed to be staring into space, perhaps into the jungle.

"Of course," Jane said, "we'd need someone to testify that he was the white hunter—Bates. Wasn't that his name?"

"Yes, Bates." Dutton's eyes now took on that peculiar gleam that Albert so often had noticed in the past when his employer was on the brink of adventure.

"Bates, yes," Dutton said dreamily. His gaze abruptly was focused upon the swinging door leading to the kitchen. "Where is Albert?" he asked.

Albert frowned. Involuntarily, his ears began to wiggle. "Good God," he muttered.

"Albert is in the kitchen, Mr. Dutton," Jane said.

"Jake . . ." Mrs. Dutton chided. "Now, Jake . . ." A note of panic entered her voice. "Jake! You can't!"

Dutton continued to stare into the future. His eyes continued to gleam. He uttered a low chuckle.

It was the peak of his daydream. For now he met Mrs. Dutton's eyes. He stared at her unwaveringly for a second or two, but then looked down. Something went out of him. His shoulders slumped. He stared down at his plate and toyed with a fragment of lemon sponge. Finally he looked up and gave Jane a smile of melancholy. "Thank you, Jane," he said. "It's very good of you, and I won't soon forget it."

"Just let me know if you decide," Jane said and withdrew, opening the swinging door and bumping into Albert, who immediately placed both hands on her shoulders, gripping them harder than was really necessary, and backed her into a far corner of the kitchen.

"Are you out of your mind?" he growled. "Are you absolutely *crazy?* Don't you realize you'd be committing perjury? I won't permit it, Jane. Have some intelligence!"

Sighing, Jane sat in her rocker before the stove and began to rock.

Albert sat on the stepladder and glared at her.

From the dining room he could hear a mumble, Mrs. Dutton's voice, punctuated now and then by a distinct "No!" from Dutton. And then once more the mumble, more insistent, uninterrupted now, and finally rising to a sharp "part of decency, Jake!"

For a while there was silence and then the tinkle of the bell. "Oh, Albert!" Mrs. Dutton called. "Jane . . . Would you both come in for a second, please?"

Albert looked at Jane. Together they went into the dining room.

"Mr. Dutton has something he wants to say to you both," Mrs. Dutton said sadly, yet with sturdy resolution. "A confession—and an apology."

"Apology!" Dutton repeated. "Who said it was an apology?"

"Mr. Dutton has no need to apologize to us for anything," Jane said.

"Of course I don't," Dutton said. "All I want to tell you is . . . All Mrs. Dutton *wants* me to tell you is . . ."

His voice faded, and he was staring hard at the table. Albert and Jane waited.

". . . the fact is, those are my Great-Uncle Jake's heads,"

Dutton muttered. "I mean *he* shot them. Fifty years ago. My Great-Uncle Jake."

"You've both been so decent," Mrs. Dutton said, "that I felt it was only right that Mr. Dutton should tell you."

Dutton's mouth was twisting, and he had a fierce grip on his fork. He looked up defiantly. "He had the same name as mine. Jake Dutton."

"But, Jake," Mrs. Dutton said gently. "He still wasn't you. He was himself. A different man."

"Okay, who said he wasn't?" Dutton demanded. "Albert, where is that pousse-café we asked for?"

Albert's fingernails probed at his palms. "I don't even know what pousse-café *is*, Mr. Dutton."

"Well, you *should* know, Albert. Anybody who's been serving table as long as you have should certainly know what pousse-café is. . . . Never mind, Albert, forget it. I don't want any now."

As Albert withdrew, he noticed that Dutton looked suddenly much older. His neck looked scrawny, and his hair gleamed like snow in the light of the tall candles.

Later, just before the Duttons left the table, he heard Jake say, "Wasn't it nice when Ike was still President? Remember, Frances? Those were nice years, weren't they?"

The lawsuit, of course, offered little difficulty—as a lawsuit. Clinker, it went without saying, was ready to call it off immediately. His purpose had been achieved. He had found an excuse to sound off in print and now would be willing to drop the case.

This much Mrs. Dutton confirmed the following afternoon.

Sitting on the bench behind the house, looking out over the lawn, she beckoned to Albert. After clearing up the matter of the lawsuit, she sighed heavily.

"Albert, there's something I must tell you. It grieves me to say it, but—we called a real-estate broker this morning and put Rear Guard up for sale."

"Oh, Mrs. Dutton!" Albert exclaimed sympathetically.

"I love it so very much. I don't think I'll be able to bear leaving it, Albert, but there was no other way. I think you and Jane understand, don't you?"

"Of course, mum. We understand, but we'll hate to leave it, and we'll hate to leave you and Mr. Dutton."

"Thank you, Albert. Thank you so much. Mr. Dutton is a strange man, as you well know."

"Oh, I wouldn't call him strange exactly, mum. . . ."

"Yes, Albert," she said firmly. "I don't like to contradict you, but he's *strange*. I've lived with him now for forty-four years, and I can say positively that he's strange."

"I think, mum, it's simply that he hears a different drummer, so to say."

"Indeed he does. But as I told him, it's simply the part of wisdom for a man to know when he's beaten. And he is beaten, Albert. He's beaten now."

"Mr. Dutton beaten . . ." Albert mused. "I can't really believe that, mum. I'd like to think of him as *never* beaten."

"He's humiliated, Albert. He made *me* call the real-estate broker. He doesn't want to talk to anybody or see anybody. He's afraid to go into town." She sighed. "I suppose in time he will get over it, Albert, yet it's clear that we can't continue to live in this area. Because everywhere he goes, people—you know what I mean, I'm sure."

"Yes, mum, I suppose I do, and I suppose I'd feel the same way in his place. Where will you go, Mrs. Dutton?"

"Back to New Jersey, I suppose, Albert, although I don't want to. I certainly don't *want* to."

"I hope you picked a reputable real-estate broker, Mrs. Dutton," Albert said.

"Yes, I think I did. Mr. Bigley, in Paxton. I've heard he's quite good . . . and of course our lawyer, Mr. Mulligan, will be seeing to our interest. He'll look out for us. I simply can't count on Jake to do much of anything. He didn't even want to discuss price, and I know that I'll be the one to call the moving-van people and *everything*."

"This Mr. Bigley—will he be able to relieve you of all the detail, Mrs. Dutton? I mean, I hope you won't be bothered with having people traipsing through the house all day long, will you? So many people just use it as an excuse to look through a house when they have no intention of buying."

"Mr. Bigley thought it would sell quickly at the price," Mrs. Dutton said. "So I don't think we'll be bothered unduly. When I talked with him this morning, he said he wouldn't be surprised if it were snapped up by nightfall. He thought we could get much more, but $69,500 was all Jake wanted. The mood he's in, he's practically willing to give it away." She sighed heavily. "I'm so sorry, Albert, but you do understand, don't you? We'll give you and Jane the most glowing references that anybody ever had."

She smiled at him bravely and rose from the bench.

"Thank you, mum." Albert could hear the telephone ringing.

"I'd better get it," she said. "I know that Jake won't. It may be Mr. Bigley."

She went inside and quickly returned. "It's for you, Albert."

"Thank you, mum."

It was a young lady who said she was calling for Mr. Merritt. "He would like very much for you to call him, Mr. Bagby. He'd like to offer you and Mrs. Bagby a job."

"No, thank you," Albert said. "Thank Mr. Merritt for me, please, but tell him I've already made other plans."

30

It was on an afternoon ten days later, the afternoon of August 28 to be exact, that Albert, neatly dressed in a dark gray sharkskin suit and fawn fedora, descended the steps from his motel eyrie and crossed the parking lot toward his modest, dust-streaked station wagon.

Jane, Beverly, and Nick were sprawled about the pool. Jane called out to ask where he was going. "Town," he called back and then, to forestall further questions, he opened the door of the station wagon, slid into the seat, started the engine and was quickly off, headed for Paxton, ten miles away.

Once there, he parked, dropped a nickel into the meter, and started walking. His destination proved to be a brick building, refurbished with early American fittings, including a multi-paned picture window with a short, sloping roof of bright copper.

He entered and was greeted by a secretary, who then ushered him into an inner office.

First to speak, characteristically enough, was Dutton, who was seated, with obvious discomfort, on an extremely low-slung sofa of yielding green leather which forced his knees nearly to head level. Mrs. Dutton sat beside him, and Mr. Mulligan, a deeply tanned, heavy-set man of perhaps fifty, sat on a corner of his massive bleached desk.

As Albert entered, Dutton glanced up and said, "Well, *Albert!*"

Mrs. Dutton's glance was filled with tenderness. "How very kind of you, Albert."

"Well, folks . . ." Mulligan said, rising.

"It's beyond the call of duty," Dutton said.

"Albert has *always* acted beyond the call of duty," Mrs. Dutton said. "And how very *nice* you look, Albert."

"Albert has always liked to be where the action is," Dutton said with a chuckle. "Eh, Albert?" He chuckled again. "Our people are late," he explained. "Ask for a quick settlement and then they're late for the appointment."

Mulligan adjusted the lapels of a capacious beige linen jacket, looking momentarily mystified. "I didn't realize you folks knew each other," he said.

"Well, of course!" Dutton said with indignation.

"All right then, folks," Mulligan said. "Why don't we all take seats at what I call my conference table here?" Snickering, he indicated a long, narrow bench about which six chairs were grouped. "Mr. Dutton, why don't you and Mrs. Dutton sit on this side and—"

"What?" Dutton demanded. He frowned. "Aren't we going to wait for the Millers?"

Mulligan frowned back. "There was no need for Mrs. Miller to be here, since there's no mortgage involved. And Mr. Miller *is* here."

Dutton looked over his shoulder and seemed, indeed, to be looking into corners and even between his feet. "Where?"

"Right here." With a smile of confusion, Mulligan waved a loose hand toward Albert.

Dutton looked at Mulligan. "Squire," he said, "you're just as crazy as a hoot owl. This is Albert Bagby, our live-in man. Where are the people who are buying our *house?*" Dutton was trying manfully to rise from the sofa, but his take-off point was so low that he was having trouble. "Here, Frances!" he commanded. "Help me up from this damned thing."

Mulligan was smiling helplessly. "Somebody around here must be crazy," he said. "Is it me?"

"It must be," Dutton said, on his feet by now.

"No, Mr. Dutton," Albert said in a vibrant, low-key voice. "No . . ."

He paused dramatically, waiting for the elation to catch in his throat, waiting for the feeling of good strong victory to course through his veins—for this, after all, was his moment, here and now, with Dutton staring open-mouthed. It was the moment when the prince returned, cast off his rags, and took his rightful place under a silvered sun.

"No," he said. "*I'm* the one who has bought your house, Mr. Dutton."

Yet, unaccountably, the elation was not there. It felt hollow.

286

"*You've* bought my house?"

Albert nodded.

"*Nonsense, Albert!*" Dutton's voice was shrill. "How *could* you have bought my house? Your name isn't Miller. It's Bagby. Some people named Miller bought my house."

Albert studied him. As yet he could not decide whether Dutton's excitement was caused by the element of surprise and his inability to comprehend—or whether it was a case of violent opposition to having his house bought by a handyman. Hoping it would prove to be the latter, Albert said, "Bagby is only my professional name, so to say. My real name is Albert Miller."

"Since when?" Dutton demanded.

"Since *when?* It's *always* been Miller. From the day I was born." Hoping to gain strength by sneering, Albert sneered.

"Well, I'll be a son of a bitch." Dutton sank exhausted upon the green leather sofa. "I don't know," he said from his great depth. "I just don't know any more. You could tell me the world was made of lemon sponge and I'd believe it. I'm telling you the truth."

Again Dutton was struggling to his feet, clawing at the air. "Here, Albert! Gimme a hand!"

After a moment of cool appraisal, Albert pulled him up from the couch. Dutton came at him, jabbing a forefinger at his chin. "Albert Bagby . . . do you mean to stand there and tell me you're prepared to give me $69,500 for my house?"

"Less the ten-percent deposit," Albert said casually.

"Well, I'll be a son of a bitch!" Once more Dutton collapsed into the soft prison of the low sofa.

"Spot cash," Albert added.

Dutton looked at the ceiling. "It must be nice. It certainly must be nice."

Mulligan cleared his throat. "Good gentlemen," he said. "I have another appointment in a few minutes, good gentlemen, so if we could get along with our business I'd be most grateful. We only have a couple of papers to sign; there's very little to it, especially with no mortgage involved."

"No mortgage!" Dutton breathed.

"There's something I'd like you both to know," Albert said to Dutton and Mrs. Dutton. "I don't want you to feel there's any hurry about getting out. I want you to feel you can take your time. No pressure."

Dutton glared at him. "I'd like to know what's going on in this country," he said. "I wish somebody would explain it to me." He spread his hands. "Well. What are you going to do?" It was a philosophical question, clearly rhetorical, but Mulligan seized upon it as an excuse to prod matters forward.

"If you'll just come over here to the table, Mr. Dutton," he said, spreading out a long sheet of legal paper.

Dutton, failing again to boost himself up from the sofa, slid forward onto his knees and got to his feet. He sat down at the table and Mulligan placed a ballpoint pen before him. Dutton seemed to be studying the document but apparently was not concentrating.

Finally he flung aside the pen. "Albert, I'm not going to *do* it. We can't do this to you. It's not fair!"

"It seems fair enough to me," Albert said. "It was the price you asked."

"I'm not talking about that, Albert."

"Ah, Mr. Dutton . . ." Mulligan said with an attempt at

tact. "You can do as you like, of course, but you don't really have any legal choice in the matter, you see. We have Mr. Miller's signature on the purchase contract, and we have your signature and Mrs. Dutton's signature—*and* we have Mr. Miller's check for the ten-percent deposit—$6,950."

"Jake," Mrs. Dutton said. "If somebody's got to have it, I'd rather it be somebody nice like Albert and Jane. . . . Really, Jake."

"You're missing the point, Frances," Dutton said. "You're completely missing the point, all of you. I just don't think it's fair to Albert. He has no idea what he's walking into. I happen to be very fond of Albert, and I don't want to see him hurt. I mean—if you just take an example . . ."

Dutton started waving his hands, groping for the example he wanted. "I mean, you read in the newspapers about people living in squalor and filth—I don't mean *you* live in squalor and filth, Albert, don't get me wrong. But you read about somebody rolling back some filthy mattress and finding a hundred thousand dollars under it. Now, those people don't take that hundred thousand and go out and buy an *estate* with it. They—" Dutton paused to look dubiously from one to the other. "They keep it right there under the mattress."

"Oh, Jake!" Mrs. Dutton said reprovingly. "That's simply awful."

"All I'm trying to say—well—" Dutton shrugged. "If you don't understand what I'm trying to say, then I can't help you. Now you take your—"

Albert interrupted him. "What Mr. Dutton is trying to say is if not to the manor born, then stay out of the manor, isn't that it?"

"Albert and I have always understood each other," Dutton said.

Albert looked at him coldly.

"Okay." Dutton shrugged. He washed his hands. He picked up the ballpoint pen and swiftly scrawled his signature in three places. "Here, Frances. Here."

Mrs. Dutton signed.

And then Albert signed.

"All right," Mr. Mulligan said. "Except for the matter of a little money, ahem, that does it. Now, Mr. Miller, if you'll write me a couple of checks, please . . ."

Deftly, Albert produced his checkbook and spread it before him.

"Did you have the title searched, Albert?" Dutton asked.

Albert nodded. "Yes, I did."

Dutton looked disappointed.

"Let's see now," Mulligan said. "The amount owing to the Duttons, you'll see by the settlement sheet here, is exactly $62,531.17, after tax adjustments. Deducted from that is the real-estate commission of $4,170. So if you'll write a check to the Duttons for $58,361.17 and a check to Bigley Realtors for $4,170, that should do it."

"Right," Albert said, picking up the pen.

With the settlement sheet before him, he wrote the checks carefully and precisely, in his very best penmanship, taking far longer than was necessary.

Finally he shoved the checks across the table to the lawyer. "There you go," he said jauntily.

Mulligan gave them a brief inspection, then put one in a folder and slid the other to Dutton, who looked at it with mild interest. "How do I know this check is any good, Albert?" he asked in a jocular way.

Albert smiled. "It's as good as gold—Jake."

Dutton's lip twitched. "Come, Frances," he said. "Let's get out of here."

They left, and as they passed down the short hall that led to the front entrance, Albert heard Dutton say in a distinct voice something about Imperial Rome and Visigoths.

Albert was on his feet. He shook hands with Mulligan and went swiftly out to the street.

The Duttons were about half a block away, headed for the bank. Albert caught up with them just as they reached the entrance. "Jake . . ."

Dutton turned, frowning.

"Visigoths, is it?" Albert asked.

"I wasn't speaking of you, Albert."

"Good," Albert said.

"Just tell me something, Albert," Dutton said.

"What?"

"Why do you call me Jake and her Mrs. Dutton?"

"I have something I'd like to say to you," Albert said. "Now, don't get me wrong—I have nothing whatever against the servant class—"

"Neither do I," Dutton said promptly. "Who does?"

"I see nothing whatever wrong with being a servant."

"Neither do I," Dutton said, "except there should be more *of* them."

"But just in the interest of accuracy," Albert went on, "I'd like you to know . . . I mean, the time has come to tell you—"

"It used to be," Dutton interrupted, "that a man could

have a servant without having his house bought out from under him. By the servant."

"Since it seems to bother you so much, you should know that I'm *not* a servant."

"Don't be ashamed of it," Dutton said heatedly. "Now, you take your servant class in Europe. In Europe, people are still raised from birth to be nothing *but* servants and they're well liked and well respected and all. . . ."

"Dammit, I'm *not* a servant," Albert shouted, "and neither is my wife!"

A man entering the bank looked curiously over his shoulder and bumped into the glass door.

"Nonsense, Albert," Dutton said. "Don't downgrade yourself. You're both excellent at your jobs. That's why I hate to see you uproot your heritage like this and tackle something that may be beyond you both. Sorry, I've got to get into the bank before it closes."

"Wait a minute!" Albert yelled.

But Dutton was opening the door and shoving his wife in ahead of him.

Albert retreated to the curb, where, after a time, he hung his head and tried to spit accurately upon a cigarette package which lay wadded in the gutter.

He looked up to see the Duttons emerging from the bank. "See you at the house, Albert," Jake called cheerfully and started off.

"Just a minute!" Albert caught up with them in front of a drugstore. "Look, I'm trying to tell you something and you refuse to listen. Now, *listen!*"

"The only thing I hear," Dutton retorted, "is the sound of a man denying his roots, and it has a shameful sound to it!"

"Listen!" Albert grabbed Dutton by the shoulder and spun him about. "I'm not a servant and neither is my *wife!*"

Dutton looked curiously at Albert's hand. "Albert," he said, "is that your hand I see on my lapel?"

Albert removed his hand. "We hoaxed you."

It was a word that finally got through. "You did *what?*" Dutton demanded.

"We tricked you. We posed as servants. We sold our house, we sold everything we owned, and we came to work for you as a live-in couple."

Dutton's eyes narrowed. "Are you telling me the truth, Albert?"

"Absolutely." Albert chuckled.

There was a long silence. "Well then, what *are* you if you're not a live-in couple?"

"What do you mean? We're not anything."

"What were you before?"

"I was an industrial engineer."

"Nonsense."

"Nonsense, hell!"

Again Dutton fell silent, as if making an attempt to comprehend. "You mean you quit your job and became a live-in couple?"

"Exactly."

"Nonsense," Dutton said, although with less conviction.

Albert saw Mrs. Dutton's eyes light up with amusement, and even perhaps with admiration.

Dutton was still thinking it over. "How about that man who sent me the reference?" he demanded triumphantly.

"Do you remember his name?" Albert asked, grinning.

"No."

"It was Miller," Albert said.

"Mill—" Again Dutton's eyes narrowed. "That was a dirty trick, Albert. How could you ever have done such a thing?"

Albert shrugged. "I was *tired* of owning things. *Tired* of being a slave to a house and possessions. Besides, look at the bargaining position it put us in."

"Oh dear, Albert," Mrs. Dutton said, beginning to laugh. "How wonderful!"

"*Not* wonderful!" Dutton turned on her. "How can you say it's wonderful? What's wonderful about it?"

"Twelve hundred bucks a month, for one thing," Albert said. "Eating your food, for another. Knowing you were paying the bills. Pool privileges. We found a pigeon."

"*Who's* a pigeon?" Dutton screamed. "Traitor!"

"What?"

"You're a traitor, Albert. A traitor to your class!"

Albert grinned.

"You shirked!" Jake yelled. "I hate to say it, Albert, because I like Jane, and I *did* like you. But I can never like you again. You gave up. You turned your back on the very world we're fighting a rear-guard action to preserve. You chickened out, Albert!"

"Oh, dear," Mrs. Dutton said. "Please don't make such a scene." She began moving away, looked back once, and headed up the block.

Dutton's voice trembled with rage. "Why should *you* have the right to quit paying property taxes? Why should *you* have the right not to own things and take care of them? What made you think *you* were so damned special, Albert Bagby?"

"Because I thought it up," Albert said.

Dutton's eyes were fiery slits. A vein showed up in his forehead. He jabbed his finger hard against Albert's chest. "Do you realize what that makes you? Do you *realize?* A *dirty communist,* that's what!" He shook his head. "Never in my life have I stood on the same sidewalk with a dirty communist! I don't propose to start now."

He turned away and started off with short, stiff-legged steps, then turned. His face was a solid red. "You dirty communist, you're even *worse* than a servant!" he flung over his shoulder, and then disappeared up the block.

Albert shrugged. Several times he shrugged, and then walked to his modest station wagon, thinking how ironic it was to be called a communist when he now owned $69,500 worth of house, pool, outbuildings, and chattels.

Ownership of which Jane still knew nothing.

Halfway home, he saw the Bentley up ahead. It was acting in a most peculiar fashion. It was weaving badly. The Bentley would go from one side of the road to the other, sometimes all the way out over the shoulder, and then back to the other side. He saw Dutton's hand leave the wheel and gesticulate. Once he saw both hands leave the wheel.

Albert slowed down and kept his distance. When he drove into the parking lot, the Bentley was there and the Duttons had disappeared inside.

He found Jane watching television. "You don't have to cook tonight," he said.

"Why not?" She switched off the set and turned. She was smiling. She put her arms about his neck and kissed him happily.

He frowned. "What's wrong?"

"Nothing. I've had some good news. You know the literary agent I sent my book to? He *likes* it. He called."

"Wonderful," Albert said absently.

"He thinks he can get somebody to publish it—and even thinks he may be able to sell it to the movies!"

"Great." Albert grinned. "I'll take you out to dinner. To celebrate."

"How about *their* dinner?"

"They said for us to take the night off. So let's go."

"I wonder why," Jane said.

Albert didn't reply.

"Maybe it's because they're sad about selling the house," Jane said. "Do you suppose that's it?"

"Yes," Albert said. "That might be it."

They drove the ten miles back to town and had dinner in a restaurant. It was about eight o'clock when he told her they were the new owners of Rear Guard.

31

"Now look, Jane, do you want me to walk out of here?" Albert tossed his napkin to the table. "Because that's what I'm going to do if you don't keep your voice down! Let's talk about this like two sensible, civilized human beings. Or else not at all."

"*Damn* you, Albert!"

"There's no subject in the world that can't be discussed sensibly."

"Oh, God! Order me a drink!" She was looking at him very much as Dutton had so recently looked at the empty beer cans littering his lawn. "A double Scotch."

When the drink came, she gulped it and moaned. "Albert, *dear Albert* . . . honest to *God* . . . You've actually *bought* it? We honestly *own* it? Surely you're kidding me. You're just kidding me, aren't you?" She reached over and patted his hand. "I *know* you're just kidding me because you've always liked to kid people, and now you're kidding *me.*"

She gulped her drink and leaned forward again. "So, let's just talk about something else." She smiled brightly, showing her teeth. "Okay?"

He nodded. "If that's the way you want it, Jane. Okay."

She sighed. "Thank *goodness*. I thought for a minute you were telling me you'd bought Rear Guard. Which would have been very stupid, and I *know* you're not stupid, so it's something you could not possibly have done."

"Right. Except that I did."

Her hand trembled as she picked up her drink.

"We'll talk about it in a civilized way," he said.

"Good," she whispered. "Indeed we will. And let me start the discussion. Okay?"

He nodded. "Go ahead, but keep your voice down."

"Albert, I'm going to talk to you as though you were very stupid, as though you were a person of subnormal intelligence. That's fair enough, isn't it?"

Albert swept the room with his eyes, feeling an impulse to get out.

"Now, if you'll remember," Jane said. "A number of months ago, you told me you had sold everything and we were going to be a live-in couple. I blew my top, if you'll recall."

"I recall. Don't yell or I'm leaving."

"Well . . ." Jane smiled pensively into her drink, as if she were a wife smiling pensively into a drink. "The strange part, Albert, is that you were right. I thought you were crazy at the time, but I found out you were right. It was brilliant. I love it at Rear Guard. I mean, this isn't something I'm just springing on you. I've told you all summer long you were right. Haven't I?"

"Yes," he conceded. "You have."

"I mean, Albert dear, I'm the living embodiment of the brilliance of your *thesis*—"

"Shhh!"

298

"I've loved having no responsibility. I've loved not having to cut a figure. I loved having so much time to myself, because you were quite right—I've had far more time for myself than I ever had back home, and less real responsibility because nothing was *mine*. Do you understand?"

He nodded.

"Furthermore," she went on, "I *love* the Duttons. It's been like living with one's parents again, or perhaps more like living with one's grandparents. Whatever. It's been so nice knowing *they* were responsible. And if that's being immature and being a little girl, then I don't care. I loved the whole thing."

"Lower your voice."

"Albert, I'm going to throw the rest of this drink right in your face."

"I wouldn't."

She looked down at the table, biting her lip. "I felt like a parasite, true, but I had the consolation of knowing that they *wanted* me to be one, and I also knew that we were giving them back a great deal in return. We did our jobs beautifully, we really *did*, Albert. And we were company for them. It was ideal. Why in God's name did you have to go and spoil it?"

"Jane, if you cry, dammit, I'm going to walk out of here. Look, if I was right once, why can't you trust me to be right again?"

"Because it's stupid, that's why. You hated the burden you had at home, with a comparatively small house and yard. Why on earth would you take on something so enormous as Rear Guard? Are you trying to punish yourself?"

"I don't regard it as punishment to own a beautiful place like Rear Guard," he said stiffly.

"Ah! Oh, the Territorial Imperative of it! Oh, the sheer maleness of it!"

"You didn't have to have that son of a bitch treat you like a lackey all summer! You didn't have to stand there and hear him say the clock was going to strike twelve for your daughter because Prince Nick was going to send her to hell back to the ashes!"

"Oh, who cares? Who really cares? Certainly not Beverly. Why should you? Why do you have to be such a self-righteous male about it? You simply couldn't *stand* for him to have something you didn't have, that was the whole thing, Albert. You figured out something very nicely with your brain six months ago, and then your stupid male ego *ruins* it."

"Double Scotch," Albert said to the waiter. "Let's change the subject, Jane."

"Change the *subject!*"

"Let's talk about your book."

"It's spoiled now."

"I think it's great. And he thinks he can sell it to the movies? For how much? Did he say?"

"Fifty thousand dollars, maybe."

"Fifty thousand dollars! Your *father?* A book about your *father?*"

"What's wrong with a book about my father?"

"Nothing, but—fifty thousand! Wow!"

She looked at him coldly. "I put in some dirty words and some dirty scenes. The agent said I should." Her voice was haughty. "Anyway, it won't do *you* any good, because I won't *be* here."

"*What?*"

"You can run Rear Guard by yourself. You honestly expect me to be mistress of Rear Guard? And have a lot of stupid parties for people who get drunk and fall on the floor at dinner? And spend my days weeding flower beds? No. I'll take my money and go off and support myself on it."

"You mean get a divorce?"

"Isn't that what you expected? Isn't that what you want?"

"No," he said. "I'm too old. Besides, we've been through a lot together."

"Maybe I'll go with the Duttons back to New Jersey and cook for them."

"Check, please," Albert said.

"You're heartless and cruel, Albert. They're miserable about leaving."

"They put the house up for sale. I didn't."

"They're heartbroken. They love us. And I love them. And I think you do, too."

"Not him." Albert shook his head. "I like her fine, but I can't stand that old bastard."

The town was quiet as it always was by nine o'clock in the evening. The streets were deserted and the air had the sweet taste of autumn.

Jane was silent as they walked to the car. She seemed to be thinking.

"Yes," she said as they headed out of town and took the

road for home. "I suppose you are right about him. He *is* a horrible old man. The world in flames and he spends his time on Jolly Dollar contests and sinking people's boats and still worries about class distinctions . . ."

Albert was silent.

"And buying frogman suits," Jane said. "And sitting in trees . . ."

"He has guts," Albert said. "He has plenty of guts."

"Yes, I suppose so, but—"

"All right," Albert snapped. "What do you *expect* him to do?"

"Me? Nothing."

"He's old. Nobody wants him. Nobody respects his opinions. Why in the hell *shouldn't* he go off in a corner by himself and do what he damn pleases? He spent his life working for the money. He started life under a set of rules. Is it his fault if the rules were changed and everything was yanked out from under him?"

Jane laughed gently. "You *are* fond of him, Albert."

"The hell I am. I think he's a reactionary old son of a bitch."

When they got home, the Bentley was gone. "Oh, God!" Jane said. "They've killed themselves!"

"Don't be silly," Albert said. "Do you seriously believe that Jake Dutton would ever kill himself?"

"Ever since you told me tonight, I've pictured him with his head in the gas oven," Jane said.

"If he ever did . . ." Albert paused. "If he ever did, it

would turn out to be an electric oven. All he'd do would be to—"

"Singe his eyebrows," Jane said.

"Yeah. Then he'd kick hell out of the oven for being the wrong kind of oven."

Jane laughed. Albert smiled grudgingly.

They went up to their room and Jane lay in bed, watching television. "Furthermore," she said, "I love this room. I adore it. It's brought me luck. I feel at home writing on that counter."

Albert sat in a chair and watched Jane watching television. Toward ten o'clock, he heard a car drive up and doors slam. He looked through the window.

"The Bentley?" Jane asked.

He nodded. "I think I'll go outside and take a turn around the yard."

"Yes," she said, eyes on the screen. "Go have a look at your property, dear. Count the trees and the blades of grass."

It was a beautiful night. The moisture of summer had gone, and the dry air of autumn let the stars sparkle as they hadn't sparkled all summer long. Breathing deeply, looking now and then at the stars, Albert walked to the outermost fringe of the property, and then walked all around the boundaries, his boundaries, down to the road, and then back up again, and then out to the river and all along the shoreline. It seemed much larger than it had ever seemed before. And beautiful, he thought, staring at the dark river. Beautiful. And it's *mine*. Looking up at the stars, he chuckled.

"What are you laughing about, Albert?"

Albert jumped.

"What's so funny?" Dutton demanded.

"I didn't see you there," Albert said.

"I've been walking around, having a look at the property," Dutton said. "While Mrs. Dutton fixes some supper. We still haven't had our *supper*."

He moved forward a few paces and they stood together on the bank of the river. "I still don't understand how you could have done such a thing, Albert," Dutton said.

Albert made no reply.

"To *me*," Dutton said. "Why would you want to do such a thing to *me*? Of all people!"

Albert remained silent.

"Was it the girl?"

"Well," Albert said, "I don't particularly *enjoy* having my daughter placed in the category of—"

"No," Dutton interrupted. "I don't mean Becky."

"Beverly!" Albert snapped.

"I don't mean your daughter. I mean the other girl. I suppose you never got over that, did you, Albert?"

"Her? I'd completely forgotten about her." Albert paused. "Who was she?"

"Hah!" Dutton chuckled. "Nobody important. Just somebody I got from the agency."

"Somebody you got from *what* agency?"

"An agency in Baltimore that supplies girls for things like that."

"Things like what?"

"Whatever you need them for," Dutton said. "I don't mind

saying, Albert—I wanted you, and I *got* you. I had you figured out just right. What's that you're muttering?"

"Nothing," Albert said.

"You may think you've turned the tables, Albert. You may have money, but that's all. I'm very fond of you in a way, but I never thought you were a person with very much class."

Albert turned away.

"Stop muttering, Albert. If you've got something to say, then *say* it. I like certain things about you, Albert, it's true, but I think you've got a common streak in you somewhere." Dutton's voice rose. "Only a man with a common streak would have done what you did. Hiring on with the idea of shacking up with your employer's wife . . . taking showers with her and whatnot."

Angrily, Dutton stomped off into the darkness. "I don't see how you've been able to look me straight in the eye!" he called back. "You haven't got the morals of a billy-goat!"

Sitting aquiver on the white bench, Albert heard the sound of tires crunching on gravel. It seemed far too early for Nick and Beverly to be home. Hauling himself wearily from the bench, he headed back across the lawn. Seeing a light on in the kitchen, he passed close to the big house, his house, his kitchen.

The kitchen door was open to the soft autumn breeze, and Jake and Mrs. Dutton were sitting at the kitchen table, with empty soupbowls before them.

As Nick entered the kitchen, they looked up and greeted him. "Home so early, Nicky . . ." Mrs. Dutton said.

"I'm going out again," Nick said. "I had to come back to get some more money. We're going up to Paxton and have a drink."

"Well, Nick, anyway . . ." Dutton dropped his soup spoon decisively into his soup bowl. "There's one consolation."

"What do you mean, Uncle Jake?" Albert heard Nick ask.

"At least now if you marry Becky, at least you won't be marrying a servant girl."

"What do you mean, Uncle Jake?"

"I mean Becky is not a servant girl. Her mother and father bought our house today."

"*What!*" Nick looked dumfounded. "Get serious, Uncle Jake. You mean—Albert and Jane are *not* servants?"

"That's right, Nick. So if you want to marry Becky, I'll not stand in your way."

"Well I'll be damned," Nick said.

"I don't like to hear you use that sort of language, Nick," Dutton said. "Anyway, I'm sure your father will feel a whole lot better about it."

"I'll be damned," Nick said.

Albert passed on across the parking lot. Beverly was sitting on the steps. "Hi," she said miserably.

"Hi, Bev. What's wrong?"

"Nick had to come back for more money. He gave such a huge tip at dinner that he didn't have any left."

"Is that what's making you so sad?"

"No. I—Daddy, I've got to get away from here. I'm going back to school early. Do you mind?"

"No, if that's what you want."

306

"He's crazy, and he's driving *me* crazy. I've never seen anybody in my life so guilty about having money."

"That's obviously a characteristic he didn't inherit from his Uncle Jake," Albert said.

"It's getting so sticky I can't stand it. He wants me to marry him and I won't. He's nice, I suppose. But I can't stand him, and I can't bring myself to hurt his feelings." She sighed and got up from the steps. "Here he comes. Good night."

"Cheer up, Bev." Albert patted her shoulder and went on in a low voice, "I may be wrong, but I think maybe you'll find it easier now—to get *rid* of him, I mean."

Just before Albert fell asleep that night, he felt Jane stir heavily beside him. "Albert . . ."

"What?" he asked groggily.

"I just realized something, Albert. It just came to me. You did the whole thing."

"*What* whole thing?"

"All of it. I'm not even sure you did it deliberately, but you did it. You engineered it. When Clinker offered us a job, you made sure Dutton heard of it. You purposely left that lion-hunting book around so he'd find it and make a fool of himself. You let him squirt those people with the bilge water. You even paid for the rocks with your own money to build up the shoreline. You did the whole thing. Poor Mr. Dutton's downfall."

"Don't be ridiculous," Albert said huffily. "Go to sleep."

He was dropping off again when he heard her say, "Albert, maybe Mr. Dutton could be *your* handyman."

"*What?*" He rose up on his elbow. "Are you out of your mind? He can't even drive a nail. If you ever saw the way he treats his tools, or the way he handles that boat of his—my God, I wouldn't let him touch anything that belonged to me. *Nothing!*"

"I do love this room," Jane murmured sleepily. "And I'd like to stay. But if you want me to stay here, you'll have to figure out some way to let them stay, too. Maybe he could pay you for their room and board. So we could all be together."

"A highly improbable family of four," Albert said stiffly.

"I don't see why. All right—take it or leave it."

"For God's sake, Jane! What are you trying to pull? Nothing would be changed except the name on the deed!"

"Who cares about an old deed?" Jane said and fell asleep.

32

The first week in October, the wild geese flew in from Canada. Mrs. Dutton mentioned them at dinner.

"Just the sight of them makes me so happy," she said. "Those long beautiful V-shaped formations flung out over the sky, like beautiful delicate tracery. They remind me of last autumn when we first moved in. Do you remember, Jake?"

"To tell the truth about it," Dutton was saying to Albert, "I've always had a good head of hair and it's not surprising, because my father had good thick hair and so did my grandfather, right up until the day they died. I think a lot of it is hereditary. You must have had some baldness in your family, Albert."

"Jake," Mrs. Dutton said. "I was telling Jane about the wild geese. They're here. Did you see them today?"

"Oh, yes," Dutton said. "Beautiful. Yes, yes, yes." In the light of the candles, his face looked serene and unusually composed. He got up from the table now and strutted about the room, patting his stomach. "Delicious, Jane. Delicious."

"Here, let me help you, Jane," Mrs. Dutton said, leaping up as Jane started to clear off the dishes.

"Albert," Dutton said. "I bought a bottle of brandy this afternoon when I was in town. Why don't we go in and sample it?"

"No, thanks," Albert said curtly. "By the way, Jake, what's the date today?"

"Today? I believe today's the fourth, isn't it?"

"No, it's the seventh," Albert said.

"Seventh, then." Dutton strayed off toward the Safari Room, with Albert dogging his footsteps. "Don't dun me, Albert. Let's get some lights on in here. It's dark as pitch."

Dutton went about the room, turning on lamps, missing none.

"I don't consider it dunning," Albert said. "I was just pointing out that today is the seventh, which is six days later than the first."

"It's getting chilly in here," Dutton said. "Don't you think it's about time you turned on the oil burner?"

309

"I'm not chilly," Albert said.

"You should turn it on a little while in the morning and a little while at night," Dutton said. "Just to take the chill off the house. By the way, have you looked at that oil burner yet?"

"No. Why?"

"You should go down to the basement and have a look at it."

"Why should I go down to the basement and have a look at it?"

"Because I think you're going to need a new one before very long. We had a lot of trouble with it last winter. The service man told me I couldn't expect much more out of it."

Dutton was bending forward, peering through the picture window, hands clasped behind his back. He turned, smiling. "I'll go upstairs and write that check for you now, Albert."

Albert went about the room, turning out all the lamps except one. Ten minutes passed. From the kitchen came the sound of clattering dishes and companionable laughter.

When Dutton still didn't appear, Albert muttered something churlish and went outside. It was almost eight o'clock, but Daylight Time would not end for another three weeks, and the sky was still pale in the west. There was a chill in the air.

Crossing the parking lot, he went up to his room and got a windbreaker from the closet. The room was a mess. The counter was littered with manuscript pages. Jane had begun a new book. Two ashtrays were filled with cigarette butts. At the other end of the long counter, the end known as his end, there were his sunglasses, a bottle of pills, and a clipping from the local newspaper telling of a general county-wide reassessment of property values.

Zipping up his windbreaker and taking his flashlight, Albert went outside and tramped all about his property. It was something he still did every evening when the weather permitted, checking for erosion along the shoreline and playing the flashlight over the limbs of trees that needed pruning, others that should be fed before winter, and then at some new potholes in the driveway, and weeds that were growing up insistently among the gravel in the parking lot. The parking lot should be blacktopped, he thought.

Albert sighed.

He saw Jane leave the kitchen by the back door and hurry across to the room, eager to get to her writing.

He heard Mrs. Dutton warm up on the piano and then break into the melody of a song which he recognized as "I Can't Believe That You're in Love with Me."

Any minute now, he would hear the sound of Dutton's voice. He waited. Instead he heard the front door open.

"Albert . . ." Dutton called.

"What!" Albert replied.

"Where are you?"

"Right here," Albert said.

"Up in the tree?"

"Yes," Albert said.

"Oh." Dutton moved up close to the trunk. "I have the check for our room and board—what do you want me to do with it, Albert?"

"I'll take it," Albert said, reaching down.

"I have it inside," Dutton said. "I'll bring it out to you."

"*Good,*" Albert said.

Dutton went indoors again. Albert waited. High in the tree, Albert looked down the river at the blinking lights of the buoys. Jane's typewriter clattered. Through the window of their room, he could see the shadow of her head, very large against the wall.

The sound of typing mingled with the sound of the piano. Mrs. Dutton was thumping out huge warm-up arpeggios. She struck a final note of introduction, and then Dutton's voice came in, loud, firm, and resonant, always a surprise.

"*Button* UP *your o-vercoat . . . when the wind is freeee . . .* TAKE *good care of yourself, you belong to me . . . Keep away from* BOOTleg *hooch . . .*"

On and on they sang and played. Occasionally, as Dutton moved off from the piano, Albert could see that he held the check in his hand.

Presently they stopped, and Dutton came outside again. "Albert . . . are you still up in the tree?"

"Yes," Albert said.

"Here's your check."

"I'll take it," Albert said, reaching down.

Dutton pulled himself up to the first branch, handing up the check. Albert grasped it firmly, folded it once, and stuck it in the pocket of his windbreaker.

Dutton took a seat among the lower branches. "I'm serious about that oil burner, Albert. You really should have it looked into."

Albert said nothing.

"Old oil burners can explode. Haven't you read about old oil burners exploding?"

Albert didn't reply.

"You can't let these things slide," Dutton said. "You've gotta keep right on top of them."

"Okay," Albert said faintly.

"I mean, I'm just as fond of you as I can be, Albert, but I don't plan to pay out *my* good money to a—to a *slum landlord*. What?"

"I said look out below," Albert said.

Douglass Wallop

Douglass Wallop is a native of Washington, D.C., and it was as a forlorn fan of the dependably listless Washington Senators that he wrote THE YEAR THE YANKEES LOST THE PENNANT, *later made into the successful Broadway musical* DAMN YANKEES. *He now lives in Oxford, Maryland, a pre-Revolutionary village in the Tidewater country, where he writes, sails, and mows the lawn. He is married to Lucille Fletcher, the suspense writer.* THE GOOD LIFE *is his eighth novel.*